KEILE'S CHANCE

Dillon Watson

2009

Bella Books, Inc.
P.O. Box 10543
Tallahassee, FL 32302

Printed in the United States of America on acid-free paper
First Edition

Editor: Katherine V. Forrest
Cover Designer: Stephanie Solomon-Lopez

ISBN 10: 1-59493-156-9
ISBN 13:978-1-59493-156-7

Acknowledgments

I'd like to thank my sister and mother for their support and encouragement, GCLS for their mentorship program, the writing group at Charis Books and More where I first felt comfortable sharing my writing and Womonwrites for providing me a safe place to share my voice.

About the Author

Dillon Watson resides in the southeastern United States. She fell in love with romances in the seventh grade, and has been writing romantic fiction ever since. Her published stories can be found in *Erotic Interludes 4: Extreme Passions* and *Longing, Lust and Love*: *Black Lesbian Stories*. When she's not writing, she's reading. For more information about her and her writing, visit www.dillonwatson.com.

Chapter One

Keile Griffen unclipped the leash and said, "Okay boy, you can take off now." She couldn't help but smile as she watched her overgrown puppy race across the open grassy field to join the dogs already at play. She shielded her light brown eyes from the brightness of the late fall sun as she made sure the other dogs would welcome her baby.

Satisfied no intervention was needed, she moved to a nearby empty bench and sank down, giving a happy sigh of contentment, grateful the unexpected warm October morning temperature only required a long sleeved T-shirt. She leaned back and rested her arms on the back of the bench, congratulating herself for picking a great weekend to finish a major project at work. Tilting her head toward the sun, she luxuriated in the rays bathing her face.

Over the past six weeks she hadn't had much time to do

anything but work. Now the pressure was off until Monday and she was determined to make the most of her first free weekend in months. She had already reestablished communications with friends and arranged to meet them for dinner.

She smiled without opening her eyes when she felt her dog rest his head in her lap. She reached down to pet Trashcan, hoping it would deter him from climbing into her lap. Her hand made contact with fur too soft and curly to belong to her pet. Her eyes opened and widened when she caught sight of the brown haired cherub resting his head on her lap. "Uh…hello. Do I know you?"

Raising his head, the toddler smiled, showing four teeth. Keile's breath caught at the unexpected pull of emotions from the sweetness of his smile. He reached out his arms and said something unintelligible. "I guess you want me to pick you up, huh?" But she hesitated. "Okay, I can do that." Once she'd lifted the child onto her lap, she looked around the open field, expecting to see someone searching for the boy in her arms. "I bet your parents are looking for you. Why don't we sit here a minute and wait for them to show up?" She used the soft tone which had worked to gain Can's trust when she first adopted him.

The child twisted his body around and gave Keile another smile, then rested his head against her chest with easy familiarity. *So this is what all the fuss is about*. She pulled him closer and took a deep breath, enjoying the unfamiliar scents of baby powder and the outdoors. Being around small children was a new experience but, surprisingly, she found herself enjoying the moment.

While the boy watched the dogs play, Keile watched for his parents. Five minutes passed, and she became agitated. Surely somebody should have missed him by now. He was too healthy and clean to be living on the streets. *What if his parents dumped him?* Her stomach churned at the thought of such callousness. No! There had to be another explanation.

Getting a grip on her overactive imagination, she turned the boy around to face her. Eyes, so like her own, were looking at her in complete trust and Keile refused to believe anyone would intentionally lose this adorable child. He must have wandered away from somewhere. *The playground!* "Well kiddo, looks like we have a mission." She gave him a reassuring smile. "We need to go find your mommy and daddy." Holding him close to her body, Keile stood up gingerly, unused to the extra weight, and whistled for her own baby. His tongue lolling, Can raced toward them at full gallop, came to an abrupt stop a few feet in front of her, cocked his head and whined.

Keile shrugged. "Hey, don't you look at me like that. It's not my fault he…" But Can wasn't listening to her explanation. His attention was entirely focused on the child in her arms. "Trashcan this is Kid, Kid this is Trashcan. But you can call him Can for short."

Boy and dog looked at each other, then without warning the boy lunged toward Can, shrieking in delight. Keile was able to latch on to his overalls before he fell out of her arms.

"Hey! Hold on now," she admonished gently and lowered the boy to the ground. He immediately toddled to Can and threw his arms around the dog's neck. Keile watched in amazement as Can sat patiently, allowing himself to be showered with soggy affection.

"Well, kiddo, now that you've met my kid, we need to go find your *mama*." Keile hoped the word 'mama' would induce a response. "Where is your mama?" she asked, speaking slowly.

The boy let go of the dog to put his arms around Keile's jean-clad legs. "Mama, Mama, Mama," he chortled.

Keile rubbed her forehead. "Uh… No, baby. I mean *your* mama." She squatted down to his level and smiled. "Your mama." She pointed at his chest.

He gave her another wide smile and said, "Mama." Draping his short arms around her neck, he nestled his head against her shoulder.

"Okay. Have it your way, Buster." Her voice was husky from the rush of emotion that felt suspiciously like longing. She kissed his soft cheek. "Come on, Can, we need to go find somebody before I start liking this." She managed to clip on Can's leash without dropping her new charge. They set out for the playground which was on the other side of the park, with Keile on the alert for signs of frantic parents.

Keile stood near the playground waiting for someone to recognize the toddler in her arms. She had been sure the boy's parents would pounce upon him immediately. Although it had probably been less than ten minutes since she'd made the tot's acquaintance, it seemed more like an hour. As the minutes ticked away, she hoped she didn't look as desperate as she felt. All she needed was someone to think she was deranged and call the police.

"The police!" She threw back her head, startling both dog and child. "Why didn't I think of that in the first place?" She pulled out her cell phone and called her friend Dani, an ex-police officer who was currently dating a cop.

"Hey, Dani, it's Keile." She raised her voice to be heard over the background noise coming from Dani's cell phone.

"You're not calling to cancel again are you? Jo will have a fit."

"No! I…I need your help."

"Wait a minute. I can barely hear you over the construction. Are you okay? You're not hurt are you?"

"I'm fine. Well…it's this kid. He found me and it's been at least ten minutes and nobody seems to be looking for him. How can you not notice a small child is missing?"

"Calm down, Keile." Dani used the same tone Keile had used on the child earlier. "Carla's on duty. I'll call and have her check into the situation. If he's been with you for ten minutes, there's no telling how long he's been away from his parents. An alert's probably been issued. Tell me where you are, I'll come keep you company."

"You're a lifesaver." Keile exhaled, and felt the muscles in her shoulders relax. "I'm at Woodson Park near the Stratton Street entrance. Look for the playground, and hey, can you bring some juice or water? He might be getting thirsty."

"And you would know this how?" Dani teased. "Never mind,

I forgot you're a mother now."

"If I'm a mother, you're an aunt."

Dani laughed. "Right. Hey, Carla might call before I get there. Give me a buzz if you have to move."

"Thanks, Aunty." Keile clipped the phone to her belt. "Okay kiddo, the lesbian cavalry is on the way. How 'bout we try out that swing while we wait?" Without waiting for a reply, Keile walked over to one of the smaller swings. She fumbled around with the seat, trying to figure out what the extra part was for. Her days of using swings were long behind her.

"You look like you can use some help."

Keile turned to find the owner of the friendly sounding voice. "Please." She admitted with a sheepish grin, "I guess you can tell I'm a rank amateur, huh?"

"I had an inkling." The curvy brunette smiled. "I'm Tina. And this little one is John," she added, referring to the baby on her hip.

"I'm Keile, and this is Buster. This is the first time I've been entrusted to bring him here by myself." Strictly speaking it wasn't a lie.

"That would explain it." Tina lifted the safety latch, motioning for Keile to place the child in the swing. "John is our third. I think that qualifies me as an expert," she joked.

"Three, huh?" Keile pulled down the latch and gave Buster a gentle push. Her head reeled from the thought of caring for three children. She could barely keep up with one dog.

"Yup." Tina sat down on one of the swings meant for bigger kids. "We're crazy like that. I take it Buster is your only one?"

"Aside from Can." Keile pointed to the black lab resting nearby in a sunny spot, then gave Buster another push. Buster grew more vocal as he swung to and fro, letting out gleeful squeals each time Keile pushed the swing. The harder she pushed, the louder he squealed.

Ten minutes later, Keile and Buster were the only ones using the swings and her arms were starting to give out. As she was considering the need to add swing-pushing to her exercise routine, Dani arrived.

"Aren't you the domesticated one," Dani teased. "I have supplies." She held up the paper grocery bag.

"I owe you big, girl," Keile said with a sigh of relief. She stopped the swing, to the protest of one small child, and attempted to lift him out. She looked at the swing in consternation. "So much for domestication," Keile muttered, remembering the safety latch. She removed Buster from the swing. When she tossed him up in the air a couple of times, his frown turned into a grin. She swung him to face her friend, a proud smile on her face. "Buster, meet Dani." She pointed to the tall, athletic looking blonde.

Buster gave Dani a shy smile before burying his face in Keile's neck. Keile was so touched by his action she almost forgot to breathe. She couldn't remember anyone giving her their trust so openly. *Maybe this feeling of euphoria is what having a child is all about.* Her cell phone chirped and she flipped it open.

"Hey, Keile. I think I have good news for you," Carla said. "Could you give me a description of your find?"

She bristled at Carla's terminology. Buster was a child, not a find. She tightened her arm around him protectively. "Light brown, curly hair, olive skin, light brown eyes," she said. "Jean overalls, a light blue, long sleeved shirt with a collar." *And he's as sweet as he can be*, popped into her head. What had come over her?

"That sounds like a match," Carla said briskly. "An officer from another precinct is escorting his mother, Haydn Davenport, to the park right now. ETA is ten minutes. I'll come meet them and we can get this situation resolved."

"That's a relief." Keile exhaled. "Thanks, Carla. I'll see you then. By the way, there's someone here you might want to see. I won't name any names but she's tall, blond and cute." She disconnected without giving Carla the opportunity to respond.

"You should never tease a cop." Dani gave her a knowing grin. "They carry handcuffs," she explained, wiggling her eyebrows.

"Please Dani, there's a child present," Keile said with mock outrage. "Now let's go get my young man some juice."

Both women became quickly acquainted with the drawback of letting young children handle juice boxes. Buster grabbed the box and squeezed, spraying juice on his face and hair and the front of Keile's shirt. Dani managed to scramble out of the way, then watched with amusement as Keile separated Buster from the juice box before he could do more damage.

When he gave a half-hearted cry, Keile relented. This time however, she closely supervised his efforts. Buster tried to push her hand away, but she remained firm.

"Have you ever thought about having kids?"

"Me?" Keile looked at her friend to see if she was joking. There was something in Dani's expression she couldn't read. "Nah. You know I'm a foster kid from way back. What do I know about being a parent? Besides, they need a lot of time and patience and I don't have either one."

"You're doing a pretty good job of it right now," Dani said quietly, her expression pensive. "Edan and I really broke up because she decided she was ready to have children and I wasn't," she admitted, a faraway look in her light blue eyes. "I really loved her, but you can't compromise on something like that."

Keile's eyes widened. She had never met Edan but she'd heard about her from mutual friends. "But I…thought it was because of your job."

Dani shrugged. "That's what I let everybody think. It was easier."

Keile busied herself wiping Buster's face with the hem of her shirt. "Do you ever regret making that decision?" She regretted asking the question when Dani grimaced.

"When I let myself, but most of the time I don't." Dani bent forward and let the long, straight strands of her hair hide her face. "It's in the past anyway. Regrets don't serve a purpose." She tucked her hair behind her ears and turned, looking off in the distance. "Hey, how did we get so serious anyway?"

"Beats me." Keile smiled, glad to leave behind the unsettling topic. "We can blame it on Buster. Nobody will punish him because he's cute."

“That he is.” Dani’s smile was almost wistful. “He also looks sleepy,” she said, watching him rub his eyes.

“It’s probably been an eventful morning for him. I wonder how far he had to walk to get here.” Keile set aside the empty juice box and adjusted the toddler so he was cradled in her arms. She dropped a kiss on his forehead and watched as his eyes fluttered shut. “He sure is sweet to hold.” She smiled ruefully, realizing what she’d admitted. “It’s so strange to feel this way, Dani. I felt it earlier when he smiled at me and called me mama. Imagine… me a mother. It boggles the mind. I’d just mess it up.”

“No way!” Dani shook her head emphatically. “Seriously, you never give yourself enough credit. He looks so natural sheltered in your arms. In fact, he looks enough like you to be your son. Your skin is a little browner but you have similar features. I mean the shape of your eyes, nose and mouth.” She grinned. “He’s a mini-you.”

“Yeah, right,” Keile snorted, holding back the sense of pleasure the comparison brought her. “Can is about all I can handle, right boy?” She stroked her faithful companion who was patiently stretched out by her side. “Besides, this little fellow is only showing his adorable side.” As she looked upon the sleeping child, she felt an unfamiliar yearning. Having children had never been in the master plan she’d mapped out as a young teen.

“There you go again. Not giving yourself enough credit. Think about how many times you cleaned up after Can when you first got him.” Dani said, pointing at her. “I won’t even ask how many Trashcans you had to rescue before you decided that should be his name. And what about that time he was sick—”

“Okay, I get your point. But that was totally different,” Keile argued. “One is a dog and the other is a child.”

“Duh! I didn’t know.” Dani rolled her eyes.

“Bite me, Dani.”

“You wish, baby.”

“Only in your dreams.” She spotted movement over Dani’s shoulder and smiled. “Oh good, here comes your girl to the rescue.” Two police cars had pulled up. “It looks like they have the anxious mother in tow," she added, as a harried-looking woman jumped out of the first squad car and looked around frantically. The slender redhead looked nothing like the sturdy baby in Keile's arms.

Dani waved to get Carla's attention. Carla nodded and pointed the woman in their direction. Haydn Davenport stopped short of reaching Keile and the sleeping child and fresh tears fell from her already swollen green eyes. "Thank God." She brought her hands to her quivering lips and greedily drank in the sight of the child in Keile's arms. "He's safe."

Keile stood and moved forward. "Hi, I'm Keile. I think I have someone you need," she said, and transferred Buster to willing arms. She crossed her arms across her chest to cover the immediate feeling of emptiness and loss.

Crying silently, the redhead held the child close to her heart. She put her head against his and rocked him unmindful of the tears spilling down her face and into his brown curls. "Thank you," she whispered brokenly, never taking her eyes off her son. "Thank you so much."

Keile tucked her hands in her back pockets and shifted from foot to foot. "It was nothing…really. He found me. Why don't we go sit on that bench?" she suggested, seeing the trembling in the mother's arms. Keile glanced at Carla to make sure it was okay. Carla nodded and turned to talk to the other officer and Dani in a low voice as Keile assisted Haydn to a nearby bench, away from curious eyes.

The mother ran her hands over her child's body as if she needed to make sure everything really was okay. "He always has been a good sleeper." She let out a sound that was between a sob and a laugh. "Oh, my sweet baby," she crooned, rocking him as her tears continued to flow. The motion seemed to calm her, and gradually her breathing became more even.

Keile bit her lip, observing the intensity of emotions evident on the woman's face. Having held Buster in her arms, she could imagine how much the mother had suffered once she realized her child was missing. For a moment she had an almost overwhelming desire to take the distraught woman into her arms and offer the safety of her broad shoulders. She placed her hand on the other woman's arm and was rewarded when Buster's mom leaned into her touch.

"Ms. Davenport, is there anything I can get for you?" Concern etched Carla's handsome face.

"No," Haydn Davenport replied softly, shaking her head. She took a deep breath, and blinked. "I'll be okay, I promise. It's just..." She bit her trembling lip. "I was imagining all kinds of crazy possibilities and to see him sleeping so peacefully...shook me up." She glanced at Keile and smiled her gratitude.

Keile was blown away by the smile, so reminiscent of the ones Buster had given her earlier. "You really are his mother," she blurted without thinking. "He gave me that same sweet smile."

"Thank you." Haydn Davenport's cheeks reddened as she dipped her head. "Thank you for everything."

"Ma'am, we need to get you back to the station." The male cop was clearly apologetic. "I know you must want to get your little one home."

"Yes, of course." With another smile and a thank you for Keile, she followed the officer to the police car.

Keile stood stiffly, watching as mother and child walked out of her life. She rubbed her arms, suddenly aware of how empty they felt and of how empty she felt inside. *Get a grip. You don't have time for a family anyway.* She gave a deep sigh and turned to her two friends with a melancholy expression on her face.

"You okay?" Dani placed a hand on Keile's arm.

"I...I really don't know," she admitted, thrown off balance by her tumultuous emotions. "Something happened...and I'm not exactly sure what it was." She felt dazed as she whistled for Can. "I'll see you guys this evening."

Chapter Two

"Forget it!" Keile dropped the brush on the counter, reached for a hair band and secured her thick brown hair, which couldn't decide if it was curly or straight, in a ponytail. Lately, she'd been giving a lot of thought to having it cut into a more easily managed style. It would certainly make life easier.

Running her fingers through the bottom of the ponytail, she sighed. Her mother had had long, straight hair. On good days, she would let Keile brush it. Those days had been much too seldom. Sometimes when she brushed her own hair, the memories of the good times would come rushing back and she'd miss the mother she hardly knew.

An image of Buster's mom looking down at her sleeping child flashed through Keile's mind. She couldn't help but wonder if her mother had ever looked at her that way—with loving intensity.

"God, what is it with me today?" Somehow her morning

rescue had stirred up memories long buried. Shaking her head, she snarled at her reflection and stuck a baseball cap on her head, a solution that solved most hair issues.

After a quick good bye to Can, she was on her way. As she drove on the tree-lined streets of her Seneca, Georgia neighborhood, Keile refused to think about anything else but the scenery—her neighborhood, with its medium-sized ranch style houses, located in one of the older parts of the city. Keile had been initially attracted to the area because of the reasonable cost of the homes and the easy commute to her job. Now that she had Can, she also enjoyed the proximity to the park.

Twenty minutes later, Keile pulled into the parking lot of The Cantina, a restaurant known for its oversized margaritas and sizzling fajitas. As soon as she walked through the door, the aroma of sizzling meat made her stomach grumble. She was scanning the crowded medium-sized room when a familiar voice called her name. Keile waved off the woman with the clipboard and crossed the hardwood floor to join her friends.

"You're a sight for sore eyes." Johanna Ocalla stood and hugged Keile enthusiastically. At five-ten she was slightly taller than Keile. "You work too hard, girl," she announced loud enough for the whole restaurant to hear. "Have you been eating right? I swear you look thinner." Her gray eyes narrowed when Keile shrugged sheepishly.

"You think everyone is skinny, Jo," Susan said with a pointed look at her partner's large, muscular frame. "Now, give someone else a chance, love." Once Johanna released Keile, Susan folded their friend into her arms. "Jo's right you know, you do work too much. You're not even thirty. You need to play more."

"I know, I know." Keile returned the full-figured blonde's warm hug. "I promise to do better in the future," she added, giving her stock answer, then bent to kiss Susan's cheek. She didn't bother to explain again that working long hours put her in good stead with her boss, and garnered her bonuses. She also didn't explain that she expected her boss to be promoted in a couple of years, and she was positioning herself to be his replacement.

"Where have I heard that before?" Jo asked dryly, pushing her hand through her short dark hair. "Have a seat, we already ordered a pitcher of margaritas."

As if on cue, the waiter arrived with the pitcher, four glasses, and chips and salsa. After filling three of the glasses, he promised to check back later. Keile asked Jo and Susan to get her caught up on what had been happening while she had been busy with work.

For reasons she couldn't articulate, Keile was reluctant to discuss her experience earlier in the day—maybe because it was still too precious to share. She had spent a good deal of the afternoon thinking of her encounter with Buster, and examining the unnerving feelings caring for him brought out in her.

Keile gave a start when a heavy hand landed on her shoulders. She looked up to see her friend Terri Ocalla grinning down at her.

"I can't believe you actually showed up," Terri said, squeezing Keile's shoulder.

"Yeah, Terri, now you owe me a dollar," Jo said with an air of superiority. "I told you she would show tonight."

"You guys are betting on me now?" Keile sniffed, and stuck out her bottom lip. "I see I stayed away too long." She stood up, only to be gathered into a bone-crushing hug. "Hey, Terri, I need those ribs," she protested.

"That's what happens when you forget about your friends." Terri loosened her hold. "I've missed your quick wit," she claimed gruffly, and released Keile, then withdrew her wallet from her pocket and tossed a crisp one-dollar bill at her sister. "That ought to shut your ugly mug up."

"At least it's not as ugly as yours." Jo made a great show of kissing the dollar bill.

"I don't know how you've been able to put up with the Boopsy twins all these years," Keile said to Susan, then rubbed Terri's buzz cut. "Nice 'do, I didn't realize you were military now."

Terri jerked her head away with a mock scowl. "Thanks, I think." She pulled out a chair and sat down. Her androgynous features and lean face went well with the new hairstyle.

"Keile, you know I only put up with them because they're pretty handy around the house." Susan gave her partner a sly sideways glance, her blue eyes twinkling.

"Thanks, honey. Maybe we should go into the construction business since we're so handy," Jo retorted sarcastically.

"What a great idea," Keile said with feigned enthusiasm. "Hmm." She put a finger to her chin. "Wait! I've got a name. You could call it Twin Construct."

Each sister folded her arms over her chest, and shot Keile identical glares. She laughed and pointed at them. "You guys better stop that if you don't want to look alike," she taunted.

Jo grabbed her chest. "That hurt."

"You? What about me?" Terri made a pitiful face and sniffed. "You'd better take it back, Keile."

"I'm sorry, it must have been hunger talking," Keile said solemnly before tossing a napkin at Terri's head. "Wipe your eyes." Her grin faltered when Terri deftly caught the napkin and threw it at an unsuspecting Jo. "Hey, you weren't supposed to do that," she protested.

"You're not helping, Keile," Susan said in her middle school teacher voice as she reached out and intercepted the missile.

Keile shrugged an apology as Dani showed up. "Hey, you," Keile said with a smile. "What happened to Carla?"

Dani's lips tightened for a second. "Something came up at the last minute. But she wanted to make sure you got this." She placed an attractively wrapped package in front of Keile.

"Thanks…I think." Keile shook the package gingerly while eyeing her friend, noting the twinkling in her blue eyes that always denoted trouble.

"What have we here?" Susan leaned forward for a closer look.

"A token of appreciation from a very grateful mother." Dani feigned surprise when everyone turned their attention her way. "You mean Keile didn't tell you about her good deed?" She turned to Keile with a smirk. "Don't tell me you already forgot about your son?"

Keile sighed, realizing Dani wasn't about to let the matter drop. "It was nothing," she insisted.

"Son?" Susan looked from Keile to Dani. "What gives?"

"Our good friend Keile played mom to a lost child this morning." Dani grinned. "I wish you could have seen her with him. She was so...maternal."

When everyone looked her way, Keile squirmed. She hated being the center of attention. "You lookin' at me?" she asked in a threatening tone while pointing a thumb to her own chest. The mobster impersonation provided the hoped-for distraction, and she relaxed when everyone laughed.

Lynn Thompson, a tall, attractive African American woman, greeted everyone warmly, then bent to kiss Terri on the lips. She picked up Terri's drink and drained it. "I'm starving," she groaned, plopping into the vacant seat between Terri and Keile.

"Looks like you're thirsty, too." Keile smiled, and passed Lynn the remains of her margarita. "All the munchies are gone, but we're about to order."

"I think Keile should open the present," Dani said after they made their selections.

Keile nodded. Carefully undoing the wrapping paper, she found a small photo of Buster in a wooden frame and a gold embossed thank you card. Keile was touched by the gift, but knew better than to let Dani know. The emotions brought on by her encounter with Buster were still too raw to withstand teasing. "His name is Kyle, but he'll always be Buster to me," she said softly, then cleared her throat. "He thanks me for saving him and his mom from disaster. And by the way, I learned how to put a toddler in one of those swing contraptions if anybody needs to know."

"Be sure to put it on your resume," Terri joked.

Keile sneaked another look at the photograph. The shot had been taken in a professional studio with the prerequisite fake seasonal background. Kyle's hair was shorter, without the curls that had tickled her chin when he rested his head against her chest. *Why am I so drawn to him?* She had no time for anyone in her life beyond Can. Especially not a cute tyke and his equally cute mother with the beautiful smile. She placed the paper on top of the photo and returned her attention to the conversation, readily agreeing that she wanted Jo to buy her a ticket to a Hexagon show scheduled for next weekend.

Chapter Three

The next morning, Keile's sleep was interrupted much too soon by a wet nose and doggie breath. "Can, a few more minutes," she pleaded groggily, and turned away from the edge of the bed.

Can barked twice and nudged the back of Keile's head. Then he ran to the utility room, got his leash and returned to the bedroom. Dropping the leash on the bed, he sat beside the bed and whined.

Keile moaned, pushed off the covers and rolled out of the bed. "Okay, okay," she grumbled at her excited dog. "Give me ten minutes to get myself together." She stretched, then wandered to the bathroom. As she brushed her teeth, she gave thanks she'd refrained from sharing the last two pitchers of margaritas. She pulled on her running clothes, stretched out her tight muscles, then raced Can to the front door.

A cold front had blown in the night before, and the brisk,

cool wind was incentive to start the run at a fast pace. As her feet rhythmically hit the pavement of her quiet neighborhood streets, Keile's mind turned to Kyle. She wondered how he was doing after yesterday's adventure. Whatever he was doing, he was probably chained to his mother's side. That's what she would do if he were her kid.

Giving in to a whim, Keile changed directions and headed to the park. She didn't expect to see her little friend or any other children at the playground—it was early and the air was too chilly for most outdoor activities. She'd be satisfied to pass by the swings and recall his squeals of joy.

Once Can realized where they were headed, he picked up his pace. When she came to the bench she'd shared with Kyle's mom, she paused, staring at the weather-worn gray wood. As she replayed the moment she'd made the connection between Kyle and his mom, she could only smile. What a goof she'd been, acting as if Kyle's mom needed her to certify motherhood status. She of all people should know mother and child didn't have to resemble each other to be related. There was as little resemblance between her, with her light brown skin and dark hair, and her fair-skinned, blond mother as there was between Kyle and his mom.

Giving the bench one last glance, Keile allowed Can to lead her down the path to the open field where unleashed dogs were allowed. She laughed when he took off at full speed, galloping across the field like some crazed kangaroo.

"Keile, over here."

Spotting the short, muscular man waving from the other side of the field, she returned the wave and headed in Steve's direction. Despite the cold, he was dressed in only a long-sleeve T-shirt that molded to his muscles and sweatpants. She guessed the large cup of coffee he was carrying kept him warm.

Steve's smile reached his light blue eyes. "This is kind of late for you isn't it? Usually you're leaving when I get here."

"Give me a break. It's the first Sunday off I've allowed myself in months." Keile covered a yawn. "Sorry. Stayed out late but Can made it clear being let out back wasn't good enough for him."

“As usual I lost the coin toss, so I got the honor of walking Buzz and picking up bagels. Speaking of bagels, I’d better go and get Charles his bagels before they run out. He sulks if I come home with only my favorite kind.”

“You forget I’ve worked with Charles. He doesn’t seem the type to sulk.”

He gave her a pointed look, then winked. “At home he’s a different person.”

“TMI.” Keile laughed, and nudged Steve with her shoulder when he looked affronted. “Tell him I said hello.”

“Will do.” He returned the nudge, put two fingers in his mouth and whistled for Buzz, a large golden retriever. “I’ll see you around.”

With his favorite playmate gone, Can trotted to Keile’s side, sat down and looked at her expectantly. “Oh, so now you’re ready to go, huh?” She patted his head and clipped on his leash. “I’m ready for some breakfast myself.” They set off at an easy pace, retracing their steps that led them by the empty playground. Feeling silly, Keile said a silent goodbye to Kyle and his beautiful mom.

Chapter Four

Keile drove to her office early Monday morning, eager to return to some degree of normalcy. She had woken up with Kyle and—if she was honest—his mother on her mind. Work had always been a good outlet for channeling her energy, and she planned to use it today.

She pulled into the parking lot of the four-building complex, one of which housed Planning Associates where she was employed. Keile's specialty was creating interactive computer queries that allowed the firm's clients to analyze and map data. She'd worked on projects ranging from new housing developments to planning for additional lanes on an interstate.

Walking up the three flights of stairs to reach her office, she weeded out any thoughts unrelated to work. Once she was in her neatly ordered cubicle, she stowed her soft-sided briefcase in the long, bi-level file cabinet which fit neatly under a section of her desk. She pulled out the tall back, swivel chair in front of the computer and proceeded to log into the company computer system and access the list of tasks that had been set aside while she'd worked on the high-profile Johnstone project.

"Hey, Keile, what's up?"

Keile swiveled her chair and took in the disheveled appearance of the short, stocky woman in front of her. Sam's clothes were wrinkled and her short, brown hair was standing on end as if she'd repeatedly run her fingers through it. "What you'd do, Sam, sleep here?"

"Had to." Sam Paxton covered a yawn. "Sorry. It was the only way to finish up my part of that new development project before starting my vacation."

"Why did you do that?" she asked, surprised. "John and I made arrangements for me to help out while you're on vacation. I made a note to check in with him this morning."

Sam's thin lips tightened. "Did Rick know about this?"

"Of course. I always keep him informed about projects that may take up a chunk of my time."

"Then I guess he has better things for you to do with your time," Sam replied dryly. "I was told in no uncertain terms to have my part finished before I left."

Keile frowned. "Then the deadline changed." She had worked under Rick Carswell's direct supervision for two of her seven years at Planning Associates, and had no complaints about him as a boss. "Someone should have told me. I would have come in this weekend and helped out."

"And that's why you weren't told," Sam mumbled under her breath. She squeezed Keile's shoulder. "Don't worry about it. I'm done and I'm going on vacation in..." She looked at the big sports watch on her right wrist. "I'll be on the way to the airport in three hours."

"Have a good time."

"No worry about that. Think about me lounging on a cruise ship while you're here slaving away," she added with a big grin.

"Rub it in, why don't you," Keile grumbled good-naturedly.

"I'll remember that when I take *my* vacation."

"Right," Sam said slowly, nodding. "I don't think you know what that word means, Keile. Maybe in another seven years you'll actually feel like you can be away from this place for a day. See ya."

"Yeah." Keile returned the wave absently, her mind stuck on her colleague's words. *She's right. Vacation isn't in my vocabulary.* She glanced around her cube, which was akin to a second home. *Neither is not working.* She'd practically lived in this space for seven years and it still looked unlived in. There wasn't one item in the cube that marked the space as hers. If she was fired today, all she would need to grab was her bag.

Her computer beeped, indicating a new message. With something close to relief, she focused her attention on answering the request for assistance, then immediately began working through the almost forgotten list of set-aside tasks. By the time she was more than halfway through the list she felt more like her old self—in control.

She was mentally checking off another item when the phone rang. "Hello. Keile Griffen speaking."

"Something came up and I need you to provide a series of maps for a presentation tomorrow," Rick said without preamble.

"No problem," she replied, reaching for a pad. No matter what the request was, she would do her best to fulfill it.

"I knew I could count on you, Keile." He proceeded to give her a list of the data items he wanted mapped. "I know I'm asking for a lot of information, but I need it done by five. This supersedes everything."

"You got it," Keile said with confidence. She was in her element, loving the thrill she got from taking what was thrown at her and returning a polished product. "Do you want paper copies, or should I send an electronic file?"

"Electronic. Thanks, Keile. Have Nicole track me down if you run into any problems. I'll be in meetings the rest of the day."

"Okay."

Keile closed her eyes briefly and visualized what she wanted the maps to look like, then fleshed out her notes. At four, when she was satisfied with the end product, she shot off an e-mail notification to Rick with the file attached, and called Nicole to let her know what she had done. She'd learned from a co-worker's mistake that it paid to cover all bases when it came to Rick.

Keile spent the next two hours clearing the list she'd been working on earlier. Rubbing her tired eyes, she decided it was time to head home.

"I'm glad you're still here," Tom Edwards said as he entered her cube. "I just noticed this in the department mailbox. I thought it might have to do with the project you've been working on all day." He handed her a large envelope. "It's from Charles Newman at JM Consult."

"Thanks for letting me know," she replied dryly, and accepted the mailer from one of her least favorite co-workers. Keile despised the way he used his good looks and boyish charm to get out of work. But that paled in light of his unofficial job as Office Crier. "I'll see you tomorrow."

"Right. Have a good evening."

Keile waited until his footsteps faded away to open the envelope. She gasped as she pulled out the large color photo of her, Kyle and Can. It had been taken when she was assisting Kyle with the juice box. Biting her bottom lip, she absorbed every detail of his intense expression. Without conscious thought, she stroked his cheek and remembered how soft his skin had felt.

What's happening to me? Feeling strangely vulnerable, Keile grabbed her bag and slipped the photo and note inside. As she walked through the mostly empty corridors to the stairwell, Keile wondered how Charles had come by the photo. In the ten months she'd been taking Can to the park, she'd only ever run into Steve. Descending the three flights of stairs, she put the whole thing down to a bizarre coincidence.

Once settled in her older model Jeep and feeling more in control, she removed the note, gave it a quick scan and set it aside. Truth is stranger than fiction, she thought. An aspiring photographer who just happened to be an acquaintance of Charles and Steve was responsible for the photo. They'd seen it in their buddy's developing tray and recognized her, of course. Charles had sent the photo to her office because neither he nor Steve knew her home address. *Really* bizarre *coincidence*, she thought as she exchanged the note for the photo. *About as bizarre as my reaction.*

Looking for clues, Keile lost herself in a study of the two faces. She was forced to admit Dani had been right—the tyke did look like her. Was that why she couldn't stop thinking about him? *Who are you, and why do we look so much alike?* She released a pent-up breath, replaced the photo and started the car. *No*, she thought as she backed out of the parking space, *the real question is why knowing about him matters so much to me.*

An exuberant Can greeted her at the door. He growled deep in his throat when Keile squatted down and gave him a two-handed rub. Eventually, that wasn't enough and he tried to crawl in her lap, knocking her over.

"Can." She laughed and pushed him off her. "Not on my good work clothes, boy. Let me change and we'll go for a walk." Keile propped her briefcase against the small table near the door and went to change.

Ten minutes later, without thinking, Keile chose the route leading to the park, the long way that took her past the playground. She knew Kyle wouldn't be there, but passing by the swing made what they'd shared seem more real. She had never believed in fate, but she had no other explanation for the connection she felt. She watched the streetlights reflect off the metal of the empty swing set and sighed.

An impatient Can strained against his leash. Jerked out of her musings, she allowed him to drag her to the doggie park. Setting him free, Keile glanced around, almost expecting her brown-haired cherub to appear. A part of her had come to believe meeting Kyle was the answer to… *What? The answer to what?*

Eventually the cold seeped through her coat. Keile whistled

for Can, ready to get away from her thoughts. "Jeez, look at me," she told him. "I'm hanging out at the park hoping for a glimpse of a baby that isn't mine. If that's not sick, what is?"

Yup, I'm certifiable. She wondered if she should begin giving some credence to fate and destiny. It would certainly help explain her sudden fascination with babies and playgrounds—things she'd never known she'd wanted.

As she walked up the driveway to her house, her cell phone buzzed. Unclipping her phone, she glanced at the caller's name. "Hey, Dani." She smiled, grateful for the distraction.

"Are you busy?"

Keile frowned in reaction to Dani's subdued tone. "Just getting back from walking Can. What's up?"

"I really need to talk to somebody," Dani said quietly, then cleared her throat.

"I can be there in fifteen minutes tops."

"Thanks, I'd appreciate it. And I'll even feed you dinner since I'm sure your fridge is empty."

"Cool. See ya."

Doling out two tablespoons of canned dog food, she wondered if Dani and Carla were fighting again. The few times Dani had called needing to talk had involved some minor disagreement. Although Keile had never been in a relationship, she was good at listening and giving common sense advice that, although Dani rarely followed it, seemed to give her some level of comfort.

She smiled, remembering how she'd initially resisted Dani's friendly overtures. She had just purchased her home and in order to save money she had been doing some of the fix-up jobs by herself. It was after repeatedly running into Dani at the hardware store that she finally agreed to join her for coffee. Through Dani, she had subsequently met Jo and Terri, and their partners.

Getting into Dani's close-knit group of friends was one of the best things that had ever happened to her. They provided her companionship and taught her some home repair basics. More importantly, they pulled her out of the shell of isolation she existed in most of the time. She was a different person because of them—a better human being to her way of thinking.

Sixteen minutes later, Keile entered an old factory building which had been converted into luxury lofts in the past year. After showing her ID to the guard, she signed in, then headed for the fourth floor. Alerted by the guard, Dani was standing in the doorway. She gave Keile a pained smile and beckoned her inside.

Keile's insides churned as she took in her friend's red eyes and nose. She'd never known Dani to cry over her tiffs with Carla. She pulled Dani into her arms and held her tight. "It'll be okay," she whispered.

Dani took a shuddering breath and leaned into the offered comfort. "Carla broke up with me for good," she said hoarsely.

"I'm so sorry." Shocked, Keile stroked her friend's back. "Do you want to tell me about it?" she asked gently, leaning back to look into Dani's eyes. She was unsure how much help she could provide—the situation didn't lend itself to sensible advice.

"She…she says she's found her soul mate. How the hell can I compete with that?" She took a shuddering breath.

Keile maneuvered them to the sofa, sat down, and pulled her friend down next to her. "That's hard to deal with," she said, frustrated at being unable to offer any words of real comfort.

"I know we've been arguing more lately, but…" Dani broke off. "I didn't realize why till today. How could I be so oblivious to her seeing someone else?" She pressed her fingers against her eyes.

"Hey, come on, you've both been working different schedules," Keile pointed out. "That makes it harder to keep up with each other, right?"

"I should have known, Keile. My girlfriend falls in love with another woman, and I don't even see it," Dani said with disgust.

"Obviously she didn't want you to see it. Those petty fights she kept starting were probably meant to throw you off."

"They worked." Dani sniffed and wiped her eyes with the back of her hands. "And to think I almost felt guilty working all those extra hours. Some investigator I am. I feel so stupid. What will people think?"

It hit Keile that Dani was more upset about being seen as a fool than she was about the actual breakup. "You're not stupid. Let's face it, Carla's a good cop and she knows how to cover her tracks. Nobody else knew, did they?"

"I still feel like a fool," Dani groaned, pulling at her hair.

"But how's your heart holding up?"

"Bent, but not broken," Dani admitted. "I'm hurt I didn't see it coming, but not devastated. After what happened with Edan I never allowed myself to think Carla could be my forever. Maybe that's why she found someone else."

"There you go blaming everything on yourself," Keile said gently. "You're not all powerful, woman. Recently I've started to believe that sometimes we have to accept things happen for reasons we may never understand." Like her encounter with a lost child.

"So now you're getting philosophical on me, huh?" Dani sniffed, letting a small smile pull at her lips. "I don't know about you, but all this bawling has made me hungry. You up for lasagna?"

Keile nodded, relieved the heavy stuff was over for now. "Can is going to be so jealous when he smells it on my breath later."

"You can always take him a doggy bag. In fact, I insist you take some with you." Dani slung an arm around Keile's shoulder. "Thanks, pal."

"Anytime Dan, anytime."

Chapter Five

"Hang on, let me check." Gripping the receiver between her shoulder and her cheek, Keile dumped her overflowing recycle bin onto the floor. She grabbed the cardboard mailer and checked inside. "You were right, Charles," she said, studying the name on the colorful business card. "I overlooked it. I'll give him a call and see if he has any information on the child. Thanks." She hung up the phone and began replacing the paper littering the floor.

"You look like you lost something," Tom commented, standing in the opening of her cube.

She forced a smile as she met his inquisitive gaze. "What do you need, Tom?"

"Rick wants to meet at three about the Johnstone project." Tom stepped closer, eyeing the mess on the floor. "You know it's funny, I thought that project was done."

"It was," Keile replied as her mind raced through the 'End of

Project' memo Rick had approved the week before. There hadn't been any outstanding deliverables. Maybe they wanted additional work. "Did Rick mention anything else?"

Tom looked up, a sly smile on his face. "No, but he didn't look too thrilled. Maybe you didn't do as good a job as everyone thought."

Keile's jaw tightened. Normally she could ignore his snide comments, but today, when she was searching for important answers, she felt compelled to respond. "You're certainly entitled to *your* little opinion. Where are we meeting?"

"Rick's office. But I won't be there. It's not my mess."

You don't do enough work to make a mess. "Then I won't see you later." Keile's eyes blazed with anger as she watched him leave, wanting to wipe the smug look off his face. She knew as soon as he left he'd be spreading rumors about her professional reputation being in question. *Why the hell did Rick send Tom of all people?* Thoroughly disgusted, she finished clearing the mess off the floor.

Before she could pull out the Johnstone file, her phone rang. "Keile Griffen speaking. How may I help you?"

"Keile, it's Carla." Her tone was all business. "I received a call from Haydn Davenport today. You may remember rescuing her son last Saturday."

"Yes." Keile gripped the receiver. "I hope he's okay?"

"The boy is fine," Carla said quickly. "Ms. Davenport would like to thank you in person. She asked me to give you her number, and to tell you that her son has been asking about you and Can. Are you interested?"

Yes! "Uh…sure. I guess that would be okay. Let me grab my cell." Keile quickly keyed in the number. "Thanks for calling, Carla."

"Sure," she said slowly. "I wasn't sure you wanted to hear from me."

"About this I do," Keile said, responding to the tenseness she heard in Carla's voice. "About anything else…well, you know where my loyalty lies."

"Understood."

"Thanks again for calling." Sitting back, Keile stared at the new entry in her phone book. Maybe now she could get some answers. She didn't have to close her eyes to see Kyle's face, so like her own, as he'd looked at her with complete trust. Or the smile he so readily gave.

She remembered how the same smile coming from his mother had affected her. Keile shook her head. There was sure to be a Mr. Davenport who had rights to that particular smile.

At five minutes to three, Keile tucked the Johnstone project folder under her arm and slowly headed for Rick's office. For once she wasn't prepared for a meeting. Instead of spending her time reviewing the file, she'd let thoughts of Kyle, and to her chagrin, his mother, fill her head. *Too late now.* With effort, Keile cleared her head of personal issues, walked past Nicole's empty desk, and knocked on Rick's partially opened door.

He looked up without giving her his customary smile, and pointed to the round table. "Come on in and have a seat. I'll just be a few minutes."

Keile entered the large corner office without a word and took a seat. After opening the folder, she surreptitiously studied her boss. In appearance, Rick reminded her of Tom with the handsome blond looks and charming smile. In the ways that mattered to Keile, he was totally different. Although Rick was only in his early forties, his proven track record for completing projects on time and within budget had led to his fast rise in the firm. Periodically, Keile heard grumbles about Rick's management style, but since she'd never had any problems working with him, she attributed the complaints to sour grapes.

"I hope I didn't keep you waiting too long." Rick stood up from his desk and stretched his fit, medium-framed body. "Nicole's out today and I'm missing her administrative skills."

"That's okay." She forced a smile. "Tom mentioned you wanted to talk about the Johnstone project."

"One little detail surfaced this morning." Rick pulled out a chair, turned it around and straddled it.

"How?" Keile's stomach dropped as she fumbled through the project folder. "I thought we wrapped everything up last week. Especially after Mr. Johnstone called and thanked me."

"When was this?"

Keile reared back at his sharp tone. "Uh…late last Friday, after I, uh…sent them an additional program to help with some data conversion."

"Next time anything like this happens, I need to know right away." Rick's thin lips tightened in the semblance of a smile. "I look pretty stupid when my boss wants to talk to me about something I don't know anything about."

"Then I apologize," Keile said quickly. "I didn't mention it because it wasn't a big deal. It took me all of thirty minutes to complete, and it made the client happy." She hugged her stomach and tried to keep her voice impassive. "I thought for this project I had the leeway to do that."

"You're right, you did," Rick said, nodding. "And I'm not criticizing you for doing the extra work, Keile, but you should have given me a heads-up about the call from Mr. Johnstone. Because he's on personal terms with one of the partners, a call from him *is* a big deal."

She didn't know whether to be relieved that there wasn't a problem, or irritated that Rick thought there was. "I apologize for not knowing that."

"It's pretty common knowledge around here, but since you work so hard, you're forgiven." He smiled as if he'd made a joke. "In that same vein, the firm received a letter from Mr. Johnstone commending us on the quality of the work that we did for his company. Since he called you out specifically, I thought you might like to know a copy of that letter is going into your file and will weigh pretty heavily at bonus and review time."

She gave a nervous laugh. "I don't know what to say. I was just doing my job."

"When you work hard, people will eventually notice. Let that be a lesson for you, Keile. You never know who's watching you, so always put your best foot forward. It *will* take you places in this firm."

"I'll keep that in mind." Keile left Rick's office feeling off-balance. Her stomach was queasy, as if she'd just gotten off a roller-coaster ride that went from goat to heroine in sixty seconds. *Take note, self, never make Rick look stupid.*

"Just do it, Griffen," Keile said as she paced around the kitchen. She'd left work before six and taken Can for a long walk. Now it was time to call Haydn Davenport and she was afraid of sounding like an idiot. Nothing she'd practiced on the walk seemed right. Taking a deep breath, she dialed the number she'd committed to memory. Her heart caught in her throat when the phone was answered.

Keile felt a pang of regret at the male voice. She'd been right, there was a Mr. Davenport. "This is Keile Griffen. May I please speak with Haydn Davenport?"

"Sure, hang on a second."

Keile heard his footsteps resounding on a hardwood floor. She heard a muted conversation before a female voice came over the line.

"Hi. Is this Keile from the park?"

"Yes it is," Keile replied, losing all nervousness at the excitement in Haydn Davenport's voice. "I got a message from Carla Hanson that Buster wants to see me."

"Buster?"

"Oh, sorry." Keile gave an embarrassed laugh. "That's what I named Kyle during our little adventure."

Haydn let out an infectious laugh. "That suits him," she declared. "I really appreciate you getting back with me. Kyle has been driving us crazy wanting to go look for you. He now thinks that every woman he sees walking a black dog, no matter the size, will be you."

"I have to confess, I looked for him a couple of times," she felt safe to say.

"Is there any possibility of getting the two of you together tomorrow morning?"

"I would really like that," Keile replied, unable to keep the excitement out of her voice. "Maybe we could meet at the park for old time's sake?"

"He'll love that. He and his dad hang out on Saturday mornings while I go into my office. Would ten be a good time for you to meet them?"

Keile dismissed another irrational pang of regret. There had never been anything between her and Haydn but gratitude. "I'll meet them by the playground. I'm kind of partial to the swings now."

"Kyle will be thrilled to see you again. I'm sorry I'll miss the reunion. Be prepared to be mauled," Haydn joked.

"I look forward to it," Keile said sincerely. "I'll see Kyle and his dad tomorrow then."

"I guess I should tell you his name is Marcus. If anything comes up, you can give him a call."

"I'll be there." Keile had too much riding on the meeting to miss it. She switched off the phone and set it down on the small kitchen table.

Making her way to the living room, she picked up the framed photo of her and Kyle in the park from its honored place on the mantle above the fireplace. "I'll see you tomorrow, kiddo." Keile didn't even castigate herself, this time, for believing there was a connection between them. Now, hopefully, she would be able to figure out what it was.

"So?" Marcus Davenport prodded as soon as Haydn hung up the phone. He'd stopped by on his way home from work to check on Kyle, as he'd done every day that week.

"She's meeting you guys by the playground. She sounded excited at seeing Kyle again." She gave her brother a fond look. She was long used to his presumption of the right to butt into her life, something he'd done from the moment her parents had brought him home and explained she had a new brother. As Kyle's father, and after her move from California to Georgia, he took a heightened interest in her life.

"Well, we both know he'll be overjoyed to see her again. Which is kind of strange."

"You wouldn't say that if you'd seen them. They looked like they belonged together. And the way she handed him to me was… It was if she knew what a precious gift she was giving me. Of course," she admitted with a rueful smile, "it wasn't one of my saner moments." She kept to herself the disconcerting sense of recognition she'd felt when she looked into Keile's eyes for the first time.

"If you say so," he said, looking doubtful. "I've got to run, but I'll be back tomorrow." He said goodbye to Kyle, who was busy playing with his toys, and ruffled Haydn's hair. "Nine sharp. I promise."

Haydn was cleaning the remains of Kyle's dinner off of his face when her roommate, Edan, ventured into the kitchen. "Hey. You getting settled in?"

"Yeah. I can't believe you and Marcus beat me here by over a month. Especially when it was my idea for us all to move to Seneca." She pulled a Diet Coke from the fridge and leaned against the counter.

"Don't blame me." Haydn gave her friend a fond look. They had known each other since their freshmen year in college, and Edan had been there for her after her world collapsed. "Your company is the one that delayed transferring you back. And you know you like already having a place to stay."

Edan's lean, sharply etched face was transformed by a grin. "Okay, you got me." She smoothed back her short dark brown hair which was normally spiked on the top. "Thanks for that and the support. I think I'm going to need lots of support."

Haydn waved away her thanks. "I owe you."

"No, you don't." Edan's dark brown eyes glittered with intensity. "We helped each other. It's like that bumper sticker says, friends don't owe friends."

"You made that up," she replied, crinkling her nose. Kyle strained against her arms and she put him down.

"He seems fully recovered." Edan gazed at Kyle with affection. "Thank goodness for the woman who found him."

"Yeah, we lucked out," Haydn said softly. She could almost feel the warm, comforting touch again. "She's agreed to meet Marcus and Kyle at the park tomorrow."

"That's so nice. Hey, was she cute?"

Haydn rolled her eyes. "I did have other things on my mind at the time."

Edan shook her head and sighed. "I see I got here just in time. You've been on the shelf too long when you can't tell if a woman is cute or not. Don't worry though, I have just the cure."

"I don't have a disease and I really don't like that smirk on your face," Haydn said, frowning. "It always means trouble. Usually for me."

"Never." Edan stretched her thin, five foot-six-inch body. "You'll like the band we're going to see tomorrow. And before the night is over, I will have taught you how to recognize a cute woman."

"Then I can save you the trouble. I know how to recognize a cute woman. Remember the two *cute* women Marcus set me up with? You know, the ones who were appalled that I had fallen for the patriarchal line and reproduced?"

Edan waved a hand dismissively. "I can't believe you took that to heart. What do they know? There are plenty of women who would want you and Kyle."

Haydn looked at Kyle. "We do pretty good on the shelf. I don't need another woman breaking my heart."

"Okay. Uh, come to the concert for me then. Please?"

"You promise no lame attempts to find me someone?"

"I promise." Edan grimaced. "Only because I'll be too busy looking for a certain someone for myself."

"I can live with that," she said grudgingly. "But you have to find the babysitter."

"Way ahead of you. Marcus has you covered. And after last week's mishap, you don't have to worry he double booked." She drained the can. "Time for the second round of unpacking."

"Wait! You just got here," Haydn called after her departing friend, "how can you possibly have made plans?"

"Hey, you're looking at a woman on a mission."

Haydn watched her leave, shaking her head. She had a feeling her life was about to be poked with a hot stick.

Chapter Six

By nine thirty the next morning, Keile could hardly stand still. She grabbed her coat, called Can, and they set out for the park. The temperature was cooler than it had been a week ago but, the sun was shining and the wind wasn't much of a factor. Keile tried to set a leisurely pace, but for once, Can was not interested in every tree or bush on the route, and he practically dragged her along in his efforts to get to the park. Once there, he resisted Keile's attempt to steer him toward the playground.

When he whined, Keile relented. "We'll stay here for now, but at five till ten we need to go find Buster," she told her pet firmly, releasing his leash.

Can shot off at full speed. His tongue hung to one side, and there was a definite bounce in his step. As usual, his kangaroo impression brought a smile to Keile's face. She gave silent thanks to Jo for badgering her until she agreed to adopt Can. He'd added a dimension to her life that she hadn't known was missing. "Maybe I should have named you Joey," she said aloud.

She was brought to attention by a voice etched in her memory. Keile whipped her head around and saw a small child running in her direction screaming "Mama" at the top of his lungs. She ran to intercept him, dropped to her knees and held her arms wide open. Kyle careened into her arms.

Keile's chest grew tight. She hadn't imagined their connection. "Oh, Buster," she whispered and dropped a kiss on top of his head.

"Mama," he said and arched back to look in her face. "Mama." He put a hand on her cheek as if checking to see if she were real.

She was completely captivated. "No. I'm Keile." She pointed to her chest. "Keile," she repeated slowly.

He shook his head. "Mama," he said, poking her chest.

She just laughed, and anchoring Kyle in her arms, she stood in one fluid motion as Kyle's father approached.

"Where are my manners? I'm Keile Griffen." Her eyes widened as she got a good look at the tall, attractive, light-skinned African American man. He couldn't be anyone other than Kyle's father, plainly. The strangest part was that anyone seeing the three of them couldn't be faulted for thinking they were closely related. "Uh… Wow!" *So this is Haydn's husband. Kyle is going to be a hunk when he grows up.* She gave a nervous laugh, positioned Kyle on her hip and held out her hand. "You—"

"Look a whole lot like you," he finished for her, shaking her hand. "Funny. You always hear you have a twin roaming around somewhere." He put a finger on his chin and gave her an appraising glance. "I have to tell you, I always expected you to be male."

Keile laughed. "Sorry. Would it help if I said I see where Buster gets his good looks?" *And his size,* she thought, assessing his broad shoulders and muscular build. At a couple of inches over six feet, he would draw a lot of attention with his stature and easy smile.

"It's a good start, darlin'," he drawled. "I guess I should say that I see you got my good looks, too. It's uncanny how much we look alike. You're not thirty-two, are you?"

"Twenty-eight."

"And I bet you weren't born in Texas either."

"Sorry. I've never even been there."

Marcus shrugged. "I guess it's just one of those things you take at *face* value."

Keile groaned. "Ha, ha. Are you always this entertaining?"

"Always. But now I have to give you my heartfelt thanks for saving my butt last Saturday," he said seriously. "I was supposed to be on duty but something came up and we used one of Kyle's other babysitters. We still can't figure out how he got out of the locked gate much less made it down here."

Keile dropped a kiss on the child's forehead. "I honestly can't take any credit. He found me." Her voice was filled with affection. "Is it okay if we go sit on the bench for a little bit? I see my dog is involved in an intense game of tag." She pointed in the direction of a group of dogs who were racing up and down the field.

"Sure. Not that there's much of a choice," Marcus said, clearly amused. "I don't think he's ready to let you go yet." He reached over and ruffled his son's curls.

"We're even then. I'm not ready to let him go either." Keile breathed in the scent of baby shampoo and outdoors. *It's almost frightening how right it feels to have him in my arms again.*

"I'm curious why we've never run into each other. Kyle and I have been coming here regularly for the past month."

"I'm usually here a lot earlier on Saturdays."

"And you probably don't hang out at the swings, eh?" he guessed.

"If I had known what I would find, I might have." Keile rested her chin against Kyle's curls.

"The two of you look good together."

"Thanks." Keile smiled proudly. "I believe Kyle is *my* twin. When that egg split in two, one really split." She laughed at her own pun.

"So I'm your daddy, too?" He sniffed, playfully wiping his eyes. "My long lost fertilized egg has come back to me," he said in falsetto.

Keile suppressed a grin. "That would explain my twisted sense of humor." She put the back of her hand against her forehead and let loose a dramatic sigh. "Daddy, I'm home," she said, doing a lousy impression of a Texas drawl.

"Dada," Kyle repeated, and pointed to his father. "Mama," he said, pointing to Keile, and grinned.

"No, Keile. Come on, you can say that, can't you, sweetie? *Keile*."

"Mama," he said with a determined jut of his chin.

Marcus gave a shout of laughter. "I tried to warn you. He's my son, but even I recognize that stubborn streak of his."

"Determined," Keile said and wrinkled her nose. "Determination is a positive trait."

"You sound just like his mother. Have you been talking behind my back?" He put his hands on his hips and sniffed loudly.

"Nope. I met your wife only very briefly last Saturday. I daresay she probably doesn't remember me that well. She had other things on her mind at the time."

"Wife?" he sputtered. "Is that what Haydn told you?"

"Not exactly," she said slowly. "I guess I did that assumption thing. You know, you're the dad, she's the mom, so that led my feeble brain to husband and wife."

"Only in Alabama," he said cryptically. "You're not from there are you?" he asked as an afterthought.

"I was born and raised here in Seneca," Keile responded, giving Marcus a quizzical look. "They don't allow people to get married anywhere else but Alabama anymore?"

"Not if you're brother and sister."

Keile's mouth formed an O, but the sound never quite made it past her vocal chords.

He laughed. "We get that reaction all the time. And before you start thinking all sorts of twisted things, I'm adopted. So when Haydn decided she wanted to have a child, I was an obvious choice. Strange relations, huh?"

She closed her mouth and nodded. "Some might see it that way," she added quickly.

"Ah, a diplomat."

Keile smiled. "I figure I should be nice if I want to see Buster, uh…Kyle, again."

"I don't think you have to worry. Kyle will see to that," he assured her.

Can chose that moment to join them. Kyle let out a joyful cry and scrambled down from Keile's lap before she could catch him. He threw his arms around Can as if he were an old friend. Can, seemingly resigned, sat down on his haunches and calmly accepted the onslaught of affection.

Keile joined them, stroking Can's back. "What a good boy," she said, praising Can for good behavior under unusual circumstances.

"Do, do." Kyle turned to grin at Keile.

"Aren't you the smart one?" Keile chucked him under his chin.

"Mama."

"Keile," she corrected automatically.

"Hey, daughter, it seems you can be stubborn too."

Keile snorted. "Determined, remember?"

"Right." Marcus tapped his forehead. "What *was* I thinking?" he asked, rolling his eyes.

"Yeah, what was your daddy thinking?" Keile reached for Kyle and scrunched up her nose. "I think we have a situation here," she said and carefully handed off the ripe-smelling child.

"And me without a diaper. I gotta run, but let's do this again."

"Definitely." They quickly exchanged numbers and Keile reluctantly bid them farewell.

Chapter Seven

Later that evening, with great anticipation, Keile reached for her favorite colorfully-striped, button-down shirt. She was meeting her friends at Hsu, a new Japanese restaurant. Afterward they would head a few blocks to Eddie's Heaven where their favorite semi-local band was playing. Her cell phone rang as she was fastening the last button. "Hello, you've reached Griffen's House of Pleasure. How may I service you?"

"What's your specialty today?"

"Well ma'am, today's special is 'name your own special'," Keile replied, keeping her voice deep and smooth.

"Oh my," Dani twittered. "You really should start a phone sex operation. You'd have more business than you could handle."

"I'll keep that in mind when I get downsized," she said in her normal voice. "If you don't want the special, Dan, what can I do you for?"

Dani exhaled. "I need a huge, huge favor. Through lesbian gossip central, I found out today that not only will Carla and soul mate be at Eddie's, but, get this, Edan and her new love will be there as well."

Shit! Keile had already heard from Terri that Edan had recently moved back to town. What she hadn't heard about was the presence of a lover. "And you want to do something else, right?" Keile guessed, stifling her momentary pang of disappointment at not getting to see the band. "I'm up for dinner and a movie. If you're nice, I'll even consent to go to a coffee shop afterward."

"Thanks, but I'm stronger than that…I think." Her laugh sounded hollow. "I'm gonna go, but you have to promise you won't let me do anything stupid, like go home with anybody, no matter what I say."

"Anybody as in Carla or Edan?" Keile felt like she was stumbling blindly, unsure of what to say or where the conversation was heading. Dealing with ex-lovers was way beyond her know-how. She didn't think now was the time to tell Dani that she'd never had a lover, let alone an ex-lover.

"Anybody as in any live body," Dani replied, her tone serious. "I know this sounds horrible, but I'm just afraid I might, you know, get depressed, start drinking and do something dumb. One ex is bad enough, but two is a little much."

"All the more reason to skip the show. Come on, Dani, Hexagon will be back in town in six months. We can see them then."

"I have to do this. If I don't show up, everyone will assume what the reason is. And let's face it, they'd be right."

But I don't care about everyone, I care about you, she thought with startling clarity and realized just how much their friendship had come to mean to her. "Okay, if that's what you need to do," she agreed reluctantly. "I solemnly swear to save you from yourself. In fact, I'll be the designated driver." She would definitely need to keep a clear head tonight.

"Even better. Come get me as soon as you can," Dani ordered. "I want to get to the restaurant early and have a drink."

"Will do." Keile closed the phone and tucked her shirt into her black jeans. Hopefully, she could talk Dani out of going to see Hexagon after Dani had a few drinks in her.

When Keile and Dani arrived at Hsu, they had to fight their way through the loud crowd to reach the bar, set off to the left from the dining room.

"How was the rest of your week?" Keile asked, once they'd positioned themselves along a wall facing the front door, drinks in hand.

Dani shrugged, looking down at the dark wood floor. "Yesterday was better than the day before, and today should be better than yesterday. I'll let you know after I see Carla with my replacement."

"You can't be replaced." Almost as soon as the words were out of her mouth, she spotted the couple in question entering the restaurant. "Uh…Dani, that's going to happen a lot sooner than you think."

"Maybe I should have started with something stronger," Dani muttered before taking a healthy sip of wine. "Let's change the subject to you. How's your day been so far?"

Keile lit up and she smiled. "Good. I got to see Kyle again. I really like that kid and lucky for me, he feels the same way."

Dani managed a smile. "How did this happen? He didn't escape again, did he?"

"No, I got his mother's number from… Well, I gave her a call. I met Kyle and his dad at the park. I got to tell you, his dad is hysterical."

Dani almost choked on her wine. "She's married to a man? I would have sworn she was family. Damn, my gaydar needs adjustment. It figures, why should *that* be any different from the rest of my life," she added, staring into her glass.

"Give yourself a break." Keile put an arm around her friend's shoulder. "Let me reassure you Marcus Davenport is Kyle's father but he is not Haydn Davenport's husband. I'll fill you in later," she said when Dani gave her a confused look. "The rest of the group is here." She pushed away from the wall and gave a quick wave. "Come on, it looks like we may be able to miss sighting Carla and Company."

"At least for now." Dani took a deep breath. "I'm ready."

They joined the rest of the group and exchanged hugs and greetings. After a five-minute wait, they were shown to their table. Keile kept an eye out for Carla as they walked through the maze of mostly occupied white tablecloth-covered tables. She was concerned not only about Dani's feelings but Jo's as well. Jo was very protective of her friends and she had been very vocal about her view of Carla following the breakup. She gave a brief thought to giving Susan a heads-up about Carla's presence.

Keile knew she was too late when she saw a scowl appear on Jo's face almost as soon as they sat down. Carla and her new lover were seated in a small booth within sight of their table. It looked like Jo was about to get up when Dani put a hand on her arm and shook her head. She leaned over and whispered something that made the glare Jo aimed at Carla less fierce.

Keile breathed a sigh of relief when Jo nodded and picked up the thick book-like menu. She mouthed 'good job' to Dani before removing her silverware from the cloth napkin. Once they placed their orders, Keile relieved the slight unease that had settled over the group by casually mentioning she'd met her boyfriend at the park. After laughing at their open-mouthed expressions, she explained about Kyle and his parents.

"What about the mom? What did you think of her?" Susan wanted to know.

Keile felt her cheeks heat up at the innocent question. Finding out Haydn didn't have a husband had given her ideas. "She ended up working late so I didn't get a chance to see her again. But after spending time with Kyle, I bet she's a great mom."

"From what Dani said, you were a pretty good mom yourself," Terri said with a mischievous grin. "When do we get to meet this son of yours?"

"Better yet, tell us what the father looks like? There was something sparkling in your eyes when you talked about him,"

Dani teased.

"I noticed it, too," Jo added. "Are you being lured to the dark side?" She wiggled her eyebrows suggestively, causing a round of laughter.

"Funny." Keile rolled her eyes. "One, he's gay, and two, it would be like going out with myself. He looks a lot like me, only taller and maler."

"That would certainly explain why your boy looks just like you," Dani said.

"Do you think you'll see your boy again?" Lynn smiled. "Seems like you're sweet on him."

"I certainly hope so."

After spending an hour and a half enjoying good food and conversation, they walked a couple of blocks to the club. Eddie's Heaven was in the basement of an older two-story building. It wasn't billed as a gay club, but on the nights when Hexagon was in town, the audience was mostly lesbian. The bar and patio area were packed with women eagerly waiting for the opening of the doors to the music room.

"Are you okay?" Keile asked Dani as they stood at the back of the long line at the bar. She had noticed the way her steps had lagged as they made their way to the club. "Just say the word and we're out of here."

Dani nodded. "Just remember your promise, okay?"

"You bet." Keile draped an arm over Dani's shoulder and looked around, taking in the special energy only a crowd of women-loving-women seemed to be able to create.

"See anything you like?"

"They all look like couples."

"Just because they're standing together doesn't mean they're a couple," Dani explained. "Look at us, we're standing here talking but we're not a couple."

Keile dropped her arm quickly. "I hadn't thought of that. You think I'm naïve, don't you?"

"No dear, I *know* you're naïve." Dani gave Keile a fond smile.

"Like a babe in the woods," Jo chimed in. "When was the last time you had a date?"

"Hey, why are we talking about me?" Keile almost squirmed, thinking about having to admit in public that she'd never been on a date. Taking an extra class load, while working two jobs hadn't left her much time for socializing in college. And after she'd graduated, her attention had turned to saving for a home. *I never did plan for beyond that.*

"Because you're so cute when you get flustered," Dani said with a laugh, and squeezed one of Keile's cheeks.

"You'd better be careful or I just might forget my promise," Keile threatened.

"Now that sounds interesting." Jo rubbed her hands together. "Do tell." She turned her attention to Dani.

Keile folded her arms across her chest and gave Dani a sly smile. "Your turn."

The announcer's voice came over the intercom to announce the doors would be open shortly, and that people would be seated according to the last name of the person who ordered the tickets.

As they followed the crowd toward the open area in front of the music room, Keile once again spotted Carla. This time she was able to get a better look at the petite brunette holding Carla's hand. Keile knew she was biased, but she couldn't see why Carla would give up Dani for this one. No accounting for taste. She gave the brunette a more thorough once-over and still couldn't see the attraction.

Keile stole a sideways look at Dani to see if her friend had noticed the couple. She was pleased to see Dani bent over saying something to Susan. Keile subtly shifted her position to block the couple from Dani's sight.

Having also caught sight of Carla, Terri came to stand next to Keile to further ensure that Dani would be able to get into the room without seeing the tall cop. "What does she see in her?" she whispered to Keile.

"I was wondering that myself. Must be some kind of butch

– femme thing that I didn't know she was into."

"You and me both. I wonder how long that was going on behind Dani's back." Terri caught Carla's eye and gave her a baleful stare, which Carla returned.

"She's not worth it." Keile grabbed a bristling Terri's arm. "We're here to have fun."

Luckily Jo's name was called, and Terri nodded. "Let's go then."

Keile kept hold of Terri's arm as they made their way through the crowd to the check-in point. *Can this evening get any worse?*

The music room was shaped like a movie theater, raised stage against the front wall surrounded by a small dance floor. The rest of the floor sloped upward, over half of which was filled with tables. The remaining floor space was covered with rows of chairs. Jo picked a table close to the front, giving them quick access to the dance floor.

Keile took a chair next to Dani and scanned the crowd for Edan. Jo nudged her.

"So Keile, show us the one woman you think is totally hot."

"What?" As she turned to face Jo, she heard a loud gasp from beside her. The stark look of anguish stamped on Dani's face had to mean Edan was somewhere nearby.

Dani looked up and met Keile's eyes before lowering her head, letting the blond strands cascade over her face like a wall.

Keile grasped Dani's clenched fist and gently rubbed it until she loosened her grip. *I should have insisted we stay away.* Frustrated, she leaned back in her chair and tried for casual as she again scanned the room. Although she'd only seen Edan in photographs, this time she spotted her right away. She was seated at a nearby table and unfortunately in their line of sight. Edan's dark brown hair was shorter and spiked on the top, drawing attention to a lean face that was more striking than beautiful. Realizing she was staring, Keile turned her attention back to Dani. "Are you sure you don't want to leave?" she asked softly.

Dani took a shaky breath and raised her head. She hooked her hair behind her ears before saying, "I'm okay. It was just…seeing her." She picked up her drink and drained it. "I'll need a couple of these to dull the ache, so flag down one of the cute servers."

"Not a problem." Keile met Terri's quizzical gaze and subtly cocked her head in Edan's direction. She nodded when Terri's eyes grew wide with surprise.

Terri nudged her sister and soon everyone at the table was aware of who was sitting across the room. Keile waved down a server.

After she left with their orders, Jo took Dani's hand. "I'm sorry this is such a rough night for you. If you need to leave, I'm with you one hundred percent."

Dani cleared her throat and blinked back tears. "Thanks, Jo," she said, her voice husky. "I want to stick this out. Besides," she added with a shaky smile, "we can't leave, we just ordered drinks and we have the best seats in the house."

"Your call." Jo let go of her hand and balanced her chair on the back legs. "Come on now, Keile, it's time for you to pick the woman you're taking home tonight."

"Wait," Keile protested, holding up her hand. "I thought the only requirement was that they be on my hot list. Nobody said anything about taking anybody home."

"Let me rephrase it then," Jo said, giving Keile a wink. "Which of these lovely ladies make you burn?"

"There you go again changing semantics. Just because a woman's hot, doesn't mean she makes you burn," Lynn argued. "And how is she supposed to narrow it down to just one?"

"Yeah," Susan chimed in. "There are so many hot women here tonight."

Jo glared at Lynn, then her partner. "You two are not supposed to be looking for hot women, right Terri?"

"Ain't nothing wrong with lookin', baby sister." Terri wiggled her eyebrows.

"Not you too." Jo sat back and crossed her arms.

"Is my wittle smookins upset?" Susan leaned over and kissed pouting lips. She hummed her approval when Jo deepened the kiss.

"All right you perverts, break it up," Dani demanded, poking Jo's shoulder. "If you don't have enough kisses to share with the whole group, then you shouldn't be doing that. And you, Keile, quit stalling and point out some chicks."

"Why me?"

"Because Jo said so," Dani replied.

"Okay, okay." She deepened her voice. "Hottie number one is standing to the right of the stage. She has on tight, low-riding jeans and a midriff top. Please note the perky, obviously unbound breasts, and the kissable lips. I'm still waiting for her to turn around to see if her backside is as good as the front."

"I don't know about you, Keile, but I'm burning now." Lynn used her napkin as a fan.

"Ditto." Terri snatched the napkin from Lynn and fanned her own face.

"Anybody want to hear about number two?" Keile asked with a wicked grin.

"I dare you to go say hi to her." The grin on Jo's face matched Keile's.

Uh-oh. Now what do I do? Keile's grin faltered until she noticed the animated look on Dani's face. "You are so on." With her grin firmly back in place, she made her way to the front of the stage. Taking a deep breath, she walked up to the woman in question and introduced herself. The ebony-skinned beauty was even more attractive up close. They chatted long enough for Keile to realize that the woman, girl really, was way too young for her. After making small talk for a few more minutes, she escaped with a lame excuse.

As she approached the table, Terri stood up and held her hand up for a high five. "You go, girl!"

"I didn't see any exchange of numbers," Jo grumbled, then glared when Susan elbowed her in the side.

"That's so not gonna happen." Keile reached for her Coke. "She's even hotter up close, but oh so young up here where it counts." She tapped her forehead.

The lights darkened and the announcer climbed onto the

stage. The crowd started clapping and whistling, eager for the show to start. She thanked everyone for coming and introduced the band. When the lights went out, the crowd surged to their feet and started screaming the band's name. With the twang of a guitar, Hexagon launched into one of their most recognized songs. Still standing, the mostly female crowd sang along.

By the third song, the dance floor was packed with die-hard fans who weren't satisfied with just standing. When the first set finished, Keile was sweating profusely and her cheeks were bright red from exertion. At some point she'd taken off her shirt, showing her tight, black tank top. Still pumped, she made her way back to her friends who had bowed out a couple of songs earlier.

"We ordered you some water and another soda," Terri said. "You wouldn't think a workaholic like you would have that kind of stamina."

"It's all the running." Keile wiped her brow with a napkin before draining the glass of water. "Thanks for the drinks." As she reached for her Coke, she realized she'd forgotten about keeping track of Dani's exes. Edan was still sitting at the same table but it seemed somehow closer. When Edan glanced in her direction, Keile quickly averted her gaze.

"Why don't we go?" Keile asked, squeezing Dani's thigh. "I can always pick up chicks some other time," she boasted playfully.

Dani threw back her head and gave a shout of laughter. "Good one, Griffen. Thanks, I needed that."

"Are you two keeping secrets again?" Susan asked.

"Nah. Keile's just cheering me up." Dani pushed back her chair. "Now I need to go join the long line for the bathroom."

Keile noticed Dani made no effort to bypass Edan's table. *She's got more guts than me*, she thought, watching Dani casually nod in Edan's direction. A flicker of movement at Edan drew Keile's attention to the other table occupant.

Instant recognition slammed into her brain. *No!* She squeezed her eyes tight and held her breath. When she opened them,

Haydn Davenport was still seated close to Edan. Some entity above sure had a damn peculiar sense of humor. Keile mumbled an excuse about needing to cool down and bolted for the door.

The cold air penetrating her sweat-soaked skin gradually filtered through her fogged brain. She shivered, rubbed her bare arms. "Oh, God, this fucking sucks," she whispered, looking at the stark outline of the first quarter moon. Her meeting Kyle was supposed to have meant something. How could it—when he was Edan's son? She couldn't do that to Dani. *Dani!* She had to have seen Haydn as well. *And I didn't go after her.*

"Are you okay?" Dani waited until she had Keile's attention before she draped a jacket over her shoulders. "You saw her too, huh?"

Keile stomped on a smoldering cigarette left by some careless smoker. "Yeah. Kind of threw me for a loop." She squared her shoulders and looked into Dani's blue eyes. "But forget about me, how do *you* feel?"

"Like I could use a pecan waffle and hash browns. Not to mention mediocre coffee."

"Sounds like Waffle House is in our future." Keile fished for her keys.

"Wait. Let's go back in for a little bit. I don't want to ruin everybody's night."

"Are you serious? God, Dani, think about yourself just this once."

"I am," Dani replied softly. "I need to get used to seeing Edan. Think of it as anesthesia."

"Okay, Dr. Knight, it's your call. Just know you're going to be looking at her from the dance floor as long as we're here."

Dani pushed her empty plate away, turned sideways and scooted in the booth at the Waffle House until her back was against the wall. She reached for her cup and cradled it between her hands. "Thanks for being there for me tonight. Without you, I would have made a complete ass of myself."

"That's what friends are for. How you doing, friend?"

"I wish I could say I was anesthetized." Dani sighed. "You'd think after three years, it wouldn't hurt so damn much to see Edan with someone else."

"It had to be a shock." Keile picked up her glass and stabbed the ice with a straw. "Especially when you saw who the other person was." *I know it was for me.*

"True. And after some of the shock wore off, any lingering anger I had for Carla disappeared."

"Carla?"

"I never loved her, so who am I to fault her for taking a chance at real love? I knew we never had that as soon as I saw Edan again." Dani's expression took on a faraway look.

"Do you think you'll ever find love again?"

"One day," Dani said with a surety Keile admired. "One day. What about you?"

"I...I don't know. It's not something I've given a lot of thought to."

"What about Buster's mom?"

"Haydn Davenport?" Keile felt her cheeks grow warm. "Why would you think that?"

"The way you looked at her that day in the park." Dani turned to face Keile. "I've never seen you look at another woman quite like that."

"Oh, that." She gave a weak laugh. "That was from seeing Kyle's smile on her face. Up until then, I thought they looked nothing alike."

"Then why were you so upset when you found out she was Edan's partner? And don't you dare tell me you weren't upset."

"It's kind of embarrassing." Keile squirmed under the intensity of Dani's gaze. "Okay. All this week I've been feeling unsettled about...my life." She took a deep breath. "I got this crazy idea that Kyle found me for a reason. But when I found out..." She shrugged and looked away. "I felt like somebody played a cruel trick because it's all come to nothing. Stupid, huh?" she asked, absently folding the paper napkin into a neat square.

"That's not crazy or stupid. Sometimes you meet someone

and everything seems to change." Dani's smile was bittersweet. "I felt that way when I first met Edan. But I'm still not sure what Edan had to do with you and Bust—uh, Kyle. Do you think she won't let you see her son because you know me?"

Keile shook her head without looking at Dani. "It wouldn't be right. You're my friend."

Dani tapped her forehead. "I get it. You're worried about me, aren't you?" she demanded, reaching across the table to still Keile's hands. She continued before Keile could reply, "Please don't let me stop you from seeing him."

Keile swallowed hard, searching for the right response. "Your friendship means a lot to me. I would never want to do anything that I know would hurt you."

"You being friends with Edan's son will *not* hurt me. What kind of bitch would I be to make you choose? Don't answer that," Dani said, forestalling Keile's response. "Meeting Kyle was good for you. Hopefully having him around will help you balance work and life a little better. I mean let's face it, you could use some help in that area."

Keile dangled the keys to her Jeep. "You do want a ride home, don't you?"

Chapter Eight

The next afternoon, Keile was sitting at her computer at home, putting the final touches on a map for Rick when her phone rang. She answered without checking caller ID. "Dani, I swear I'm not working."

"Is this Keile Griffen?" asked a voice Keile couldn't quite place.

"Yes it is."

"This is Haydn Davenport. Kyle's mom."

Keile's heartbeat sped up without her permission. "Sorry, I thought you were a friend. How are you doing?"

"I'm fine," Haydn replied with a hint of laughter in her voice. "I'm sorry to call at the last minute, but I'd like to invite you to dinner tonight. Marcus has gotten it into his head to cook a big dinner, and he insists you simply *must* join us."

Keile laughed. "I bet he said it just like that."

"You know him already," Haydn replied dryly. "He was going to call you himself but he's much too involved with this new dish he saw one of the TV chefs make. I hope you don't mind being a guinea pig?"

"No. I pretty much eat anything. Is there anything I can bring?"

"Just come prepared to entertain a certain young man. He's been asking for you."

"He has?" Keile's grin stretched her face. "If someone wanted to bring, say, a little gift for him, what should that be?"

"Any truck or car that's designed for children under three. He's obsessed with them already."

"I can do that. What time should I be there?"

"I'm sure Kyle would like you to be here now," Haydn said. "Judging by the state of my kitchen we're not going to eat for another three hours, so anytime between now and then is fine."

Two hours later, Keile parked her Jeep on the street in front of Haydn's house and stared at the pale blue siding. *Maybe this isn't such a good idea*, passed through her mind. *No, this is fine.* The excitement she felt had everything to do with seeing Kyle and Marcus, and nothing to do with seeing Haydn. *It's just a harmless crush*, she told herself, glancing in the rearview mirror and patting down a few loose strands of hair. Haydn was unavailable. Keile snagged the gift from the passenger seat and made her way to the front door.

She rang the doorbell, and grinned when she heard a squeal, followed by rapid footsteps. Marcus opened the door, then stepped aside to allow Kyle access to Keile. She dropped to her knees, and enfolded the toddler in her arms. "Hi, Buster." After giving him a kiss, she drew back so she could gaze at him. He looked cute in a long-sleeved dark top and matching pants covered with trains.

"I feel so superfluous." Marcus sniffed, smiling down at the pair.

Keile stood up with Kyle in her arms. "Hey, Marcus. Something smells really good. So wonderful of you to think of me while you were slaving away in the kitchen."

"Smart-ass." He put his hands on his hips and tsked. "What? No hug from my newly found daughter?"

Keile hung her head in shame. "Sorry, Dad." She grinned and put her free arm around him, squeezing tight.

"You need to take this show on the road," Haydn said and her eyes widened when they looked at her. "Wow! Triplets. I have to get a picture of this. Don't move," she commanded before rushing off.

"Is this a house tradition?" Keile whispered once Haydn left the room.

"No, it's more of an anytime-you-get-near-Kyle-she-whips-out-the-camera tradition. A word of warning, my sister is ruthless with a camera."

After Haydn snapped more than a dozen photos, Keile was led to the large family room. It had a lived-in feel. One corner was obviously Kyle's domain. An overflowing toy box sat next to a raised train set, which was complete with buildings and people. The entire assembly was perched on a slightly raised platform.

Kyle squirmed to get down, and ran to his toy box. He began pulling out toys, babbling all the while. With a cry, he pulled out a large dump truck, and ran back to Keile. Grinning, he held it out to her and said something she couldn't begin to understand.

Keile *oohed* and *aahed*, hoping she was expressing her appreciation in the correct manner. She lowered herself to the floor and pushed the truck over the plush carpet, causing squeals of delight from Kyle. She added truck noises, and was soon on her knees, chasing him with the truck, much to his delight.

"I can tell you've been around kids a lot," Haydn commented.

"Not really. It's the kid in me coming out, I guess." She smiled. "Or it might just be this little guy here." She raised him above her head, evoking more squeals of excitement.

"Quick, sign her up for babysitting," Marcus said, entering the room with a tray of drinks and snacks.

"Keile, did you enjoy the show last night?" Haydn asked.

Keile nodded, holding her glass away from Kyle's grabby

hands. "Hexagon is one of my favorite local bands. I've missed them the last two times they've been here because of work, so last night was even better for me."

"They put on a good show. Kyle, you know you can't have that. Where's your cup?" Haydn looked around for his spill-proof cup.

"I saw Hexagon at a pride weekend in Florida, about four years ago," Marcus said. "It was amazing to see the sheer number of lesbians come out of nowhere to rush the stage."

"We were definitely out in full force last night." Keile scooted closer to the coffee table and placed her glass out of Kyle's reach. She grabbed him quickly as he dove for the snacks.

Marcus announced that dinner would be ready in fifteen minutes and excused himself to go take care of the final preparations, declining any offer of help.

Kyle finished gnawing his cracker, handed Keile the soggy remains and wiggled off her lap to fetch a fuzzy black bear from his toy box. Toddling to his mother, he held up his arms. "I think the excitement of seeing you wore him down, Keile," Haydn said as she settled him onto her lap. "Good job."

While Keile enjoyed the sight of mother and child, she was a little disconcerted at the intense heat building in her stomach. Before she had a chance to put a name to what she was feeling, she heard the front door open. How could she have forgotten about Edan? Her body tensed as the footsteps, resounding off the hardwood floor, came closer.

"Hey, I found this by the front door," Edan announced as she entered the room waving a package. "Isn't it a little early for Santa?" She lowered the package when she noticed the newcomer. "Oh, hi."

Keile jumped up and wiped her hands on her jeans, sure she looked as guilty as she felt. "Hello." She flashed an uncertain smile. *She looks like she didn't know I would be here.* Resisting the urge to look at Haydn for direction, Keile tucked her hands in her back pockets. "I'm a friend of Kyle's. From the park," she added as Edan continued to stare at her.

"You're right," Edan said without taking her eyes off Keile, "she looks even more like Marcus close up."

"I'm sure Edan doesn't mean to talk about you as if you weren't in the room," Haydn said dryly. "We're still working on her social skills."

Edan blushed. "I'm sorry. Maybe we should start over again." She placed her bag on the back of the sofa and held out her hand. "I'm Edan Richardson."

Keile smiled, returning the firm grip. "Keile Griffen. Nice to meet you."

Edan cocked her head and asked, "Hey, didn't I see you with Dani at the concert last night?"

"Yeah, that was me," Keile said. So Edan had been as aware of them as they were of her. *Interesting.* "We were just talking about the band," she said for lack of anything else to say. Now was not the time to blurt out, *I've heard so much about you.*

Luckily, Kyle reached for the brightly wrapped gift Edan was holding. "I really did find it on the porch," she said.

"It's for Kyle," Keile said shyly. "I must have dropped it earlier when I picked him up. Well, I hope he likes them."

Kyle opened the present with help from his mother. He grinned and babbled when a truck and a car were revealed.

"Go thank Keile." Haydn set him down and pointed to Keile. "They're from her."

"Mama!" With a cry of delight, he ran to Keile, throwing himself against her legs. Keile sat down and pulled him into her lap, accepting his sloppy kiss. She helped him remove the vehicles from the packaging while listening intently to his garbled speech. "One day I hope to understand you, little man."

"Give it time." Edan smiled mischievously as she looked at Kyle and Keile. "I know you're not his mother, but are you sure you aren't his dad? I think Kyle looks more like you than he does Marcus."

"What?" Keile looked up, her eyes wide. "No! I...I just—"

"Edan, leave Keile alone," Haydn interjected. "She doesn't know you well enough to realize how twisted you are."

Edan laughed. "Sorry again, Keile. I couldn't resist. But it was more a dig at my crazy friend here." She elbowed Haydn playfully, then quickly dodged away from a retaliatory elbow.

"Friend?" Haydn scoffed. "Please don't listen to her ramblings, Keile. She's more like a charity case than a friend."

Friends? Keile dared to hope as she watched Haydn and Edan act more like friends than lovers. "That's okay, Haydn. Buster and I look alike because I'm his twin sister." She grinned. "Marcus thinks I'm his long lost fertilized egg."

"That sounds like my kooky brother," Haydn said with a snort. "In this case though, I don't blame him. You do look like brother and sister. I can't wait to print out the pictures I took earlier."

"You should e-mail them to your mom," Edan said. "She'll freak."

Haydn nodded. "It's a good thing Keile is too old to be a by-product of Marcus's misspent youth."

"I heard that," Marcus said from the doorway. "It wasn't my fault high school textbooks don't tell you that being promiscuous doesn't cure homosexuality."

"So what's your excuse now?" Edan asked.

He gave her the look. "Don't make me hurt you, girly. I don't have time, because dinner is served."

"That's a relief," Edan muttered as she left the room to go put her things away.

"Keile, there's a bathroom right down the hall if you want to wash up," Haydn said. "I'm going to run upstairs and change Kyle."

Keile slipped into the bathroom and shut the door. *Well, that went rather well.* As she washed her hands, she couldn't help but grin. They were only friends. She had a chance now. "I... What am I thinking?" Keile couldn't think of the last time she'd spent this much energy thinking about a woman. She stared at her reflection in the mirror, searching for any signs of the change that seemed to have occurred a little over a week ago. There weren't any. She still looked the same on the outside, but inside was a different matter.

Taking a deep breath, she turned away from the mirror. *Change is good. I can do change.* She opened the door and let her nose lead her to the wonderful smell of food.

Chapter Nine

Keile paced around her living room, phone pressed to her ear, waiting impatiently. She tightened her lips when her call went to voicemail. "This is Keile. Call me as soon as you get this message. I don't care what time it is." Keile plopped down into an overstuffed chair which had seen better times, feeling as if the wind had gone out of her sails. She had been looking forward to sharing some good news with Dani, and surely finding out earlier that Haydn and Edan weren't a couple qualified.

The restlessness that had plagued her the past week had returned. She wandered over to the stereo cabinet. Smiling, she ran her fingers almost lovingly over its dings and scratches. She'd been so proud when she'd saved up enough money to purchase it from a thrift store eight years ago. It didn't look pretty, but it had been cheap and it still served its purpose. Most of the components were newer, picked up at various yard sales that dotted her neighborhood during the spring and fall.

After placing a couple of CDs in the player, she returned to the chair. Some of her restlessness abated as the smooth jazzy sounds of Miles Davis filled the air. Leaning back, she let the music waft over her, filling her senses. Had anyone written a dissertation on the relaxing properties of jazz music? If nothing else, it would be a great project to research, and in some ways more interesting than the graduate level projects she had worked on. Just not as profitable.

A rueful smile touched her lips as she propped her feet on the edge of the wooden coffee table. Money had long been a driving force in her life. At thirteen, while living in foster care, she had gotten word of her mother's death. After a good cry, she vowed to never again be at the mercy of anyone else. That meant going to college and getting a good job. She'd thrown herself into her schoolwork at the exclusion of everything else, getting good grades the focal point in her life. As long as she was successful in school, being moved around to different foster homes, and ultimately to a group home, didn't matter.

And she had been successful, graduating at the top of her class and earning a full scholarship to attend college. She continued to push herself and was able to graduate early. Soon after she started working at a small company, she realized she needed more education to command the type of money necessary to make her feel secure. In two years she added an advanced degree and landed her current job.

So why wasn't that enough anymore? She sighed and slipped off the chair down onto the soft carpet. Her small circle of friends had been enough to satisfy her need for human contact. In the past six months, she'd even allowed Dani to get closer, despite her deeply ingrained fears. Life in foster care had nailed down the notion that nothing lasts forever. Just when you got comfortable with a family, it was time to move and leave most everything behind. In a way, it had been kind of a relief to be placed in the group center where older children stayed until they were eighteen and no longer the responsibility of the state.

There were no expectations that the perfect family was going to find you. You were mostly on your own, and she had thrived in that environment.

Or did I? Now, sitting alone in her own home with money in the bank, she wasn't so sure anymore. Tonight she had gotten a glimpse of the kind of family life she'd never experienced, and she had liked it. All the adults had pitched in to help get the food on the dining room table. Then they sat at the table and made conversation without the need to talk over the loud noise of a restaurant. Even Kyle had chimed in now and then.

Keile smiled and thought about her favorite part of the night. While Haydn, Marcus and Edan were cleaning up the kitchen, she had been upstairs with Kyle. She'd stopped reading him his favorite bedtime story only because he had fallen asleep.

As she'd sat gently rocking the freshly bathed child, many thoughts jumbled their way through her brain. Kyle, innocent that he was, hadn't yet learned the danger of giving his heart away freely. She brushed a curl off his forehead and wished that he would never have to learn that particular lesson. "But you have a sweet mommy to help you when you do, Buster," she whispered softly. Having spent time with Haydn, she didn't doubt for a minute that Haydn and Marcus would always do their best with Kyle.

She smiled, thinking about Haydn—funny, a little shy and a lot beautiful. Keile had found herself wanting to see if Haydn's shoulder-length, vivid red hair felt as warm as it looked. She'd also wanted to kiss the cute upturned nose that crinkled when Haydn laughed.

"Hey, I think you can safely put him in his crib now," Haydn had said softly as she entered the room. "You did a good job of knocking him out."

Keile smiled. "He'll probably be more comfortable in his bed, too. It's just…nice to hold him." After giving him a butterfly kiss, she gently placed him in his bed beside his stuffed train. Along with Haydn, she watched him flip onto his stomach and settle back into sleep.

"He's almost too sweet," Keile whispered.

"Wait till you catch him in one of his cranky 'I'm so tired, but I don't want to sleep' modes. Then tell me he's too sweet," Haydn said, stroking his back. Despite her words, the look on her face was one of intense love. "But all in all, he's pretty special."

"Like his parents," Keile said shyly, sneaking a quick look at Haydn. They were standing almost shoulder to shoulder, and Keile felt her body heat up at Haydn's closeness.

"Thanks." Haydn looked up and smiled.

Keile couldn't help but return the smile that she wouldn't soon forget. Her heartbeat sped up and her stomach tingled as she looked into Haydn's sparkling green eyes, noticing for the first time the tiny golden flecks. For a crazy moment, she was tempted to pull Haydn into her arms, kiss the freckles on the bridge of her nose, then move to her soft-looking lips.

Placing her hands behind her back, she swallowed the sudden obstruction in her throat. "I need to get home and rescue my dog," she said, though she wasn't ready to end this moment with Haydn. With one last glance at Kyle, she followed Haydn downstairs. "Thank you for inviting me to dinner. I had a great time."

"You'll come again, I hope?" Haydn asked as she stepped onto the front porch.

"I'd love to," Keile said eagerly. "Or, maybe next time all of you can come to my house," she heard herself saying.

"You don't know what you're getting into," Haydn warned. "With Kyle, nothing is safe."

"There isn't much in my house that Can hasn't already had his way with," Keile replied and shrugged. "I'm not worried." *I just hope you can overlook the fact that my place isn't as attractive as yours*, she thought with not a little panic. *Shit! What was I thinking?*

"Okay. I'm sure Kyle would love to see you again. Marcus, too."

But what about you? Keile wanted to ask, sensing Haydn was backing away from the closeness they'd shared minutes ago. "I'll call you and set something up. If that's okay with you," she added hastily.

"That would be fine."

Keile swallowed disappointment. She wasn't sure what response she'd expected, but surely, given the moments they'd shared earlier in Kyle's room, it should have been something more. Something to suggest Haydn wanted to see her again.

Keile's musings were interrupted when Can licked her chin. "I guess this means you forgive me for leaving you alone all night." She scratched his neck. "I certainly hope you're not going to get bent out of shape if I start going out more. Humans do that kind of thing," she explained. "Trust me, it's way past time for me to start, boy."

Can's response was to roll over on his back, silently commanding her to rub his tummy. He growled in the back of his throat when she complied. Keile smiled. "You can be sweet when you want to." She lay down beside him and rested her head on his chest.

Later that night, as Keile completed her bedtime routine, she glanced at her still silent cell phone and sighed. She was still eager to tell Dani about her earlier conversation with Edan.

Haydn had taken Kyle upstairs for a fresh diaper and Marcus had excused himself to make a phone call, leaving Keile and Edan temporarily alone. "You looked like you were having a great time last night," Edan had said, then added as if it were an afterthought, "Dani, too."

"Yeah. It was fun."

"So, what's Dani up to these days? I assume she's still the super cop."

Where is this going? Keile regarded Edan carefully. "No. She quit a couple of years ago. She's a dick now."

"What?"

Keile noted Edan's startled expression, not sure if Edan's reaction was due to the word *dick*, or that Dani wasn't a cop. "You know, private eye type?"

Edan looked down at the thick, gray carpet beneath her feet. "You two looked awfully chummy. Are you dating?"

"Eww." Keile shook her head violently. "That would be like dating my sister."

"Is…Is she dating anyone?"

"Why do you want to know?" Keile countered.

Edan pressed her hands over her eyes and rocked back and forth before answering. "She once meant a lot to me. I'm interested in knowing how she's doing. If she's okay."

"Why now after three years?"

"It's not as if I haven't been keeping tabs on her in my own way," Edan shot back, sounding defensive.

"I probably shouldn't tell you this, but it hurt Dani a lot to give you up. She doesn't deserve to be hurt again," Keile said quietly.

"I don't want to hurt her." Edan dropped her hands, showing tear-drenched eyes. "I want to stop hurting."

Keile, believing Edan was sincere, had awkwardly patted her knee and said, "She's not dating anyone right now."

Keile jumped when the phone rang. She quickly snatched it up from her bedside table. "It's about time you called me back."

"No wonder you don't get return calls if you greet everybody like that," Dani said. "What's your news?"

"I had dinner with Kyle and his family tonight. Oh, Marcus is a fantastic cook by the way."

"The point, Keile. I know you didn't call me to tell me how good a cook Marcus is."

Keile suppressed a laugh. "Okay, grouchy. I just thought you might like to know that Edan and Haydn are not involved. In fact, Edan seemed extremely interested in what *you* were up to." The silence that greeted her pronouncement surprised her, and made her worry she'd misread the situation. "Dani, you still there?"

"You're kidding."

Keile rubbed her forehead, confused at Dani's subdued tone. "I would never kid you about something like this. I know it's too important for that."

Dani gave a loud sigh. "What did she ask?" She sounded as if she were afraid of the answer.

Keile thought carefully before she replied. "I think the most important thing for her was whether you were dating anyone." Once again there was a long pause and Keile tightened her grip on the phone. She had been so sure this would be welcome news.

"I'm not sure I want to hear this," Dani said slowly, as if the words were being forced out of her. "I'm not sure I'm ready to think about how many times I've dreamt about this. Wanted this very thing to happen." Her voice sounded like she was fighting back tears. "It was so hard for me to let her go last time. I just… I…"

"Oh, God, I'm sorry I brought it up," Keile said into the silence, remembering the anguish she'd seen on Dani's face. *Was that only last night?* "Dani?"

"It's just it hurt too bad last time," Dani finally said.

"I'm coming over," she said firmly. "Give me fifteen minutes."

"You don't have to." Dani's protest was unconvincing.

"You're wrong, my friend. I'm on my way."

She was dressed and out of the door within minutes. Although it was fairly late, there was still more traffic than she had anticipated. *This town just keeps getting bigger and bigger*, she thought, waiting her turn at a busy four-way stop. Soon Seneca would be a city with all a city's problems. She sighed and pulled up to the stop sign.

But traffic conditions or the size of the town weren't the crux of the matter. How was she going to make things right for Dani? She didn't have any experience with being in love, or relationships. Hell, she'd never gotten past longing, so what did she know about helping Dani open herself up to love? This was a woman who'd been strong enough to let love go.

Keile hit the steering wheel. "I'd be a great one to talk about letting someone into your heart." But somehow, she knew she had to do just that. Images of Haydn and Kyle flashed through her mind. "They're why I have to figure this out," she whispered, and pulled into the parking lot.

Keile walked into Dani's building still not knowing what she was going to say. She checked in and took the elevator up, toying with the slight hope it might get stuck, giving her a temporary reprieve. "Don't be a chickenshit," she told herself sternly as the doors opened. The quiet hallway seemed to get longer with each step. Assuring herself she would know what to say when the time came, she rang the bell.

Dani opened the door, and they stared at each other wordlessly.

"I'm sorry. I should have kept my big mouth shut." Keile swallowed nervously. "Forgive me?" she asked softly.

"I would if there were something to forgive," Dani replied, wrapping her arms around Keile. "You didn't do anything wrong." She leaned back and smiled before moving Keile aside to shut the door. "I know I told you, you didn't have to come over, but I'm glad you're here."

"Me, too." Keile was confused by the seemingly calm, smiling Dani standing before her. Cocking her head to the side, she said, "You have me totally confused. Shouldn't you be weeping, drinking and ranting and raving right about now?"

Dani gave a half-hearted chuckle and motioned Keile in the direction of the living room. "Women don't weep anymore," she said.

They sat on the sofa. Dani said, "I can't say I haven't missed having Edan in my life. I can say that I don't know if we can go back to the way things were before the whole baby issue came up." She rubbed her eyes. "And I sure as hell don't know if we can go forward."

"I guess next time I'd better do a better job of feeling you out before I pass along good news, huh?"

She shrugged. "Good news can be subjective."

"Yeah, I'm sorry," Keile said with a pained smile. "If I had a clue about relationships, I might have known you wouldn't necessarily be overjoyed at her return."

"It does raise a lot of questions in my mind. Kids were very important to her, so why doesn't she have any? What if she wants me back because she hasn't found anyone else? What if I'm, like, her last resort?"

Keile reached for Dani's hand. "No way could you be a last resort."

"You're prejudiced."

"Maybe. But I talked to Edan, and so should you."

Dani pulled a face. "If I say I'll think about it can we talk about something else? Like, how was the rest of your evening?"

"It…it was good."

"What are you trying to hide from me?"

"Nothing," Keile said and turned away from her friend's inquisitive gaze. "I should go. Work tomorrow." Before she knew it, she was confined in a headlock. "Hey, let me go!" She struggled to no avail.

Dani laughed and tightened her grip. "Give or we'll be here all night."

"Okay, but let go first."

Dani smirked. "Come on, you know you want to spill your guts."

Keile shoved her shoulder. "You big goofball. I don't know what you're talking about."

"Wait! I get it. This is about the mom, isn't it? You tried to deny it, but I could tell you were interested in her."

"So maybe I am. I don't think she's interested in me," she admitted glumly. "We seemed to be hitting it off, then bam, it was like she put a wall between us. Maybe I rushed her."

"What did you do, try to kiss her?"

"No!" Keile looked horrified. "Nothing like that. She invited me over again and I said they should come to my house next time. It seemed like the right thing to do." She pulled at her hair. "Dani, what the hell was I thinking? How would I know what the right thing to do is? All I know is how to study hard and work even harder." The last was added with disgust.

"I know we've never really talked about this, but you *have* had a girlfriend before, right?" Dani asked gently.

Keile looked down at her lap. "Well…um…not really."

"Define not really."

"There was this girl freshman year. We kind of fooled around. She would touch me, but she wouldn't let me do much beyond kissing. This is so embarrassing." Keile covered her eyes. "I thought it was because I didn't know what I was doing, so I kind of gave up. After that, it was easier to focus my attention on graduating early. Then there was work and..." She shrugged.

"Time got away from you?" Dani suggested.

Keile nodded and uncovered her eyes. "Walking up to that girl at Eddie's last night was way out of my comfort zone. I'd never done anything like that before." She didn't add that she'd never had an incentive before—like taking Dani's mind off Edan.

"Lesson number one," Dani said, holding up her index finger. "It's always easier to be bold when you're with a group of friends. But that's a good thing. Lesson number two. It's even easier with alcohol. But that's a bad thing."

"That I don't have to worry about. I never get drunk."

Chapter Ten

The next morning came much too soon for Keile. "Okay, Can," she mumbled, sitting up without opening her eyes. She stretched, then had to use her fingers to open her gummy eyelids. Last night it had felt good to talk to someone about how she was feeling, but now she almost wished she had stuck to the short version.

Keile was brushing her teeth when Can ran into the bathroom, the leash in his mouth. He sat down, knowing he had to wait for her to finish before they could leave.

"Good boy," Keile mumbled around a mouthful of toothpaste. She looked at her reflection and once again considered cutting her hair. She surprised herself by wondering what Haydn would think of the idea. "Much too early to be thinking like that, Griffen. You still have to figure out if she's even interested." She sighed, remembering all the instructions Dani had given her the night before. "Let's go before my head explodes," she told Can, and ran for the front door.

During her run, Keile's mind returned to her conversation with Dani. They had talked way into the night about women, love and relationships. At some point, she had decided that romance was where she wanted to go with Haydn. Keile's stomach tingled as she saw herself pulling Haydn into her arms. She would rest her cheek against Haydn's silky red hair, breathe in the slightly sweet scent she exuded, then kiss her. *Please let her see me as more than just Buster's rescuer. I know if given a chance, I can be so much more.* Huffing and puffing, invigorated by hope and the brisk morning air, she turned around and headed for home.

She was finishing up her breakfast when the realization sunk in that she had voluntarily invited Haydn and family to dinner. She looked at her small beat-up table and couldn't help but compare it with the one she'd eaten on the night before. "What the hell was I thinking? I can't have her over here." Keile gnawed on her lip. The last time she'd invited anyone over, they ordered pizza and watched a football game. All she'd needed to keep her guests happy was snacks and beer. Somehow she didn't think that would work with Haydn and her family.

Frowning, she put the dirty dishes in the sink and stared out the window overlooking the backyard. She barely noticed the small, empty patio or the well-kept lawn as she contemplated her options. You didn't invite a woman you wanted to impress for dinner, then open up a jar of spaghetti sauce.

Who was she trying to kid? Haydn wouldn't want to be impressed by someone like her. And why should she? She probably had plenty of women interested in her who had more to offer. The thought hurt.

With a deep sigh, she packed her briefcase and left for work. By the time she pulled into a parking space, thoughts of wooing Haydn had moved to the fringe of her consciousness. She arrived at her cube, mostly ready for a day's hard work. The folder in her chair cleared her mind completely.

Turning on her computer, she picked up the folder. Her

interest was piqued as she read through the scope of her new assignment. Initial research always gave her a thrill. She viewed it as the most important piece to the success of the project. Her next step would be to collect the necessary geographic data from different sources and make them fit together.

Grabbing a pad, she jotted down notes she would use to develop a project schedule. She worked steadily, only stopping for caffeine. By six thirty, she had a decent outline with tentative due dates. Satisfied with what she'd accomplished so far, she called it a day.

Once in her Jeep, she rubbed her rumbling stomach. Food was starting to sound like a good idea. "The dinner!" What should she do about that?

"Dani!" Unclipping her cell phone from her pants, she dialed Dani's number, then drummed her fingers on the dashboard while she waited for the voicemail message to finish. "Hey, it's Keile. I need your help again. Call me." She dropped her phone on the passenger seat and pulled out of the almost empty parking lot.

On the drive home, she brooded over how an innocuous invitation had mushroomed into something terrifying. The light turned to red, forcing her to stop near a large, run-down apartment complex. As she looked around, she couldn't help but notice the number of kids, running and screaming. Despite the darkness, everywhere she looked she saw kids.

Why have I never noticed them before? The complex was on her regular route, so she passed it frequently. The light turned green and she moved forward slowly, taking one last look at the children illuminated by the streetlights. She wondered derisively if not noticing the complex, or the kids, was her way of ignoring her meager beginnings. Twenty or so years ago, it could have been her playing outside in the cold and the dark without parental supervision.

"Okay, Griffen, you're all over the place," she admonished herself, gripping the steering wheel. "One problem at a time, please." She drove the rest of the route trying to visualize a scenario where she could have Haydn over to her house for dinner and still impress her. When she pulled into her driveway twenty minutes later, she was still searching for that scenario.

As always, she was welcomed by an exuberant Can. While she was taking him for a walk, her phone rang. Slipping the phone from her coat pocket, she checked the caller ID. "Hey, you."

"Don't tell me you've picked up another child, Keile," Dani said by way of greeting.

"Bite your tongue. What gave you that idea?"

"Your message. You said you needed my help again."

"Oh. Well, it's more like advice."

"Go on," Dani urged.

"Remember I mentioned inviting Haydn and family to my place for dinner?"

"Yes, and?"

"I think I made a big mistake. Looking back, I can see I was too stupid to recognize she was only being polite. So now my question is, should I pretend like I never asked her over? She would want that don't you think?"

"I think you're tying yourself into knots." Dani was clearly amused. "Where are you now?"

"Almost home. Why?"

"Duh! You obviously need help. Expect me in twenty. I'll bring dinner."

"Dani, you don't have—" Her protest was heard by the dial tone. "Can, I'm in for another lesson." Keile gazed down at her furry pal as she pocketed the phone. She was sure to get more advice than she'd bargained for. As she made her way home, she wondered why Dani, with her take-over mentality, wouldn't want to have kids. They were the perfect outlet for that type of activity. She laughed, imagining what Dani would say if she dared to voice these thoughts out loud.

Once Can was fed, Keile studied the living room critically, trying to see it the way a stranger would. With the second hand furniture and the stark white walls, a person couldn't be faulted for thinking she was strapped for cash. But what the hell did it really matter? She'd never cared what others thought. It had always been enough that she had a house and the means to keep it. But now that it wasn't enough, where did that leave her? Did she really want to go down that road?

She stopped in front of the rectangular mirror above the mantel, studying the face reflected back at her. "I look the same, so why is everything inside me so different?" She brushed back the strands of hair that had escaped the confines of her French braid and paced around the room.

By the time Can barked to announce incoming, Keile's nerves were stretched thin, but her mind was made up. For Haydn's sake, the dinner was off. The doorbell rang before she had time to analyze the feeling of disappointment at the bottom of her stomach. Before she made it to the door, she heard the key strike the lock. Dani was taking no chances. She smiled in wry amusement, crossed her arms over her chest and waited for her friend to enter. "You really didn't have to do this."

"Just like you didn't have to come to my house last night, you mean?" Dani shut the door with her shoulder and held up a large paper bag with the logo of a nearby Mexican restaurant. "I have food, so you have to let me stay."

"Okay, but you should know I've already made a decision and you're not going to talk me out of it."

"Fine. Let's eat."

Keile made a face before retrieving plates from the cabinet. "I decided dinner is so not happening. The woman probably thinks I'm a bore, and my place isn't exactly up to entertaining standards."

"We'll talk about your place later," Dani said as she removed two Styrofoam containers from the bag. While they ate the laden taco salads, Dani amused Keile with tales of the sleuthing she had done in the early morning hours. "And this despite not getting a lot of sleep," she said, pointing her fork at Keile.

"Sorry."

"I can tell. But it didn't matter because the guy made no attempt to hide what he was doing. I almost feel guilty for taking the poor wife's money. She could have followed him herself."

"It's one thing to know, but far harder to see, I think."

"She asked for pictures."

"I would hate for something like that to happen to me."

"Don't we all. But let's remember, you can't be cheated on until you actually *have* a girlfriend."

"What a comforting thought," Keile said and closed the empty container.

Dani smirked. "I do my best. Now can we discuss the whys of your decision?"

"If you insist." She sighed at Dani's nod. "It's simple. She doesn't want to do it, so I don't want to do it."

"Look. All you did was ask Haydn and her family, mind you, to dinner. Look at this as an opportunity to socialize with Haydn and her brother, and to see Kyle again. Quit making it more than it is."

"Maybe if you joined us—"

"Nope, not gonna happen."

The look on Dani's face forestalled any request for an explanation. "What do I do about the house? Look at this table. It's not exactly designed to seat four people and food."

"You have a point there." Dani pursed her lips. "It doesn't have to be a sit-down dinner. Be creative."

"Easy for you to say," Keile mumbled. "I have about as much creativity as my dog. Too bad it's winter, or we could do a picnic at the park," she added as an afterthought. "That would be easy enough."

"That's it!" Dani's face lit up with enthusiasm. "What if you had the picnic in your living room? You could move back the furniture, put a blanket down in front of the fireplace and serve picnic type stuff. Come on, let's go check it out."

Giving her friend a dubious glance, Keile complied. She entered the room and looked around, trying to see it as Haydn might. "I don't know," she said, frowning. "It's just not...you know?" She shrugged, unable to think of the right word.

"This *will* work," Dani clapped her hands together. "Trust me, Keile. This room has enough space to spread out a blanket, plus you could bring in a small table to put the food on. And if anybody didn't want to sit on the floor, they could pull up one of the chairs."

"It would be simpler than getting a dining room table delivered in the next few days," she conceded grudgingly. "And I wouldn't have to buy a set of matching plates or glasses either," she added slowly, beginning to warm up to the idea.

"You don't have a set of matching plates?" Dani regarded her friend with raised eyebrows.

Keile stuffed her hands in her pockets and looked away. "I haven't gotten around to it yet. Besides, with just me it doesn't really matter."

"I see I'm going to have to sic Lynn on you," Dani said wryly. "You don't have to live like you did in college anymore."

"I know, I know. I just haven't...well, gotten around to it." She hung her head like a scolded child. "I'm trying to be frugal."

Dani snorted. "Sure. So when are you having this shindig?"

"We didn't set a firm date. I said I'd call and set it up."

"You should do that today, so she'll have time to plan."

Keile swallowed, feeling butterflies flapping their wings against her insides. "Yeah," was all she could manage.

"Don't be scared."

"I'm not scared." She took a deep breath and let it out slowly. "Nervous. I'm nervous. I've never called anybody for something like this before. God, that sounds so lame."

"Remember this is not a date." She patted Keile's shoulder. "All you're doing is getting back with her to confirm something you already set up. But if it will make you feel any better, we can practice."

Keile's eyes widened. "Practice?"

"When you give a presentation at work, don't you practice it first?"

"Well...yeah."

"This is no different from that. I'll be Haydn and you can rehearse different lines with me. Then when you get her on the phone, you'll know what to say and you won't sound nervous."

"How do you know all this stuff?"
Dani grinned. "Practice."
She threw her head back and laughed. "I love you, Dani."

Chapter Eleven

"Wednesday at six thirty. We'll see you then." Haydn turned off the phone and looked at her brother. "There it's done. Are you happy now?"

"Yes I am," he said seriously. "Come on, it won't kill you to go to dinner."

"Why do you care?" She leaned back against the gray slate kitchen counter and crossed her arms over her chest. "I could be wrong, but this feels like you're trying to set me up again. Didn't you learn your lesson the last time?"

"I admit I made a mistake when I set you up with Claudia."

"And Justine. We can't forget Justine, the boy-child hater."

"Okay, I get the point. Much like I did when you reamed me a new one for not checking to see if they had an aversion to sticky fingers and runny noses. But that's why Keile's perfect."

"Nobody is perfect," she shot back, disgruntled. She didn't

need her brother to tell her what she'd already been denying.

"Why must you be so difficult?"

"I'm not being difficult. I just want you to stay out of my love life."

"What love life?" he asked, throwing his hands in the air before taking a deep breath. "Do you really want to be alone the rest of your life? Someday you're going to have to move on."

"I tried that. Remember the two women we were just talking about?" She looked out of the window above the sink. It was dark and clear outside, the half moon shining brightly in the sky. "I have Kyle. He's enough for me. I don't need to go looking for a woman who's going to rip out my heart and stomp on it."

Marcus crossed the room and put his arm on her shoulder. "You lesbians always think a date equates true love."

Haydn snorted. "Not funny."

He smirked. "It was, but that's beside the point."

"What is the point?"

"That we're talking about dinner with a lesbian who already knows you have a child. A *male* child, whom she spent an evening entertaining. And once you add in the fact that Edan and I will be there as well to make sure Keile doesn't try to take advantage of you, it's a win-win situation." He let out a sharp breath when Haydn elbowed him in the ribs.

"That's what you get for trying to be funny." She ran her fingers along the thick ridges of her corduroy pants. "The real point is that I think she wants more than I have to give," she said quietly. "Her face lit up like a Christmas tree when I said she should come again."

"Maybe it was the thought of seeing Kyle again that did it. She seems very attached to him."

Haydn's jaw tightened. "Don't be ridiculous. I could see it in her eyes. It's been a long time since a woman has looked at me that way, but I still remember what that's like," she said with a touch of bitterness. "If this were only about seeing Kyle, she would have made arrangements to meet you in the park."

"I don't get this," he said, clearly frustrated with his sister.

"You have an attractive woman, who also finds you attractive, wanting to go out with you and you *don't* want that? Where's the logic in that, Haydn?"

"You would have to put it that way." She hung her head. "It does seem—"

"Moronic?"

She couldn't stop a reluctant chuckle at his outraged expression. "A little scary." She rested her head on his shoulder. "I'm not ready to feel any of this."

"That I can understand. But remember, before we moved here you said you were going to start over. This is your chance. Nothing may come of it, but it is a start."

"I guess you're right," she said after a long pause. "And I guess I'm glad you're my brother."

"I know you are," Marcus said smugly, then pushed her away before she could elbow him again. "Now let's go see what you're going to wear."

Keile turned away from her computer monitor and absently answered her office phone. "Hello. Keile Griffen speaking."

"How did it go?" Dani asked, not bothering with a greeting.

"Kyle caught a stomach thing and they had to cancel at the last minute," she said, trying to mask her disappointment.

"Bummer. I know how much you were looking forward to it."

"It's okay, really. Haydn did say she would call me back to reschedule once she figured out how serious his illness is."

"That's a good thing. It shows definite interest if she's already thinking about setting something up."

"Oh yeah?" Keile's mood brightened. "I was thinking of giving her a call to see how Kyle's doing, but I don't want to seem like a pest. Especially if she was only being polite again."

"What is it with you and polite? Just do it, girl. She knows you're crazy about her son, so I don't see how she could take it the wrong way."

Keile pulled on the top of her turtleneck sweater and swallowed hard. "I guess."

"Call her right now and see if she needs anything. And even if she doesn't, it's Thursday—"

"I know that."

"If you'd let me finish, I would have added that it's close enough to try to set something up for this weekend."

"I don't know about that, Dani. I could offer to share the food we didn't eat last night. If she's been dealing with a sick kid all day, surely she'd welcome a ready-made dinner."

Dani laughed. "Perfect. You just don't know how adorable you sound."

"Thanks, I think. I'm going to owe you big-time when this is over."

"You betcha."

Keile disconnected, then immediately dialed the number she knew by heart. She caught her breath as the phone was answered on the first ring.

"Hi. It's Keile. I just called to check on Kyle and see if there's anything you might, uh, need me to pick up for you."

"Kyle seems to have picked up a minor stomach bug. He'll probably be back to normal by tomorrow."

"Uh, good. That's good. Are you holding up okay?"

"The only pain I have is my nose. You don't want to know how many diapers he's gone through in the past twenty-four hours."

Here goes nothing. "I don't have much experience with that, but I'm more than willing to come over and learn."

"You don't know what you're getting yourself into. Runny diapers are not for the faint of heart."

Keile wasn't sure if she was being encouraged or discouraged. "My heart can take the strain," she replied with more confidence than she felt.

"Don't say I didn't warn you."

To Keile it almost sounded like a challenge. She could do challenges. "I won't. Is it okay to bring the food I was going to serve last night? You wouldn't want it to go to waste now, would you?"

Haydn chuckled. "Okay, Keile Griffen, you and your food can come by at seven."

"I'll be there," Keile said quickly. "Do I need to pick up diapers?"

"That we have covered. Thanks for calling to check on Kyle."

Keile held the receiver long after Haydn hung up. She'd actually done it. And more surprising, Haydn had responded the right way. God, she was going to owe Dani a fortune. *But it's worth it,* she thought with a smile and dropped the receiver in its place.

Haydn glanced at the receiver before returning it to its base and wondered when she'd lost control of the conversation. How did she go from giving an update on Kyle to giving in to Keile's invitation?

"What's with the look on you face?" Edan asked as she joined Haydn in the kitchen. "You look happy-confused or is it confused-happy?"

"I just told Keile she could come over and help me change diapers."

"Is that all?"

"All? You call that all? All she did was get me so confused I didn't even realize what I was saying." She ran her fingers through her hair and shook her head. "I didn't plan to see her again and before I knew it, I agreed to have her come over and bring food! So don't say is that all."

"She's bringing food? What a good date."

"Dinner. No, it's not even dinner."

"Haydn honey, if it wasn't more than dinner, you wouldn't be freaking out. It's okay to admit you're looking forward to seeing her again."

"Okay, maybe a tiny bit." She used her fingers to demonstrate. "But like I told Marcus, I'm not sure I'm ready for any of this. For her."

"You will be after a nap. Now go."

"Sure I will," she said, sounding anything but sure.

Upstairs, Haydn stopped by Kyle's room. Once satisfied he was comfortable, she walked to her spacious master bedroom at the end of the hall. Falling into the softness of the maroon comforter, she couldn't remember how long it had been since she felt so off balance because of a woman. *Too long maybe*, she thought, staring at the white ceiling. *Or maybe not long enough*. She had the feeling dinner with Keile might force her to come up with the answer.

Feeling more excited than nervous, Keile rang the doorbell. The ornate, red door opened to reveal Haydn. She was beautiful, dressed in a tight-fitting green shirt and worn jeans that hugged her hips. Keile was glad she'd taken the time to change from her work clothes to casual attire. "Hi." She swallowed, caught off-guard by the intensity of her emotions.

"Hi. Come on in." Haydn stepped back to allow Keile to enter. "The worst seems to be over. You might even get out of diaper duty," she said with a glimmer of a smile.

"Too bad, but I still have food." Keile held up a large paper bag by the handles.

Haydn led Keile to the kitchen. "Oh. Marcus and Edan aren't here, so…well, it's just the two of us for dinner."

The nervousness in Haydn's voice caused Keile to pause in the act of removing the containers from the bag. She looked up, catching Haydn's eyes and gave her what she hoped was a reassuring smile. "I hope that's okay with you. I wouldn't—"

"No, it's fine," Haydn said, then looked away from Keile's gaze. "I thought you should know."

"It's fine with me too," she said evenly and returned to emptying the bag. "This was a last-minute thing."

"Looks like you have a good selection," Haydn said, setting out plates and silverware. "You must have slaved all day," she joked, sounding far more relaxed.

"I did," Keile replied solemnly. "I used the store's containers because I didn't have enough of my own."

Haydn raised one auburn brow. They shared a laugh before dishing up the food fit for a picnic. Keile, with input from Dani, had purchased two types of chicken salad, potato salad, cucumber salad, coleslaw, deviled eggs and crisp French rolls. As they ate, the sound of babbling seemed to come from near the fridge. Startled, she looked around for Kyle.

"It's the baby monitor. Kyle just woke up." Haydn's lips twitched as if she were trying to hold back a smile. "I'll go get him."

"I'll tag along, if it's okay?" Keile was halfway out of her seat before Haydn nodded.

They found Kyle standing in his crib, clutching the guardrail and babbling away. He shrieked when he saw his mother, holding out his arms. "Mama," he said, placing his head in the crook of her shoulder.

"Look who's here to see you," Haydn told him, rubbing his back.

"Hi, Buster." Keile changed her position so she was in his line of sight.

"Mama!" He reached for her with a wide grin.

Keile wrapped him in her arms, inhaling his clean baby scent. She sniffed him playfully. "He sure does smell good for a pooping baby. Can he come downstairs and eat with us?"

"Eat, no. Drink, yes. He's on a liquid diet for now."

They went back downstairs to their interrupted meal. Kyle strained against his mother when she tried to put him in his high chair. Giving in gracefully, Haydn settled him on the floor and handed him his spill-proof cup. He took a few sips before toddling over to his big yellow truck. Sinking to his knees, he slowly pushed the truck back and forth, making sounds.

He still appeared lethargic to Keile's untrained eyes. She turned to Haydn for reassurance. "He will be okay soon, right?"

"I promise you that by tomorrow afternoon he'll be running around at his normal pace," she said with a smile.

"I'm glad. I was worried about him." Keile was comforted by the sudden warmth in Haydn's eyes. "It must be really hard on you when he's sick and you can't make it go away."

"Yes, but with something like this I have the advantage of knowing how to treat it. It's all part of getting that motherhood badge I'm shooting for." She picked up her fork, turning her attention to the food. "So tell me where you work," she prompted, then listened while Keile tried her best to explain her job. "Sounds more interesting than what I do."

"And that is?"

"I'm your run-of-the-mill accountant. I do the books for a number of small companies across the country."

"Does that mean you travel a lot?"

"Lucky for me most of my business meetings take place over the computer. I do have an office near Tenth to impress potential local clients."

"You've impressed me. It must be difficult to run a business *and* take care of Kyle."

"Before I had Kyle, I was a financial manager for a big company and having that job while trying to raise Kyle would have been very hard. Once I decided to have a child, I realized I needed a change of pace and luckily my bank account allowed it. So no, it's hasn't been that hard. And Kyle's started going to day care for part of the day since we moved here and I work some at home when he's sleeping. Plus Marcus takes him Saturday mornings and helps out if I get in a bind. Compared to other working mothers I have it easy, believe me." She pushed back her chair and began gathering dirty dishes.

Keile jumped up. "Let me help you with that." Working together, they cleared the table and repackaged the leftovers.

"Time for Kyle to have more liquids." Haydn retrieved his cup and refilled it. "Do you have time to stay a little while?" she asked as she closed the refrigerator door with her hip.

"Sure." Keile reached for Kyle, who was tugging on her jeans, and put him on her shoulders. "I haven't had a chance to compliment Kyle on his trucks."

Haydn looked from Kyle to Keile and gave a ghost of a smile. "We wouldn't want you to miss out on your fix. You go ahead, I'll be right there."

When Haydn entered the room, Keile was trotting around in circles and whinnying with Kyle still on her shoulders. And although she didn't want to be affected by the sight, she was. She tore her gaze away from the joy on her son's face and settled on the sofa.

"I'm officially worn out," Keile announced and swung Kyle to the floor. "Your toys are going to have to do for now." She took a seat next to Haydn and looked surprised when Kyle leaned against her knees and held his arms out. "Up with you then," she said and lifted him onto her lap. "I thought for sure he would go to his toy box."

Haydn watched as Kyle rested his head against Keile's chest. "Looks like he wants to cuddle. He's probably getting sleepy again."

"I'm curious, why does he call me mama?"

"I really don't know. He went through a short phase a couple of months ago when he called everything mama, but I thought he was over that. It sounds a little different when he calls me mama than when he calls you mama...have you noticed?"

"Well...no. I imagine it'll take me awhile to be able to understand him as well as you do." She stroked Kyle's cheek with the back of her hand. "Although by that time he'll probably start calling me Keile."

"It'll take some more development before he'll be able to pronounce that," Haydn said, unable to hide her amusement. "Keile's not the easiest name to pronounce."

"Maybe I can help with that. I'm pretty determined when I set my mind to it." She smiled. "Although I have to admit that my friend Dani likes to call it stubbornness."

"Then maybe you and Kyle *are* related," Haydn said. "According to Marcus, Kyle is stubborn."

"He tried to tell me that, too. But Kyle and I know we're very determined. Isn't that right, Buster?" Keile looked down to see that he had fallen asleep. She gave him a fleeting kiss.

Haydn felt her breath catch in her throat. The sight of her baby being held so tenderly was almost too much to bear. *Why does she have to be so damn likable?* She took a deep breath.

"Can I help you put him to bed?"

Haydn swallowed, trying to ease the lump in her throat. "Sure," she said, her voice slightly husky. "I'll even allow you the pleasure of carrying him upstairs."

Keile grinned and stood, careful not to jostle Kyle. She followed Haydn up the stairs, placed him on the changing table, then watched carefully as Haydn changed Kyle's diaper and put on his pajamas, all without waking him. "I'm impressed," she whispered.

"Then you're easily impressed." She looked up and was momentarily taken aback by the intensity of Keile's gaze. Her smile faltered. "I'll let you put him to bed," she said and looked on as Keile lowered him into his crib as if he could break. "He's tougher than he looks, even when he's sick."

"I'll keep that in mind," Keile replied softly, watching as Kyle turn onto his stomach. "I guess I should go. You probably need your sleep as well." When they returned downstairs, Keile refused to take the leftovers, insisting they were for Marcus and Edan. "If they don't finish them off, I promise to come back and get them."

"See that you do," Haydn said, her emotions ranging from panic to excitement at the thought of seeing Keile again. All these feelings on top of the sleep deprivation were making her slightly dizzy. She swayed and would have fallen if Keile hadn't caught her.

"Are you okay?" Keile put a hand on Haydn's back to steady her.

"I'm fine…really," Haydn said with an embarrassed smile. "My body just reminded me of how little sleep I got last night." Worrying about Keile's imminent arrival had kept her from having a restful nap. That was the only reason she could think of when, instead of stepping away, she leaned into Keile, drawing from her quiet strength.

Keile gathered her even closer. "You sure you're okay?" she whispered after a few moments.

"I am now," Haydn replied, fairly humming with contentment as excitement won over panic. "I see now why Kyle likes to be held by you."

Keile chuckled lightly. "These arms are available any time you need them."

Haydn leaned back and looked up into Keile's face. She almost cried, seeing the warm concern directed her way. She wasn't used to this kind of attention. "Thank you," she said softly, and kissed Keile's cheek.

Keile slowly released Haydn. "I hope to see you soon." This time, she led the way to the front door. She put on her coat, lightly kissed Haydn on the lips, then left.

Slipping into bed, Keile was still on Haydn's mind. She hadn't wanted Keile to be so charming, or so damn nice. A part of her had been waiting for flaws to emerge, giving her a reason to truthfully say she wasn't attracted to her. The opposite had happened, and now she could still feel Keile's arms around her, making her feel like she was special. It had been comforting to know she could shift the burden to someone else's shoulders, if only for a little while.

But there were dangers attached to giving up even a little bit of control. And she wasn't sure she wanted to let another woman deep inside. Haydn rolled over onto her stomach and closed her eyes. Sighing, she clutched her pillow. Although she was tired, sleep was long in coming.

Chapter Twelve

Keile walked into her cube the next morning at seven, the kiss she'd shared with Haydn still fresh in her mind. If she breathed deeply she could smell Haydn's scent clinging to her coat. With a bemused smile, she stowed away her briefcase and pulled out her chair. *I kissed the girl.* She hugged herself and laughed out loud. *Life is good.*

As she twirled around in her chair, she noticed the bright yellow note attached to her computer monitor. She grabbed a notebook and hustled to Rick's office as requested.

Rick looked up with a smile. "Come on in. Sorry to have to harass you so early this morning. Do you need coffee?"

You'd think he'd know by now that I don't drink coffee. Keile quickly dismissed the uncharacteristic churlish thought. "I'm fine." She sat in one of the two chairs in front of Rick's desk. "I assume this is about the Crawford project," she said, opening her notebook.

"I got word last night that he wants to meet this afternoon and see a preliminary schedule. I know that doesn't give you a lot of time, but what else is new? What can I do to help?"

"I have most of the schedule finished." She handed him her copy. "I'm still waiting for word from Alex to finalize everything. Maybe you could give him a buzz to speed things up. He usually gets in around eight. I also need to double check a couple of other supporting background data. What time is the meeting?"

"Two was the latest I could get Mr. Timmons to agree to." Rick checked his watch. "If Alex gets you the information by nine, can you can be done by then?"

"Sure," Keile replied with confidence. She hadn't gotten to where she was by telling the boss no. Whatever needed to be done, she would do.

She worked steadily throughout the rest of the morning. She wasn't surprised to get a message from Alex at ten minutes after eight with the information she needed. A call from Rick always sped things up. At one, she sent the presentation to Rick for approval, then leaned back in her chair and waited for word. Keile was shocked when the phone rang almost immediately. Too soon for Rick to have gone through the presentation, which meant he didn't like what she had done. She picked up the phone.

"Hello, Keile Griffen. I'm calling to make sure you have us on your calendar for Thursday after next," Jo told her.

"Of course. Now remind me again what I'm doing Thursday after next."

"Turkeys, pilgrims and lots of food. Ring a bell? Remember, you already promised Susan you'd come."

"Is it that time already?" Keile looked at her calendar, surprised at the date. "Far be it for me to stand Susan up. Uh, do I already know what I'm supposed to bring?"

Jo laughed. "How 'bout I put you down for beer?"

"I can do that. What time?"

"We plan to eat around three. But since you're bringing the beer, come early for God's sake. Feel free to bring as many guests as you want."

Why do I think she's talking about more than Can? With a rueful smile, Keile replaced the receiver. Maybe Dani had been talking? For once she didn't mind if she was the focus of conversation. *Hmm, I wonder what Haydn's doing for Thanksgiving.* She stared at the phone and fantasized about having Haydn and Kyle with her on Turkey Day. What a pipe dream. She was glad when the computer dinged, bringing her mind back to work. The new message was from Rick, letting her know the presentation was good to go.

At ten minutes to two, she headed to the conference room nearest Rick's office. She was happy to note that the projector was set up. All she had to do was plug in her flash drive and copy the presentation to the laptop. Promptly at two, Rick entered the conference room with Mr. Timmons in tow. Keile stood up and walked over for introductions. After a couple of minutes of small talk, Rick began the presentation. Mr. Timmons interrupted a couple of times with questions, but for the most part was silent.

"Good work, Keile," Rick said, stepping back into the room after seeing Mr. Timmons off. "I can tell he was impressed. Here's what we need to do next." He waited for Keile to grab her pad before he proceeded to give her detailed instructions. "I need this by midday Monday. I have a feeling we'll be hearing from them sooner than later."

"Sure, no problem." *No problem, except I actually wanted to have kind of a life this weekend!* The amount of work Rick was asking for would take up a good bit of both days. "I'll get right on it."

"Thanks. We'll sit down Monday and see about getting you some help for the rest of the project."

Why not now? Irked, Keile could only nod in acknowledgment as she gathered her papers.

By the time she returned to her cube, she was over her temporary spate of anger. It was unreasonable of her to expect Rick to treat her any differently from the way she'd shown him she could be treated. She was the one who willingly worked weekends and nights to make a deadline. And she had bonus money sitting in her financial accounts, making her feel secure and successful, to show for it.

"So get over it," she told herself sternly and plopped down into her chair. Pulling herself to the computer she began evaluating the data that would best support the project.

"Is he asleep?" Edan asked when Haydn entered the family room and placed the baby monitor on the coffee table.

She nodded, covering a yawn. "Finally. If I had to sing that inane Muffin Man song one more time, somebody was going to get hurt." She plopped down on the sofa next to Edan and pulled her legs under her body. "So where did you end up last night, young lady?"

"Not where I wanted to be." Edan's expression was glum. "I looked everywhere, but contrary to inside info she was nowhere to be found. So I gave up and came home to my lonely bed. Tell me you had a better time."

"Surprisingly I did," Haydn admitted with a small smile. "We didn't do anything exciting, but…there's something about her presence."

Edan tilted her head and motioned for Haydn to continue.

"She kissed me. It was almost over before it began, and if I hadn't been so tired, I would have pulled her back for more."

"And that scares the shit out of you, doesn't it?" Edan said gently.

Haydn sighed, running her fingers through her hair. "What scares me more is how safe and secure I felt when she held me." She gave a humorless laugh. "She's too perfect, like some heroic figure. I mean, come on, real people have flaws and they hurt you."

"I won't argue with you about people having flaws. But it doesn't sound like Keile can win with you. She's too heroic and therefore doesn't show you her flaws, or she shows you flaws and you reject her."

Haydn beat her head against the back of the sofa. "I never said I was rational," she whined. "You're supposed to be my friend, Edan. If I can't be unreasonable with you, who can I be unreasonable with?"

"Oh. Forgive me for trying to help out my best friend. What *was* I thinking?" She threw Haydn a challenging glance. "Listen, if I can make a fool of myself by hanging out in public places in hopes of spotting Dani, you can call Keile and invite her over. Don't look back in a couple of years and feel regret," she added softly. The *like me* was left unspoken.

"Maybe you should take your own advice and call Dani."

"I don't have a number."

Haydn shook her finger. "Not good enough. I'll get it for you." She gave Edan a sly smile. "If I have to do it, you have to do it."

Edan quickly stuck out her hand. "You've got yourself a deal."

It wasn't until later that Haydn realized she'd been set up.

Keile groaned, arching her tired back. She rubbed her eyes and squinted at the clock on the monitor. "Seven! No wonder it's so damn quiet." She'd meant to leave at six, take Can for a long walk, then continue working on the project at home.

Hooking up the company-issued portable hard drive, she copied samples of the huge land use data files. The program she was developing needed them to be able to assist the client in selecting the best site for new commercial development. There was still much to do before noon on Monday. She sighed and tried not to think of what else she might have been doing instead of work. With her arms filled with work, Keile made her way to the deserted parking lot.

Once home, she changed out of her work clothes and took Can for a walk. Breathing in the crisp night air, she threw off her earlier frustrations and enjoyed the relative quiet of her neighborhood streets. Things weren't so bad. She still had a good job and a roof over her head. Maybe she needed to consider taking a break. Keile smiled. Of course, her life had changed since then, and she hoped Kyle and Haydn would factor into her plans somewhere down the line. But for that to happen she had to do a better job with this courtship thing. "Okay, Can, I need to call Haydn and ask her out on a real date."

Can chose that moment to stop and look back at her.

"What? You think I don't have the nerve to make that call?" She could have sworn she saw her own doubt reflected in his eyes. "Let's go home and I'll prove it to us." She pulled on his leash, forcing her reluctant pal to turn around and head back home. Her cell phone rang before she could unlock the front door. "Hey, what's up?"

"The rumor mill has it I'm being stalked. You know anything about that?" Dani asked.

"Are you serious?"

"Sort of. Three women have made it a point to let me know Edan was asking about me last night."

"So, do you want to be found?"

"That's why I'm calling," Dani said after a pause. "I need you to plant a suggestion for me."

"Ah," she said slowly as she began to understand where Dani was going. "So you do want to be found. But you don't want her to know that, right?"

"Something like that. I need her to make the first move this time."

"In my humble opinion, she already has." Wedging the phone against her shoulder, Keile unlocked the door, and stepped aside for Can to enter. "Not only did she go looking for you, she told people she was looking for you. What do you want the poor woman to do, buy a billboard?"

Dani snorted. "Maybe I do. Anyway, I need you to let her know that you and I are going to be at Daily's Pub getting an early drink tomorrow, say, around five."

"We are?"

"Pay attention, Keile, you're talking to a deranged woman," Dani said with a hint of desperation. "You and I will go have a drink. Edan will come in, we'll get to talking, then I'll take it from there."

"Does that mean I silently bow out of the picture at that

point?"

"It…depends. We'll see how it goes."

"Is it okay to invite Haydn?"

"Yes. That would be even better. Why didn't I think of that?"

"Because I'm smarter than you?" *And because I think about Haydn all the time.*

"Whatever. Just call!"

"Will do. I'll let you know as soon as I've made the arrangements."

"Sorry I snapped, Keile. I'm…I just…" She exhaled sharply.

"I understand."

"Thanks for making the call."

"Hey, I owe you." And she really did. Now she had a perfectly good reason to call Haydn. Smiling, she hung up her coat, doled out dog food, then made the call.

Her pulse raced at the sound of Haydn's voice. "Hi, it's Keile."

Haydn's laugh was rich. "You don't sound so sure. How are you?"

She swallowed. "I…I'm doing good." *Except your laugh made me lose my train of thought!*

"I'm glad you called. You saved me from having to call you."

"Oh yeah? Great minds and all, I guess. I'm calling for two reasons really," she said, gripping the phone tightly. "First, this friend of mine found out that a friend of yours is looking for her."

"Yeah? Is your friend interested?"

"She wants me to let your friend know that she and I will be at Daily's Pub tomorrow around five."

Haydn laughed. "This sounds like Super Sleuths. I guess both of our friends are allergic to phone calls."

"Just to phoning each other. But don't tell Edan or Dani I said that. So…I was wondering if you'd like to, you know, join us?"

"I need to see if Marcus can watch Kyle."

"It's okay to bring Kyle with you. I've seen plenty of kids in there. It's more of a restaurant than a pub and they don't allow smoking."

"That's a good fallback, but I'll still see if I can get Marcus to help. It's been awhile since I've gotten to be just an adult."

"I hope you can make it. I'd really like to see you again." Keile held her breath as she waited for a response.

"Edan and I will be there. We'll see about Kyle."

"Good." Keile closed her eyes and took the dive. "I was also wondering if you'd like to go out on a date sometime. You know, just the two of us."

"That…that would be okay."

Keile bit her lip at the hesitation in Haydn's voice, but decided to forge ahead. A yes was a yes. "Would Tuesday night work for you?"

"I need to check on a sitter and get back with you," Haydn said slowly.

She wondered if she'd misread the situation once again. "Sure. If you have to postpone, I understand. Kyle comes first."

"It's good you get that. I'll see you tomorrow night."

Keile frowned. After the kiss they'd shared, she'd been sure things were moving along. Now, she wasn't sure. Haydn didn't say no to the date idea, but she hadn't been enthusiastic either. Maybe that yes had been no. She sighed. Dating was nothing like work where following through on goals actually got you somewhere.

Chapter Thirteen

"You're sure she's going to show?" Dani asked for what seemed to Keile like the thousandth time. They were leaning against the bar at Daily's, waiting for Haydn and Edan to arrive. At five o'clock the large pub was relatively quiet.

"Yes," Keile replied, drawing the word out. Her frustration faded away as she took in her friend's panicked expression. "I know you're nervous, but remember she's as eager to see you as you are to see her."

Dani took a deep breath and let it out slowly. "You're right. I do need to calm down." She ran her hands down the sides of her nicest jeans. "I almost feel like I'm going out of my mind because she's all I've been thinking about lately. It's worse than it was when she left before."

"Welcome to the club." Keile put a hand on Dani's shoulder. "Considering she was stalking you, the feeling must be mutual."

"God, I hope so," Dani said fervently. "And if you tell anyone about this, you'll have me to deal with," she added, shooting Keile her tough cop look.

Haydn and Edan were approaching. "Hey," Keile said to both women, though her eyes were drawn against her will to Haydn. She stuffed her hands into the pockets of her jeans to keep from reaching for Haydn's hand.

"Hey yourself," Haydn replied with a smile. "This place looks great."

"Dani and I like it," Keile said with a pointed look in Dani's direction.

Dani pushed off the bar and mustered a smile.

"Hello," Edan said, breaking the silence between them. "I've been looking for you," she admitted, then caught her bottom lip between her teeth.

"So I hear," Dani said hoarsely, then cleared her throat. "Can I buy you a drink?"

Edan smiled. "Sure," she said, stepping closer. "How 'bout a hug for old time's sake?"

"Okay." Dani gingerly put her arms around her former lover and closed her eyes.

Keile looked away from what appeared to be an intimate moment and found Haydn watching her. "You ready to sit?"

"Yeah. Who knows how long they can go."

Keile tapped Dani's shoulder. "We're going to grab a table. Come when you're ready."

Dani gave Edan a final squeeze and let go. "We're ready."

"Yeah, Dani owes me a drink," Edan joked before she gave Keile a hug and hushed thanks.

After leading the way across the room and up a short flight of stairs to an empty booth, Keile stood back to allow Haydn to slide in. She slid in beside her, careful to leave enough space between them, then watched in surprise as Dani mimicked her actions. After the hug she just witnessed, she wouldn't have been surprised to see Edan sit on Dani's lap. "It occurs to me that Dani and Haydn have never been introduced," she said, and did so.

Conversation was stilted until they found a subject they could all agree on. Trashing the Defense of Marriage Act over beer and burgers led to numerous other topics, making the next couple of hours fly by.

"I hate to break this up, but I need to get back to Kyle," Haydn said after a glance at her watch. "He was acting a little cranky when I left. Any chance you could give me a ride, Keile?"

"No problem," Keile said.

"I hope I didn't put you on the spot," Haydn said once they'd left the noise of the pub. "I thought Edan and Dani needed more time together." She looked at Keile out of the corner of her eye, wanting to gauge her reaction. It hadn't been hard to pick up on Keile's seemingly cooler manner and she knew where the blame lay.

Keile rushed ahead to unlock the passenger side door, then held it open. "You're in luck. I cleaned out the Jeep last weekend."

"You didn't have to. Having a small child, I'm used to messy." Haydn fastened her seatbelt as Keile slid the key into the ignition. "And speaking of kids, I have a babysitter for Tuesday night. You do still want to go, right? I wouldn't blame you if you changed your mind."

Keile turned to look at her, surprise written on her face. "Why would I do that?"

"You don't have to make it sound like I'm crazy. It is flattering though."

"I would love to take you out Tuesday night." She bit her lip and traced the steering wheel with her finger. "I…I thought you didn't, you know, uh, want to go out with me," she admitted softly. "And I can understand that."

Ouch, Haydn thought and grimaced. "I'm sorry I gave you that impression. I'm a little rusty with the whole dating scene."

"I'm a little rusty myself."

"You?" Haydn's eyebrows inched up her forehead. There was no way someone as attractive as Keile wasn't swamped with offers.

"You don't have to sound as if I'm crazy. It is flattering though," she added, mimicking Haydn's tone exactly.

Haydn pursed her lips to keep from smiling. "Smart-ass."

"I've been called that before." Smiling she said, "Let's go check on a cranky Kyle. You did warn me he wouldn't always be sweet."

They were met at the door by a cranky father and son. "Thank God you're here," Marcus said, looking worse for wear. "He has been one unhappy camper." He all but shoved a pouty-faced Kyle toward his sister. "I need a drink," he declared to no one in particular.

"You should have called. I'd have come home sooner." Haydn frowned as she felt Kyle's neck with the back of her hand. "He does feel a little warm." She should never have left him.

"I checked. He has a low-grade fever and he started filling up diapers again. I abandoned the bananas and applesauce."

"Need me to go pick up anything at the store?" Keile reached for Kyle's hand, and smiled. "Hello, Buster."

"No, we're stocked up on diapers and Pedialyte," Marcus replied. "But since you're here, daughter of mine, you're next in line for stinky diaper patrol," he said as if doing her a big favor.

"I'll have you know I already volunteered." She leaned forward and stroked Kyle's reddened cheek. "My poor baby," she said, and held out her hands to take him. She dropped them quickly when he shrank back against his mother.

Marcus clapped her on the shoulder. "He gets that way when he's sick. I promise your time will come. Now let's go fix some drinks."

"Go light on the alcohol," Haydn said as they followed Marcus to the kitchen. "I have a feeling I'll need my wits about me with this one." She kissed Kyle's temple.

Marcus put his hands on his hips. "And who says *you* can have any?"

"It's *my* house, remember?"

"You guys are funny," Keile announced. "I bet it was laugh-a-minute at your house."

"Wait until you meet our parents," Marcus said, spreading his arms wide. "Of course you're no slouch yourself. Do your parents know how hilarious you are?"

"I don't have any." Keile's response was matter-of-fact. "My mom died when I was a kid."

"I'm sorry to hear that." Marcus was clearly upset. "What about your father?"

"Never had one. All I got from the owner of the sperm was my name. Well, sort of." She snickered. "It's kind of funny. My name was supposed to be Kylie because his name was Kyle, but my mother misspelled it on the form for my birth certificate. And when a nurse commented on how pretty sounding my Hawaiian name was, my mother decided to keep it. So in the end, all I got from him was Griffen."

"Your dad's name is Kyle, too?" Haydn busied herself trying to get Kyle to sip some water. "So is ours. Hence my Kyle."

"I would never refer to that man as my dad," she replied with a touch of bitterness. "He's done nothing to earn that title."

Marcus busied himself collecting the other ingredients. "Did you ever…look for him?" he asked, his back to her.

"Why would I bother? I think it's obvious he had no interest in me."

"Maybe he never knew," Haydn said gently.

"He knew," she said. "I asked my mother about him a couple of times. She claimed he wanted to be with us, but couldn't. I stopped asking and after awhile it was like he never existed."

"Again, I'm sorry I brought this all up," Marcus said. "I hope I didn't upset or offend you in any way."

"Hey, don't worry about it." She waved a hand in dismissal, though Haydn wasn't entirely convinced the subject didn't sting Keile a little bit. "It was so long ago and I could hardly expect you to know about any of this. Unless you read minds."

He grimaced. "Still, *I*, of all people, should have known not to assume everybody grew up with parents," he said, pointing to his chest. "Lord knows, I was lucky in that regard."

Haydn looked from Marcus to Keile, her expression

thoughtful. She addressed Keile. “How did you grow up?”

“I lived with my mother off and on, then with a couple of different foster families, and finally in a group home until I was eighteen.”

“So you actually knew your mother?” Marcus said intently.

Haydn glanced at her brother, taken aback by the intensity of his gaze and the longing in his voice. Was he was thinking of the woman who had given him up for adoption? And why hadn’t the subject been broached before? She hadn’t known this was important to her little brother. She was learning new information about someone she thought she knew very well.

“As much as a young child can know a parent,” Keile said and shrugged. “I do remember that her hair was long and blond.” Her fleeting smile was wistful. “Sometimes when she was in a good mood, she’d let me brush it. I’d do twenty strokes and she’d do eighty.”

That wistful smile tugged at Haydn’s heart. She gave a quick thanks to her parents who had always been available even when she didn’t want them to be. “I’m glad you have some good memories.”

Keile crossed her arms. “Those times were never enough, but they were very special.” She looked away, blinking rapidly. “How about you, Marcus? Have you ever looked for your birth parents?”

He shot Haydn a quick sideways glance before replying. “When I was going through a rebellious teen stage.”

“What? Why didn’t I know?” Haydn was surprised and hurt. Why had this never come up in any of the tell-all conversations they’d had over the years? “I don’t remember you ever talking about it.”

“Because I didn’t. One of my friends and I did it for kicks. Hell, we were young and stupid back then. When I found out she’d passed away a couple of years before, I figured nobody needed to know I was interested.” He added tequila to the blender, spilling some in his haste.

“I’m sorry,” Keile said. “I know that must have been hard

even though you didn't know her."

"I'm going to sound callous, but it didn't bother me that much at the time. She wasn't real to me. Later, when I finally got around to reading the letter she left me, I thought it would have been nice to reach out and say thanks for giving me to a wonderful family."

"Still, I wish you'd told me," Haydn said quietly. "I could have done something."

"Like I said, I was okay. Besides, I still had you guys to drive me crazy."

"I don't know about Mom and Dad, but I know for a fact it was you driving me crazy. Always sneaking into my room and going through my stuff. But I'm sure that's nothing compared to what you went through, Keile. Having to live in a group home must have been tough."

"At times. But what isn't? And I am a stronger person for it."

"You're to be commended for surviving intact," Marcus said. "I know. I did volunteer work when I was in college. It was sad to see kids get lost in the system."

"Lucky for me I was in a place where getting an education was stressed."

"I doubt luck had much to do with your success." Haydn shifted a drowsy Kyle to her left hip. "Aren't you the one who said you're determined?"

Keile smiled. "Touché."

"I'm determined. Determined to have a drink that is," Marcus declared, and turned on the blender.

"Sorry it got so serious," Keile whispered to Haydn under the cover of the blender noise. "Is he okay?"

She shrugged. "I never knew any of this about his birth mother. I always thought he didn't care. I can't believe he never told me."

"Maybe he feels guilty for wanting to know about her when he had a perfectly good home environment. Or maybe he thought he'd hurt your parents' feelings."

Haydn watched her brother and the closed look on his face.

"He shouldn't feel guilty for wanting to know his roots. He and I are going to have a talk."

"The poor guy doesn't know what he's in for, does he?"

"Nope."

"Okay ladies, I've finished my concoction." Marcus walked over to the cabinet and pulled out three glasses. "Let's drink."

"Does he always sleep with his knees drawn under his stomach?" Keile asked as she and Haydn descended the stairs after putting Kyle to bed.

"Pretty much." Haydn smiled. "But for some reason he only does it when he's in his crib. I blame all his little quirks on Marcus."

"I'm sure he loves that." Keile paused as they reached the bottom of the stairs.

"Can you stay for a little bit?"

Keile spared a brief thought about all the work she needed to do, then nodded. She would gladly make do with less sleep. Being with Haydn was worth that and more. "I'm not ready for the night to end, either."

"Good. Can I get you anything to drink?"

"No." She patted her flat stomach. "I'm good."

"I'm going to grab some water. Make yourself comfortable."

Keile eyed the sofa and finally decided to sit on the end, so she wouldn't seem presumptuous. When Haydn entered, she sat in the middle and turned so she was facing Keile. Keile swallowed and pulled at the turtleneck, which felt like it was shrinking. She glanced at Haydn, then quickly looked away.

"Alone at last, huh?"

Keile nodded and gave a nervous laugh. "I'm nervous all of a sudden." She ached to scoot closer to Haydn, put her arm around her shoulder and bury her face in Haydn's neck.

"Me, too. Why is that?" She tilted her head to the side, considering the problem. "It's not like we haven't talked before."

"This feels different." Keile rubbed her damp palms along the side of her pants. "I feel different," she added softly.

"How so?" Haydn asked, looking into Keile's eyes.

"Different expectations, I guess," she said slowly. "I… It feels much more like a date, and I want to make a good impression."

Haydn scooted over and placed a hand on Keile's thigh. "You've already made a good impression. This is you and me getting to know each other better."

"I can do that." She smiled, enjoying the warmth radiating from Haydn's hand. She could almost feel it in her heart. "What else do you want to know?"

"Everything," Haydn replied. "And I want to tell you everything about me."

"But you already know all about me," Keile said, wishing she had something exciting to reveal. "I'm really a simple person."

"You're right in a way. I do know the important things. You rescue runaway kids in the park and you're obviously strong-minded."

"Are you calling me stubborn?" Keile stuck out her bottom lip in a playful pout.

Haydn laughed. "If the shoe fits. But no, I'm talking about overcoming your upbringing. No matter what you say, I know it must have been a struggle."

"The important thing is that I made it. So you see, determination is a good thing."

"I'll try to remember that when I'm dealing with Kyle. Now tell me something else."

"I'm good at setting goals and following through." Keile studied the freckles dotting the bridge of Haydn's nose, knowing she had to proceed carefully. "Up until two weeks ago, my main goal was to feel financially secure. I'm sure you can guess why," she said wryly. "Then I met a little charmer and my perspective shifted, or maybe I finally left the insecure teenaged Keile behind. Whatever the reason, I have a new goal. I know it's going to be an uphill battle because I'm sure you're rusty at dating for a good reason, but I've done uphill before. I guess what I'm trying to say is that I want a chance to show you I'm worth the risk."

"Straightforward. I like that." Haydn tightened her hand on

Keile's muscular thigh. "I want to give you a chance. I do. But I haven't felt this way in a long time and I need to take this slowly. For me and for Kyle and for you."

Keile cupped Haydn's face. "I can accept that," she said softly. "Hopefully some day you can tell me about what happened. Until then, we take it slow. I can do slow."

"I know you can," she all but whispered, her voice tremulous. She smiled, trapping one of Keile's hands between her cheek and shoulder. "I know you can."

"I'm glad." Keile kissed Haydn's forehead, then circled her arms around Haydn's waist. She was in heaven. Resting her cheek against the top of Haydn's head, she felt her heart swell. Holding Haydn was enough for now.

Chapter Fourteen

Tuesday evening, Haydn checked her appearance in the mirror for what she promised herself was the last time. Tucking her hair behind her ears, she peered at the bridge of her nose. *I guess I don't need to try and cover my freckles.* She smiled, thinking back to Saturday night when, as they had continued to cuddle on the sofa, Keile had admitted how much she liked her freckles. She hadn't believed it until Keile gently traced the bridge of her nose and said one day she was going to try to kiss every one of them. For the first time in a long time, Haydn had felt beautiful and desirable. What a rush. What a woman. After brushing a speck of lint off her blouse, she left the closet, ready to go wait for her date.

"Wow! Don't you look good." Marcus gave an appreciative whistle as Haydn stepped into the family room. He and Kyle were on the floor playing. "I told you that shirt would bring out the color of your eyes." He sat up, giving her an appraising look. She was wearing a green silk blouse with the top buttons undone and black pants that hugged her curves. "You look hot, sis. Maybe Kyle and I should tag along as chaperones," he teased.

"Don't even think about it," she retorted with a mock glare. "I'm nervous enough as it is."

"But you just went out with Keile Saturday."

"That was different." She gave him an impatient glance. "Edan and Dani were there. Tonight is a date and it's only the two of us."

Marcus walked over to his sister. He put a hand under her chin, and raised her face. "What are you really worried about?" he asked gently.

"The truth?" she asked with a sigh. "I'm afraid I'll like her even more after tonight. I'm afraid she'll hold me and kiss me, and I won't want her to stop." She drew in a shuddering breath. She had spent the entire day thinking about being with Keile, vacillating between anticipation and anxiety. As a result, her tiny office had felt claustrophobic and she'd barely gotten any work done.

"Do you want me to pull her aside and read her the riot act?"

"Don't joke," she pleaded, resting her head against his chest. "This is too…" She was unable to describe the turmoil her senses were in, mostly because she didn't understand it herself.

"I won't." He patted her back. "It's only a date. Just enjoy yourself. No need to pack the U-Haul."

"One day I'm going to get you for disparaging lesbians," she said, poking his chest.

"Yeah, yeah. Now admit you feel better."

The ringing of the doorbell sent Kyle rushing out of the room. He stopped at the front door and rapped his knuckle against it, as if that would make it open.

Haydn was seconds behind him. "That's not how we open the door, sweetie." She pulled him aside and looked through the peephole. Taking a deep breath, she opened the door.

Keile stood on the welcome mat, smiling shyly and holding up flowers. "Hi."

"Hey." Haydn's heart hammered as she accepted the flowers and stepped back. She took a moment to appreciate the fit of Keile's charcoal pantsuit.

"Mama!" Kyle held up his arms.

"Keile," she said, pointing to her chest before she obligingly picked him up. "Keile."

"Mama," he chortled, clutching her neck.

"Told you he was stubborn." Marcus smirked. "And can we say you dress up nicely, daughter of mine?"

"We can."

"I'll go put these in a vase." Haydn hurried to the kitchen. Leaning against the counter, she took a couple of deep breaths and let them out slowly. *Why does she have to look so good?* She considered banging her head against the counter. Bruises on her forehead would clash with her blouse.

"Are you okay?" Keile asked softly. She stepped up behind Haydn and rested her hands on Haydn's hips. "If this is too fast, we can stay here and order pizza."

Haydn turned around and smiled at Keile's earnest expression. "I want to go out with just you and me. Really," she said and realized she meant every word. While she might still harbor some apprehension, she realized it was time to take this first baby step. She peered at Keile suspiciously. "Or are you just trying to get out of paying for a fancy dinner?"

Keile's eyes zeroed in on Haydn's pouting lips and she swallowed. "You found me out," she said, her voice husky. "You look great tonight." Unable to resist, she dropped a quick kiss on Haydn's pink lips.

"Thanks. So do you." She blushed under the scrutiny of Keile's appreciative gaze.

"Thanks back. Shall we?"

They endured a prolonged goodbye from Kyle before departing. Keile opened the passenger door of her newly detailed vehicle and assisted Haydn into the seat. On the drive to the restaurant, Keile brought up the remarkable improvement in Kyle. "And he was so cute, not wanting us to leave."

About like you when you talk about Kyle, she thought, feeling ridiculously pleased. "Kids bounce back quickly."

"I guess I dodged changing dirty diapers again." Keile released an exaggerated sigh of relief.

"There's still time," Haydn warned, patting Keile's thigh.

Keile gave her a quick smile as she pulled into the busy parking lot of the restaurant. "I hope you like The Prado. It was highly recommended by one of my co-workers," she said.

"When I lived in San Francisco we used to eat out all the time. But it's funny," Haydn said with a smile, "I find I don't miss it as much as I thought I would. I'm happy eating at home watching Kyle play with his food. Don't get me wrong, I appreciate you taking me out someplace special, but I want you to know I don't need this all the time."

The Prado was designed to look like a mini Southern mansion, with a wide covered porch offset by four white columns. Keile opened the opaque glass door. They were immediately greeted by a hostess, who escorted them to a small booth. "This is nice." Keile glanced around, taking in the understated elegance of the room and most of the occupants. The tables were spaced far enough apart to give a semblance of intimacy. She fingered the smooth leather covering the thick bench.

"And it's so quiet," Haydn whispered. She'd grown accustomed to restaurants geared for people with kids. "I can actually hear myself think. I'll let you know later if that's a good thing." She shot Keile an impish grin and opened the thick menu.

"Good evening, ladies. My name is Sean. I'll be your server this evening. Would you care for something to drink? We have an excellent selection of wines."

Keile deferred the choice to Haydn, who ordered a chardonnay.

"How long did you live in San Francisco?" Keile asked once Sean left.

"A little over seven years. I enjoyed it out there. It's a lot different from Texas and Georgia."

"I can imagine. Seneca is getting bigger because it's close to Atlanta, but even Atlanta is no match for San Francisco. Can I ask why Seneca?" Seeing the contemplative look on Haydn's face, she quickly said, "You don't have to answer if you don't want to."

"I was just thinking." Haydn smiled. "First, Marcus applied for a job in Atlanta. Then Edan started making noise about trying to get back to Seneca. The next thing I knew, they ganged up and started working on me. And I realized there was nothing to keep me there with them gone." *Nothing but bad memories.*

"I've lived here all my life, so it's hard to imagine someone willingly moving from California to Georgia." Keile closed her menu. "I'm just glad you did."

"I'm glad I moved here, too. Don't tell Edan or Marcus, but they were right, I needed a change." Haydn shut her menu decisively. "As difficult as it is, I think I've narrowed it down to one entrée."

"That was delicious," Haydn said as they exited the parking lot. "I'm stuffed. Next time you have to eat more of the dessert."

"Hey, I thought I ate my fair share."

"Not even close, Keile. I took up the slack for you this time but I don't know if I'll be up for the task next time," Haydn said, giving Keile a sideways glance.

"That's a small price to pay for the pleasure of your company," was her smooth rejoinder.

"You're not playing fair," Haydn complained. "You're supposed to be slipping up and exposing your flaws."

"Sorry," she said, "I didn't get that e-mail."

"Ha, ha. I guess I can put down smart-ass in the flaw column." Haydn pretended to take notes. "What else?"

"I don't really like coffee, and I'm a recovering workaholic."

"That would explain the trillion packets of sugar," Haydn said. "So you don't like coffee. I can see I'm going to have to think very hard before saying yes the next time you ask me out."

"That doesn't include Thanksgiving does it?"

"No. Since I've already accepted, that date is grandfathered in."

"Good," Keile said with satisfaction. She was looking forward to introducing Haydn to the rest of her friends. After pulling into Haydn's driveway, she hurried around to help Haydn out of the vehicle. "But you know I would drink coffee for you, don't you?"

Haydn stroked Keile's cheek. "You're going to make me cry." She leaned forward to kiss the spot her hand had been stroking.

Keile looked into Haydn's eyes. "I don't want to do that. Never that," Keile said seriously. She gathered Haydn into her arms and closed her eyes. *I can do slow, if it feels as wonderful as this.*

"Do you want to come in for coffee?"

"Depends," Keile replied, her mouth against Haydn's ear. "How much sugar and milk do you have?" She kissed her ear. "I'm taking it slow," she said, more for herself than Haydn, and nibbled on Haydn's neck. The ensuing shiver caused a tightening in her abdomen. With a groan, she pulled back, her breathing shallow and rapid. "About that coffee?" she asked with a rueful smile.

Haydn exhaled, her eyes slightly unfocused. "I guess it is safer."

Keile could hear the reluctance in Haydn's voice. *It's a good start.* Giving a silent prayer, she took Haydn's hand in hers. *It's a very good start.*

Chapter Fifteen

"Okay Dani, I want a piece of whatever it is that put that look on your face."

Dani smirked. "Sorry Griffen, no can do. This is strictly a one-on-one deal. Now can I come in or you just going to stand here and pout all night?"

A few minutes later she was sitting with Dani on the worn, blue couch. She reached for the bottle of beer sitting on the coffee table. "Tell me about you and Edan."

"We're good," Dani said with a big grin. "Real good. I can't believe how easy it's been to be with her again. We've seen each other every day since Saturday."

"Judging by your grin, you've spent some nights together as well."

"Keile Griffen, I can't believe you're trying to get me to kiss and tell."

"Fine. Keep your secrets, Knight." Her smile slipped. "What about, you know?"

"We haven't had a chance to talk about that yet. We haven't had a chance to talk about much of anything. The non-verbal communication has sort of taken over." Dani flipped her ponytail over her shoulder. "What can I say? She wants me."

"There's nothing wrong with that. I just think you might want to bring it up at some point."

"I will. Come on, she came back to me. Doesn't that tell you something?"

"That you're good in bed?"

"There is that. But I was talking about kids. She's knows how I feel, so maybe she's decided parenting isn't for her."

Keile gave Dani a sharp look. "Do you really believe that? I don't and I've seen her with Kyle."

"We'll get there, okay? Right now we're in the honeymoon phase."

"I'm just saying. You were just crying about Carla, so be careful, okay?"

"Okay. Noted and appreciated. How are things going with Haydn?"

"Good. I think good."

"You don't sound so sure."

"Haydn's a little...well...hesitant I guess that's the right word. The more I think about it, the more I worry I may never be enough for her to get over whatever's holding her back."

"But what if you are?" Dani grabbed Keile's arm. "It's early, Keile. Give her time to get to know and trust you."

"As if I know how to instill trust." Keile pushed away her empty beer. "I was so sure I knew what I was doing." She tried to smile but it came out more like a grimace. "What an idiot I was. I can set goals, but the problem is that I'm not in control of the outcome. I'm not so sure I like that. It seems like such a big risk."

"What's the alternative? Would you want to go back to where you were before meeting Kyle?"

"No! I've never felt this alive. It's strange, it's almost like I never knew myself. There are these big chunks of me experiencing feelings I never have before." *And it scares me.*

"You're not alone. It's just another stage and with each stage there's growth. It's a good thing."

"If you say so. Frankly, at this point I would just like to be able to pretend I knew how this love thing works."

"Nobody knows that. It's all part of the whole relationship black box. You put things in and hope it all ends up right."

"Are you telling me I can't search the Internet for a solution?"

Dani laughed. "My advice is to run like hell from any person who tells you they have it all figured out. Now I have to run, I have a job to do."

"So do I." Keile sighed, thinking of the burgeoning Crawford project. It was going to be a long night in front of the computer, and that was on top of the hours she'd put in over the weekend. She'd only taken breaks to call Haydn, let Can out and sleep. Rick had yet to mention his offer of help again and she was loath to bring it up. But if things continued at the rate they were going, she'd be forced to. "Thanks for the pep talk."

"That's what friends are for."

With a huff of disgust, Haydn closed the folder containing the report she'd been staring at for the last thirty minutes and pushed it away. It was already Thursday and she was behind in the work she had wanted to complete this week because of Kyle's illness and because she couldn't force her brain to stay on monthly accounts of Garvey and Sons Plumbing. She had a clear picture of the cause of her trouble. Keile Griffen, who with a kind deed, had turned her life into a swirling vortex. Haydn wasn't sure if she was up, down, back or front anymore.

I am officially pitiful. She placed her hands on the desk and stood, knowing that she wouldn't get any work done until she settled her internal issues. Striding to the kitchen, she filled the kettle and placed it on the stove. While the water heated up, she wandered around the kitchen, aimlessly wiping off clean counters. The activity did nothing to relieve the anxiety churning in her stomach. She knew Keile wasn't to blame for her problems. No. The main reason for her anxiety and doubt about opening her heart belonged to Reagan Marie Darrow.

Her lips twisted in a bitter smile as she thought about her former lover. Reagan had been her high school sweetheart and her best friend. They'd started out as adversaries at the beginning of tenth grade, then somehow ended up as friends, then, two years later, more.

Her brain still clouded with memories, she grabbed a cup, filled it with powdered hot chocolate mix and added the hot water. Absently stirring, she sat down at the table.

Remembering again the almost crippling pain she'd felt when Reagan abandoned her, her chest tightened. How had their eleven-year relationship disintegrated with her being none the wiser? Three years later she still felt like a fool because she hadn't had a clue the end was coming. She took a sip of the chocolate, letting it warm her insides. No matter how many times she relived the last month with Reagan, she came no closer to understanding what had happened. Now that her heart was awakening, she was scared she'd repeat the same mistake. The one she hadn't even known she made.

What if she made that same mistake with Keile? This time it would be more than her heart at stake. This time Kyle would also be left wondering what had happened, why Keile hadn't come home. A note that didn't even begin to explain the problem wouldn't be enough for him. *Or me*, she thought bleakly.

Tightening her grip on the cup, Haydn forced her thoughts away from failure. An image of Keile holding Kyle popped into her head and the tightness in her chest loosened. Keile, with her gentle understanding ways, was slowly making her believe again. Haydn raised the cup to her lips, but didn't take a drink. It was time for a talk. Time to explain. Maybe then she could get beyond the doubts that held her back.

"I really am sorry I can't make dinner tonight," Keile said for the third time.

"Really, it's okay." Haydn clamped the phone between her cheek and shoulder and checked the baking chicken. She wasn't sure if she was disappointed or relieved to have the talk postponed. "It was a spur-of-the-moment invite anyway. You are still on for tomorrow night, right?"

"Definitely. That's part of why I want to knock out a lot of work tonight. It'll give me more time with you and Kyle this weekend." She paused. "Maybe I shouldn't be so presumptuous."

Haydn caught the hesitation in Keile's voice. "You think ahead, that's good. I'll let Kyle know you're working now so you can play with him tomorrow."

"Don't talk me up too much. I wouldn't want to disappoint."

She smiled. "There's no such thing in Kyle's mind."

"And I would like to keep it that way. I want you and him to know I'll do my best to see that he's safe from disappointment."

"I'm beginning to realize that very thing. I hope it's not too slow for you."

"Progress is always good. I'll see you tomorrow."

"I look forward to it." Haydn hung up with a smile, then pulled together a salad to accompany the chicken. The doorbell rang as she was finishing up.

Marcus draped his coat on the coatrack. "How are things?" he asked, following Haydn to the kitchen.

Haydn joined Marcus at the table, carrying two bottles of water. "It's still chugging along if that's what you're asking." She plopped one of the bottles in front of him asking, "That is what you're getting at, right?"

"I thought Keile was supposed to be here and since she's not..." He shrugged, twisted off the top of the water bottle and took a deep sip.

Haydn shot him a glare. "For your information, little brother, she couldn't make it. Some big project at work is keeping her busy."

"Damn. I was hoping to catch her."

Her eyes were drawn to the way his grip dented the plastic bottle and her stomach sank. "What's really going on here? Don't tell me she has a girlfriend."

"Huh?" He looked at her as if she was crazy. "Where the hell did that come from?"

She placed a hand over her beating heart and took a deep breath. "Ignore that. I don't know what came over me."

"If you say so," he said slowly, giving every indication he was reluctant to drop the matter.

"I do," she said firmly. "Now tell me why you want to see Keile."

"It's nothing, really. I just had a couple more questions for her." Looking away from Haydn's gaze, he took another sip of water.

"Still trying to figure out if you're related?"

Marcus nodded. "It's crazy I know, but I can't get the thought out of my mind."

She placed a hand on his arm and gently squeezed. "Given your resemblance, it's not unreasonable to think you might be related to Keile in some way."

"Except we were born on different sides of the country."

"I can't believe you said that." Haydn gave him an amused look. "People have been known to move from Texas to Georgia," she said. "I can think of at least two people right off the top of my head." She waved off his glare. "You know I'm right," she taunted and smirked when he gave her the finger. "But what do you think you're going to find out by quizzing Keile some more? She doesn't know anything."

"Did I ever tell you what an annoying big sister you are?" He crossed his arms over his chest and leaned back. "I'm looking for new ideas. I did a search on the Internet for Kyle Griffen, and the number of hits I got was obscene. I need something to narrow it down."

"How did you find your birth mother?"

"Remember Larry?" She nodded. "Let's just say we spent a lot of time looking at files we had no business seeing."

"It doesn't surprise me that Larry-the-geek was a hacker, but you?"

Marcus shrugged, the picture of innocence. "Technically, I was a victim of circumstances, Your Honor. You won't find my prints on the keyboard."

Haydn snorted. "I doubt Keile knows anything about the man, but she and Dani are coming over tomorrow to play with Kyle while Edan and I do shopping therapy. You know, maybe you should talk to Dani. She searches out information for a living."

He shook his head. "I'm not ready for anybody but you to know what I'm doing. If nothing comes of it, so be it. And I don't know how Dani would feel about it going behind Keile's back."

"What is it *you* want?" Haydn asked gently.

"To fill in some blanks." Marcus ran his fingers through his hair. "Look at you. You know who you look like. I don't. I know my hair is brown and curls if I let it get too long. What I don't know is if it's from my birth mother or birth father. If it turns out that Keile is my half-sister it won't tell a whole lot about the people that brought me into this world, but it will let me know that yes, I got my looks from my birth father. And for some reason, that feels like a good start. Is that so wrong?"

"Not at all. I can't help but wonder what brought this on."

He hesitated. "Keile talking about her sperm donor, as she calls him. Maybe he's a hit-and-run kind of guy, and maybe he hit my birth mother, too."

"Crudely put."

"You know what I mean. What if Keile is part of my family? I didn't get a chance to meet my birth mother. I don't want to wait and look back with regret."

"Like you do now," she said softly. "I get it. I hope you find what you're looking for."

Chapter Sixteen

Keile resisted the urge to yawn as she watched Rick navigate through the demonstration program she'd spent more time developing than she wanted to remember. The program was designed to help the client distribute future population and employment growth in a user designated area. Although she knew she'd done an outstanding job, she felt too numb to take any pride in her accomplishment. She was tired, and more than a little bit angry that the help Rick promised a week ago had never materialized. At some level she knew her anger was irrational, fueled by having to pass up dinner with Haydn last night. That didn't stop her from being pissed.

"This is excellent work as always." Rick looked up from his computer screen with a satisfied smile. "It's good to know I can always count on you to help me look good. I certainly appreciate the hours you put into this."

"Thanks, Rick." She looked at him and remembered the moment she'd realized that the possibility of a bonus couldn't make up for the time she'd lost out on with Haydn and Kyle. At first she'd been shocked that such a thought would cross her mind. Then as she'd really looked at her situation, the future stretched out in a narrow road that led to work and more work. Now that she had a taste of something different, she didn't want to go back to being one-dimensional.

She took a deep breath and squared her shoulders. "You're right about the hours. I could really use the help you were talking about getting for me last week. This project is growing exponentially every day."

Rick leaned back in his big, leather chair and crossed his arms. "I thought you thrived on the extra work." His voice seemed deceptively mild.

Keile fought against the desire to look away from his penetrating gaze. "I've been doing this so long I feel burnt out. I'd like to scale back to a fifty-hour week and have a life outside of work." She smiled, willing him to understand.

"I see." Rick tented his fingers under his chin and nodded. "I have to admit I'm a little disappointed, Keile. I thought you were a team player."

"I'll still be doing more than my fair share of the work, Rick." Keile hated how defensive she sounded, and at that moment she was angry at him for putting her in this position. "I'm just asking for someone else to take part of the load. You yourself commented on how the scope has been expanded."

Rick glanced at his watch. "I have a meeting in a few minutes. We'll come back to this later. In the meantime, please start working on the tasks we outlined."

"Certainly," Keile said, giving no hint of the frustration mixed with anger she felt at Rick's clear dismissal of her and her concerns. With a tight smile that barely moved her lips, she left quietly. The farther away from his office she got, the angrier she became. She wasn't asking for much, and there were several of her co-workers who could step in and help out. Rick had certainly let other managers use her in that capacity before.

Keile ducked into the bathroom, glad to find it empty. She paced around until the anger gradually dissipated, allowing her to think more clearly. She wasn't being fair to Rick. He just needed more time to get used to not having her at his beck and call at all hours. Once Rick saw the benefit of adding another person to the team, he would come around and their relationship would return to normal. She didn't want to think of the alternative.

"Thanks for tonight," Haydn said softly, and before she could stop herself she pulled Keile closer for a kiss. Keile had been sporting a proud smile for her first successful babysitting gig and she looked irresistible.

Keile hummed in pleasure and leaned back enough to gaze into Haydn's darkened eyes. "If this is my fee, I'll be happy to do it every day, ma'am."

Haydn's smile was bittersweet. "Be careful what you promise," she said half-jokingly and pulled back. "Parenting is hard work. I wouldn't want to stick you with it every day." Damn, she thought and winced as some of the light went out in Keile's eyes. Why did she keep botching things up? She knew she needed to explain, but not tonight. There wasn't enough time and she wasn't mentally prepared to bare her soul.

"I should go."

"I want you to know how much I appreciate what you did tonight. It's not easy to get an inexpensive *and* experienced babysitter on a Friday night," she added playfully.

"I'll admit I'm cheap," Keile said with an easy smile. "But experienced? I don't think so. I barely muddled along."

"Don't sell yourself short. For me or for anyone." Haydn poked her chest. "You have a lot to offer."

"Is this the part where you say you don't want what I have to offer?" she asked, looking pained.

"No!" They both turned to the crib when they heard Kyle stir. "Let's go downstairs."

Haydn berated herself for being so clumsy all the way down

the stairs. She plopped down on the sofa and pulled a throw pillow tight against her stomach. "I'm sorry. I'm not usually so inept with words," she said as soon as Keile seated herself out of touching distance. "Contrary to how that sounded, I'm not trying to give you the brush-off. Hell, I like you. I more than like you."

"And that's a problem?" Keile perched on the edge of the recliner, all of her attention focused on Haydn. "What did I do?"

She gave a sad laugh and rubbed her eyes. "Do? You did nothing but be you. I'm the one with the problem. You must think I'm a real bitch, the way I blow hot and cold. I sure think I am."

"No. I think you're scared. I'm not stupid enough to think I can promise to never hurt you, but I can promise to do my best not to."

Looking at Keile's solemn expression, Haydn thought her heart would crack. Keile had done nothing but prove her worth. Surely it was time to stop tarring her with Reagan's brush and give her a real chance. "You're incredible, you know that? Why some woman hasn't grabbed you up I'll never know."

Keile shrugged. "Are we okay?"

"That depends. Do you think you could spare Kyle and me some time tomorrow?"

"I did promise him I would come and play with the race track I bought him."

"Well, I guess that will have to be enough for now." Haydn rose gracefully and held out her hand, smiling. "On that note, I'll let you go."

She let herself be pulled up. "I'd be happy to spend time with you and Kyle tomorrow." Her eyes drifted to Haydn's lips. "I'm dying to kiss you goodnight." When Haydn wrapped her arms around her neck, Keile said, "Non-verbal. Good." She brushed her lips across Haydn's, then more firmly.

Haydn's breath hitched as their tongues met, searching, caressing. She pulled Keile closer, wanting to be inside her. For a moment she forgot about everything but the feel of Keile's mouth on hers as desire blazed through her body.

Keile pulled back, breathing hard. "Now I'd really better go before I lose my head completely."

She let her go reluctantly. "That is the smart thing to do." She exhaled, still feeling the imprint of Keile's soft lips. At the front door, she gave Keile a quick hard kiss, still wanting more. "Take care on the way home."

"I will. Need to get back here tomorrow." Keile smiled. "There's a race track in my future. Pleasant dreams."

Haydn locked the door and leaned her back against it. Pleasant dreams? How was she ever going to sleep with the blood still pounding through her veins?

Awakening later than usual the next morning, Keile took Can for a short run, then stopped by the park to let him play with the other dogs. Jogging in place to keep warm, she looked around the grassy area, finding the bench where she'd been sitting when the direction of her life changed. *Was it only three weeks ago?*

"Mama!" Keile swung her head around at the sound of Kyle's voice. Dropping to one knee, she held her arms wide and reeled back under the onslaught of an excited little boy. Smothering his face with loud kisses, she held him close until he squirmed. "Hey ya, Buster."

"I tried to warn him you'd have him arrested for stalking," Marcus said, watching the interaction between Keile and Kyle intently.

Keile stood up with Kyle in her arms, suddenly aware of Marcus's close scrutiny. "Is everything okay?"

"I was once again struck by our resemblance."

"It is pretty amazing. Hey, I thought you were flying to Texas today?"

"Later. I thought I'd give Kyle another dose of my magnetic personality before I left."

She grinned. "That's what I like about you, Dad. You're always thinking of everybody else's well being."

"Yup. That be me," he said with a thin smile.

"Do! Do!" Kyle pointed at the group of dogs.

"That's right. Dogs," Keile enunciated slowly. "Dogs." She whistled for Can, who came flying over with his tongue hanging out of the side of his mouth. When Kyle strained to get down, she lowered him, placing a hand on Can's head in case the energetic boy startled him. She needn't have worried. Can sat patiently while Kyle showered him with affection.

"I wish Haydn was here to take pictures," Marcus said.

Keile whipped out her cell phone and took a few shots of Can and Kyle. "Will this do for now?" She handed him the phone so he could view the pictures. "Haydn can take some more Thursday at Jo's. Too bad you're going to miss our first Thanksgiving together, Pops. I would have liked to show you off to my friends."

"Yeah? So you're not upset with me for barraging you with questions about Kyle Griffen?"

She hadn't been upset, but she had spent some time trying to figure out why he would be asking her questions about a man she only knew as a name on her birth certificate. If Kyle Griffen had ever been in her life, it had been when she was very young because she had no recollection of him. She hoped Marcus wasn't trying to find Griffen as a favor to her. Seeing or getting to know that man was something she hadn't wished for in a long time. First as a teen, then an adult she'd come to despise a man who would impregnate, then abandon an emotionally fragile woman like her mother. "Why would you think that?"

Marcus shrugged, looking away.

"Look, I just hope you're not wasting your time searching for him as a favor to me."

"I'm not." He sighed when she gave him a look of patent disbelief. "Okay. I have this crazy idea we're related. I thought if I could find him he might be the connection."

Keile's eyes grew wide. "Are you serious?" She punctuated every word as her voice rose an octave.

"Look at us, look at Kyle. I think it's more than just a

coincidence. And I really have to know."

She put her hand on his arm. "This is important to you, isn't it?"

He nodded. "Please don't tell Haydn, but I was real broken up when I found out my birth mother had died. I mean, I do love my mom and dad, it's…it was like I missed this great opportunity I could never get back." He ran his fingers through his hair. "For awhile, I blamed my parents. I got over it but there's still a part of me filled with regret."

"And you don't want that to happen with me," she said softly. "That's sweet and I understand. Do you really think it's possible?"

"I think it's probable. How would you feel if we were related?"

"I think it would be great. I never imagined I would have a family." She looked down as Kyle tugged on her pants. She picked him up. "After living in foster care I thought it would never happen to me. And I confess I have a hard time letting myself believe it will."

"You will," he said assuredly.

She wanted to say no, but didn't. Lucky for Marcus he really didn't have a clue what impermanence was like. In foster care toys were never yours for long, and neither were friends, and certainly never your new so-called family. But he didn't need to ever know that. "How will you find out?"

"I'm still working out the details," he admitted with a rueful smile. "Don't look so skeptical. I have faith and so should you."

You can afford to have faith, she thought. But said, "I'll try."

Chapter Seventeen

Early Thanksgiving afternoon, Keile pulled into Haydn's driveway, glad the cold morning rain had moved on. She hurried to the door, trying to keep the biting wind from seeping through her heavy coat. The door opened before she had a chance to ring the bell. Keile's heart gave its customary start at the welcoming smile that lit up Haydn's face.

"Hi." Haydn gave Keile a quick kiss. "Come on in."

"Hi." Keile wiped the moisture off the bottom of her shoes before entering. "Has it only been two days since I saw you?" She took off her gloves and put them in her coat pocket, admiring how good Haydn looked in the thick green sweater and form-fitting jeans.

"According to the calendar." Haydn closed the door and turned to face Keile. "It felt longer than that to me."

"Much longer." Keile gathered Haydn into her arms and

rested her cheek against Haydn's silky locks. "We have to work on that calendar," she whispered, her voice husky.

"Mama! Mama!"

Keile raised her head at the strident call. She smiled at the adorable picture Kyle made, dressed in his winter coveralls. "Buster!" She let go of Haydn and held out her arms to him. He toddled over to her unsteadily, obviously still getting used to being bundled up. She swung him up into an embrace and kissed him on the forehead the way she had each time she visited these days. "Are you ready for our trip?"

He smiled and patted her cheek.

"While he may not be ready, his paraphernalia is." Haydn pointed to the large bag and stroller sitting by the door. "I'll go grab my coat and bag and we can load my car."

"Can and the beer are already in the back of mine," Keile explained. "I would just as soon not expose your nice sedan to Can's messiness yet."

"Then I need to get Kyle's car seat out of my car."

"Sorry." Keile shot Haydn a look of apology. "I hadn't thought about that."

"And why would you," Haydn said with an easy smile. "It's not something you've had to deal with."

"I'll remember it next time. I'm a quick study."

Haydn ran her finger along Keile's arm. "I know you are."

Within ten minutes they pulled out of the driveway, en route to Jo and Susan's house.

"Now you're sure it's okay to bring Kyle? I don't think they know what they're letting themselves in for," Haydn said with a frown.

"Relax." Keile threw her a quick smile, aware Haydn was nervous about meeting the rest of her friends. "Unlike me, Jo and Susan have dealt with young children. If it makes you feel better, I promise to watch him like a hawk."

"Famous last words," she mumbled, glancing out of the window.

"And if he messes something up, it'll just be payback for all the cleaning I had to do when I first got Can."

"So which one convinced you to take Can, Jo or Susan?"

"That would be Jo who hounded me, pun intended," Keile said with a quick grin. "I feel kind of guilty that I haven't been back before now."

"Why haven't you been back?"

"Because I get so tied up with work that I barely do anything else," Keile admitted. "I may be slow, but I've finally figured out that all work and no play makes me a bad friend, among other things."

Jo and Susan lived on the south side of Seneca, in a neighborhood that, unlike Keile's, was still in the early stages of gentrification. It wasn't unusual to see recently renovated homes next to ones in ill-repair. But even the fixed up houses were cheaper than could be found elsewhere, and they were starting to attract a lot of first-time buyers.

"This really looks nice," Haydn commented, looking up at the house. They were halfway to the house when the front door opened. Susan stepped out onto the glassed-in porch with a big, welcoming smile.

"I'm so glad you made it. Do you need any help?"

"We got it," Keile replied with an answering smile. "Is it okay to let Can…" She stopped since Can had already entered the house.

"As if you need to ask. I live with the dog lover, remember?" Susan said. "He can go out in the back and hang around the smoker with the other dogs."

They stepped into a large open area and warmth. Keile put down the stroller and caught Susan in a one-armed hug. "Thanks for inviting us for Thanksgiving dinner." She stepped back and reached for Haydn's hand. "I want you to meet…" She paused, not sure what to say. "Haydn Davenport and her son Kyle."

Susan held out her hand. "Hi, I'm Susan Barfield. It's good to meet you."

Susan walked them through the house to the back door. Jo, two white Labradors and Can were in a small area sheltered from the wind by a partial wooden fence. Keile performed introductions, and this time Kyle, excited about the dogs, deigned to give Jo a big grin. "Mama, do."

"That's right, three dogs," Keile said slowly. "Dogs."

"Do." He pushed against Keile to get down. She set him down, but kept a hand on the back of his coat, ensuring he wouldn't get in over his head. The other dogs were used to getting attention from the neighborhood kids and welcomed Kyle with plenty of doggy kisses. He giggled, covering his face with his hands. The dogs immediately backed off at Jo's command.

"It's about time you brought your son to see us." Jo slapped her friend on the back. "So this is what you've been working on so hard," she added with a wink at Haydn.

Keile laughed despite her heated cheeks. "Be nice."

"Ignore her, Haydn, she never grew up," Susan said, giving her significant other a pointed look. "If you've finished playing with the food, Jo, you could come in and entertain our guests."

An hour later, most of the guests had arrived and were spread throughout the house. Keile, Haydn, Edan, Dani, Terri, Jo and a couple from the neighborhood were seated in the heated glassed-in side porch. Kyle and Jake, a youngster near his age, were on the floor in a corner playing. Keile noted with interest that for them playing together meant sitting next to each other and playing separately. The boys didn't fight over toys, but there was a definite sense of ownership. She smiled, seeing the customary look of concentration on Kyle's face. He took his trucks and cars seriously.

Draping her arm around Haydn's shoulder, Keile turned her attention to the conversation flowing around her. It felt good to have a special someone beside her while she listened to the bull flying around. The knowing glances from Jo, Terri and Dani only added to her pleasure. That, and the warmth coming from Haydn's hand on her thigh.

Susan called for everyone to gather around the table. Keile picked up Kyle and followed Haydn to the small dining room directly adjacent to the kitchen. The group arranged themselves around the oval table filled with turkey, ham, dressing, side dishes of every variety and desserts. Susan thanked everyone for coming, then turned to Lynn, who said a few words of thanks for the food and friendship.

Keile stood with an arm around Haydn and Kyle on her hip, and wondered if she could stand so much joy. She was part of a family within a family—something she had no recollection of experiencing. Closing her eyes briefly, she sent her own thanks into the universe.

Later, after dessert, Jo asked Keile to join her in checking on the dogs. Keile gave her friend a quizzical look then agreed. After handing off a sleepy Kyle to Haydn, she followed Jo to the backyard. The sun was going down, dropping the temperature.

"So how are things going with you? You seem happy."

Keile stuck her hands in her jeans and rocked back on the heels of her shoes. "That's because I am. The past couple of weeks have been a real eye-opener for me. I've had to go back and reassess what's important."

"That's a good thing, right?" Jo prodded, bumping her shoulder.

"Yes, but not without growing pains," she admitted. Her mind flashed to the situation at work and just as quickly let it go. She was here to spend time with friends and family, enjoying herself. There would be time to brood over work later. "But I expect it to be worth every twinge."

Jo nodded and squared her shoulders. "I don't want to meddle, but I can tell you from past experience it's hard to work all the time and keep a family." She blew on her fingers, and seemed to wait for Keile's reaction.

"Sure you want to meddle," she said with a smile. "But don't worry, I've already talked to my boss about my hours. Working all the time isn't all it used to be."

"You *are* serious about her," Jo said, her eyes wide in surprise. "Does Haydn know?"

Keile looked away from Jo's searching gaze. "Yes, but it's

complicated."

"Love always is. But as long as you're willing to work on it, anything can happen."

"I want to be with her and I'll do what it takes to win her love."

"I hope she realizes what a bargain she's getting." Jo shot Keile a playful elbow.

"Ouch!" Keile rubbed her side. "Can we go in now? I'm starting to freeze," she complained, rubbing her arms.

"Wimp." Jo threw an arm around Keile's shoulder. "Let's go rescue your woman from the inquisition."

"Inquisition?"

"You didn't think Susan and Lynn are going to let this opportunity go by do you?" Jo laughed at the look of panic on Keile's face.

"Damn, I hope I'm not in trouble. Why can't I just take a class about all this relationship stuff?"

"The class is called life." Jo made no attempt to hide her amusement. "Don't worry. I'm sure Haydn expected your friends to vet her."

Chapter Eighteen

Keile pulled into Haydn's driveway, triggering the floodlights. She switched off the ignition and turned to Haydn. "Did you have a good time?"

"Yes." Haydn leaned over and gave Keile a fleeting kiss. "Thanks for inviting me. It means a lot that you wanted to introduce me to your friends."

"I can't tell you how much it meant having you with me."

"And you did a wonderful job of keeping track of Kyle." The kiss she gave Keile this time was anything but fleeting. "Do you have time for coffee?"

Keile laughed. "Do you have milk and sugar?"

"I guess that's a yes."

Keile got the honor of carrying a sleeping Kyle upstairs and getting him ready for bed. Haydn put on the kettle for hot chocolate before joining them. Stopping just inside the door, she leaned against the wall and observed Keile gently undress Kyle. Her breath caught in her throat when she noticed the intense expression on Keile's face that she'd seen many times on Kyle's face.

"I got his clothes off, but you're going to have to help me with the diaper." Keile looked up and met the warm gleam in Haydn's emerald eyes. "I'm doing okay, right?"

"Yes," she said huskily, "you're more than okay." A warm feeling settled over her when Keile favored her with a radiant smile.

"Uh…diaper?" Keile fairly trembled under Haydn's blazing scrutiny. "Diaper," she repeated hoarsely.

"I guess it's time for that lesson," Haydn said, her voice laced with amusement at the flustered look on Keile's face. *You have no idea how adorable you are,* she thought and bit her lip to keep from laughing. And as luck would have it, neither did the other lesbians in Seneca.

"Lessons…yeah," she muttered, turning her attention to Kyle.

Haydn moved to stand next to Keile. She felt drunk from the sense of power coursing through her veins. She wondered how she could have forgotten the rush of emerging love. *Did I think love?* Not ready to delve any further, she talked Keile through a diaper change. When the last tab was fastened, she remembered the water she put on to boil. "You're on your own with the pj's. I've got hot chocolate to make." She gave Keile a promising smile and hurried downstairs.

Left to her own devices, Keile dug through the drawers beneath the changing table until she found pajamas. She pulled out the top pair and managed to get them on a seemingly boneless Kyle without waking him up. She was cradling him against her chest when Haydn returned. "All done," she said, smiling proudly.

Haydn, who had spent the time downstairs getting her emotions under control, felt them ricochet right back out. "You're incredible," she said, leaning against the doorjamb.

"I want you to think so."

"I do," Haydn said softly. She walked across the room until she was standing in front of Keile. "I really do."

Keile reached out and ran the back of her free hand down Haydn's cheek. "I'm glad," she whispered.

Haydn smiled. "The hot chocolate is getting cold. Let's put Kyle to bed and go enjoy."

Keile nodded, seemingly unable to speak.

They walked down the stairs holding hands. Haydn had already taken the time to start a fire in the gas fireplace in the family room and placed the mugs of cocoa nearby. She picked up a few cushions off the sofa, arranged them on the floor in front of the fire, then beckoned Keile.

"This is nice," Keile said, sinking to the floor. "The perfect way to wind down." She picked up a mug and took a sip.

"Keile," Haydn began, then stopped abruptly and gazed into the fire, seeking courage, guidance or a combination of the two. "I'm ready to tell you about my past."

Keile put a hand on Haydn's shoulder and squeezed. "Thank you for trusting me."

Haydn felt some of the tenseness leave her body. "Reagan and I were together for eleven years. We were high school sweethearts who thought we had it made. We stayed together through college, graduated together and made the joint decision to move to the West Coast. After we'd been working for a couple of years, she decided it was time for us to think about having a family. Don't get me wrong, I was more than agreeable because I wanted it too." She exhaled sharply and tightened her lips.

Keile scooted closer and placed an arm over Haydn's shoulder. Haydn leaned into Keile, grateful for the additional warmth suffusing her body. "I don't know why I'm getting so upset. I want you to know that I am over her, and over the disillusionment."

"Can you tell me what happened?"

"I'm not really sure. We had all these great plans and... then one day we didn't." She blinked her eyes rapidly, trying unsuccessfully to stave off tears. "I can't tell you how devastating it was to come back from a business trip and find her gone. She left a letter, but it wasn't enough. After all we'd been through together, I deserved more than that. I did." Her voice broke and tears coursed down her face.

"You did. That and so much more."

"I mean, we were planning to start a family and she pulls this. I was a wreck for longer than I want to think about. She shattered my trust, my self-confidence, my everything. It took me a year to get over losing her, and much longer to regain confidence."

"I'm so sorry you had to go through that," Keile said, the sheen of tears in her eyes. She rocked Haydn, much like she did Kyle, until the tears stopped. "That woman was an idiot to let you go. I'm not an idiot."

"I know. You're nothing like her." Haydn managed a watery smile and wiped her eyes. "Thanks for taking up for me. You're good for my ego." She should have known she'd only get concern and understanding from Keile. Keile, who didn't deserve to pay for Reagan's mistakes. "Thanks to you, I'm ready to believe again."

"It wasn't me. It was in you all the time."

Haydn shook her head. "My heart was locked up tight before I met you. You," she pointed her finger at Keile and smiled, "you blew right past it, almost as if it didn't exist."

"Not true," she said. "I prefer to see it as chipping away. It all goes back to determination."

"I guess you're right about determination." Haydn nestled closer. "It is a good thing."

"Please know I will always be determined when it comes to you and Kyle," Keile said solemnly.

"I know you will." And in truth she did. A part of her had always sensed Keile could be trusted. Maybe it started when she'd found Kyle safe and sound in Keile's arms. Haydn sighed, at ease and happy. Her eyes gradually drifted closed and she fell into a light sleep.

Keile gave a silent laugh when she heard Haydn's even breathing. "I love you," she whispered. "And your heart will always be safe with me."

Haydn's eyes fluttered open thirty minutes later. "Oh. I'm sorry I conked out on you."

"You're okay. I enjoyed holding you. But now I think it's time for me to go. I'm betting that Kyle has no respect for how late you stay up."

"I hate to see you go," Haydn crawled to her knees and stretched, "but you're right about Kyle."

Keile stood and helped Haydn to her feet. Hand in hand, they walked to the front door.

"I want to see you again. How about you come over after you get off work?" Haydn asked.

"Why don't you and Kyle come over to my place? We never did have that picnic."

Haydn smiled and shook her finger at Keile. "Okay, but the warning about inquisitive toddlers and what they can do to your possessions still stands."

"I'll take my chances." Keile reached out and brought the wagging finger to her lips. She grinned at the sound that rumbled from Haydn's throat, then kissed her palm.

"Hmm." Haydn moaned louder.

Keile cupped Haydn's face between her hands and proceeded to kiss every freckle she could reach. "I love your freckles, but I think I love your lips more." She leaned in and touched her lips to Haydn's, her body trembling at the contact. She increased the pressure and slid her hands to cup Haydn's behind, deepening the kiss as their bodies melded.

Haydn threaded her arms around Keile's waist. She spread her legs, nestling their centers, and her breathing became erratic as rational thought left her mind. All she could think about was the hardening between her thighs and the slick wetness building in her center. She pulled back from Keile's sweet mouth, needing to breathe and unsure that her legs had the strength to hold her.

Keile took a shuddering breath, resting her head on Haydn's. "I'd better go," she said, full of regret and took a step back.

"Tomorrow."

Haydn nodded, still trying to get her treacherous body under control. "Tomorrow," she said, her voice shaky and took a deep breath. "And it can't come soon enough." Then almost against her will, she pulled Keile's mouth to hers for one last kiss.

Chapter Nineteen

Keile spotted a familiar car in her driveway as soon as she rounded the block with Can in the lead. Her pulse quickened and she picked up her pace. "Come on Can, let's run," she urged, unwilling to be without her future family for a second longer than she had to. She slowed to a walk as she approached the silver sedan and knocked on the window.

Haydn smiled and rolled down the window. "Hi. Hope I'm not too early."

Keile poked her head into the car and kissed Haydn thoroughly before she could reply. Then she grinned, taking in Haydn's dazed look. "Let me unlock the door, and I'll come back and help you with Kyle's paraphernalia." She looked in the backseat with a ready smile for her pal. "Uh…Haydn? You didn't leave him on the bus, did you?"

"No silly, he's in the trunk."

"Does this mean what I think it means?" Keile's grin grew progressively wider.

"If you're thinking you're stuck with just me for company, you'd be correct. Dani and Edan are womanning the fort, so to speak. If you ask me, Edan's desensitizing Dani to kids."

"I'm thinking that's a good thing," she said, knowing Dani had yet to talk with Edan about the very subject that had torn them apart. She hoped being with Kyle would help Dani broach the subject. She ushered Haydn inside. As she took Haydn's jacket, Keile noticed her inquisitive glance down the hallway. "How 'bout a tour? I should warn you, it's pretty…well, spartan."

"I'd love one. I really like the outside, especially the screened-in side porch and the swing."

"We can try it out when it gets warmer," Keile said as they moved into the living room. She gestured around the room. "Here's where I listen to music and watch TV."

"I like how the room is centered on the fireplace. Gives it a homey feeling." Haydn looked at the mantel and her eyes widened. Crossing the room, she plucked the photo off the mantel and studied it carefully. "Where did you get this?" She turned to Keile with a look of wonder. "It's adorable."

"Oh, yeah." Keile tapped her forehead. "I've been meaning to make a copy of this for you. A friend of an acquaintance took it. Apparently this guy is an aspiring photographer, so he goes around taking shots for practice. Friends saw it and sent it on to me."

"I'd say he's more than aspiring," Haydn said, studying the photo.

"The expression on Kyle's face is priceless. It makes him look so alive."

"Looking at this, I would have never guessed you just met." Haydn pointed to the photo. "Even though he's concentrating, I can tell by his body language that he feels completely comfortable with you."

"Well, he didn't hesitate when he held out his arms for me to pick him up." Her eyes brightened as she relived the moment.

"Then he leaned back against me as if it was something we did every day. It was a pretty special feeling having his complete trust. I knew then I had to look out for him." Keile lowered her head and studied her shoes. "You probably think I'm crazy."

"No." Haydn replaced the photo. "I think you're someone with a big heart." She lifted Keile's chin so they could see eye to eye, taking in her reddened cheeks. "Don't ever feel embarrassed for being sweet, okay? I like it."

Keile nodded as a heat borne of pleasure and possibility unfurled in her stomach. She closed her eyes briefly, marking the moment. It was much too wonderful to let go.

"I'll be as sweet as you want," she said, reaching for Haydn's hand and bringing it to her lips.

"Good." Haydn's voice was husky. She brought their lips together for a kiss, which quickly threatened to spiral out of control. "About that tour?" she asked, after she pulled away, breathless.

Keile's knees went weak at the sight of desire on Haydn's face. She cleared her throat. "Shall we?" She gestured to the opening that led to the dining room. "Through here is the dining room, which leads to the kitchen. As you can see, I use it more as a home office right now."

"I do see you're going for the minimalist look in here," Haydn teased, taking in the bare white walls, the chair tucked under the old, beat-up desk, which held a computer, and a dented, gray file cabinet topped with books.

"I call it my work in progress. And don't you dare ask me how long I've lived here," she cautioned, a smile creasing the corners of her mouth. "Now let's go look at the kitchen. It's my favorite room. Not because I like to cook, but because it gets a lot of sun and it's *not* a work in progress."

Once in the kitchen, Haydn did a full turn around, lightly brushing her fingertips over the granite countertops. "I like it," she declared as she peered at the dials on the grill cooktop. "Your cabinets look especially nice. I like the reddish tint in the wood."

"Thanks. I got them through Terri and Jo's supplier, and they even helped me install them."

"Now I'm really impressed, Ms. Griffen. I'm going to need to add some additional information to your bio."

"Don't be too impressed. Most of the credit belongs to Terri and Jo. I never could have done it without them."

"Don't sell yourself short. Even with their help, I couldn't have done this."

At that point, Can wandered into the kitchen and walked over to his bowl. He nudged it with his nose, then looked up at Keile.

"I think Lassie is trying to tell you something, Timmy," Haydn said in a stage whisper.

"What is it boy? Is it a dead body?" Keile asked before breaking into laughter. Crossing the room, she gave him a quick scratch behind the ear, then retrieved his food from the pantry. "Would you like something to drink? There's plenty of stuff in the fridge."

"I'll go get the bottle of wine I set on the table in the foyer."

Keile washed her hands and pulled the foodstuff that needed prep work out of the fridge. She ran through the list of items she'd bought to make this a special meal. As much as she enjoyed Kyle's company, she was going to make the most of this time alone with Haydn. *All alone*, she thought and her eyes blazed with excitement and desire.

The sound of a drawer opening caught her off guard. She looked up to find Haydn, corkscrew in hand, regarding her with a breath-stealing smile. "Do you need any help opening the wine?"

"I was just itching for my camera," she said and concentrated on removing the cork. "That was some expression you had on your face. Care to share?"

"Maybe later," she said, hoping her embarrassment didn't show in her face. "Is it okay if we finish the tour later? I thought I should go ahead and get dinner pulled together."

"That's fine with me." Haydn picked up the filled glasses.

"Anything I can do to help?"

After they finished dinner, they took the wine and moved to the living room. Keile quickly moved the coffee table and spread a blanket in front of the fireplace. She started the fire, pulled a few pillows from the sofa to the floor and joined Haydn on the blanket.

"This is nice," Haydn said, sitting upright with a pillow in her lap. "I talked all through dinner, now it's your turn."

"You don't want to hear about my boring life," Keile protested. "It's mostly filled with school and work."

"That can't be all."

"Well…it was up until about two years ago," Keile amended. "Then I met Dani, who refused to let me be a complete hermit anymore. It was one of the best things that ever happened to me. And through her I met the rest of the gang," she added with a fond smile. "And of course, Can." Can's ears perked up at the mention of his name, but he didn't move from his warm spot near the fireplace. "Yeah, we're talking about you, big guy."

"I've been meaning to ask you about his name. Why do you call him Can?"

"It's short for Trashcan." Keile grinned. "It took me six months to train him not to dig in the trash. I said trash can around him so many times, he started answering to it. Now I only call him Trashcan if he's in trouble."

"That must not happen a lot. From what I've seen, he seems well behaved."

"I have Dani to thank for that. She found me this great obedience class through one of her clients. She's a good friend, and a great source of information."

"I'm glad I finally had a chance to get to know her. I was prepared to dislike her because of Edan," Haydn admitted. "But I realize what happened between them can't be laid on anybody's doorstep. I'm happy they're working things out. Edan was miserable without Dani."

"I don't think Dani let herself realize how much she missed Edan. I'm glad she's happy now. But," Keile said, setting down her glass, "I'm ecstatic they're giving us this opportunity to be alone. There's something that's been on my mind since last night."

Haydn's lips twitched. "And what would that be, Ms. Griffen?" She set her glass down and allowed herself to be drawn toward Keile.

"Your freckles." Keile framed Haydn's face with her hands and rained it with kisses. Then she nibbled on her lips, slowly sucking the bottom one in her mouth. Her body tensed at the sound of Haydn's moan. Pressing her advantage, she fully covered Haydn's mouth with her own and deepened the kiss. Keile shivered as desire sprang full-blown between her legs. Thrusting her tongue forward, she searched the sweetness of Haydn's mouth.

Haydn moaned deep in her throat, pushed Keile backward onto the floor, then slowly crawled on top of her. She slipped a thigh between Keile's legs and resumed the kiss, but only for a moment. Haydn dragged her lips away from Keile's, despite Keile's murmur of protest, and moved on to her vulnerable neck. "God, you feel so good," she ground out against Keile's tender throat. "I want you so much."

"I'm yours," Keile replied, placing her hands on Haydn's backside to bring them closer together. She picked up the rhythm of Haydn's gyrating hips. "I think I'll die if you don't kiss me."

Haydn complied, thrusting her tongue in Keile's mouth in tandem with the thrust of her hips. When Keile groaned Haydn pulled back and gazed at her. "I need to see you." She rolled on her side and reached for Keile's shirt.

"Can…can we take this to the bedroom?" Keile grabbed Haydn's hand and brought it up to her lips. At Haydn's assent, she stood and pulled Haydn to her feet.

Keile swallowed hard when they entered her bedroom. She turned on the light, but she was too nervous to worry about what Haydn would think of the starkness of the white walls or the queen-sized bed with no headboard. She took a deep, steadying breath. "Haydn, there…there's something I have to tell you before we continue," she said slowly.

Haydn looked at Keile in concern. "What's wrong? Am I

moving too fast?"

"I..." She faltered as her voice cracked. Keile cleared her throat. "I don't have a lot of experience," she whispered and covered her face with her hands. "I don't want you to be disappointed."

Haydn exhaled. "God, Keile, you had me worried. And wasn't that you driving me crazy a minute ago? How could you possibly think I would be disappointed?"

Keile let her hands fall and shrugged, looking anywhere but at Haydn. "It's easy from my perspective."

Haydn laughed softly. "You won't disappoint me." She wrapped an arm around Keile's waist. "We'll take it nice and slow." Threading her fingers through Keile's hair, she applied pressure, pulling their lips together. The kiss was intended to be more about reassurance, but quickly turned to passion. Haydn broke away with effort. "Let me love you. Is that okay?"

"I'm not a complete idiot." Keile hugged her closer. "I want to love you, too. And I want to see all of you," she said shyly, pressing her face in Haydn's neck.

Haydn's laugh was full and sexy. Turning her head, she caught Keile's lips in a sizzling kiss. "I want to see you, too." Taking a step back, she slowly unbuttoned Keile's shirt and stroked her taut stomach.

Keile moaned, exhaling sharply against the throbbing of sensitive, swollen flesh. She was afraid the warm fingers drawing lines on her stomach would make her lose control. She wasn't ready for that just yet. "Wait! I want to feel your skin against mine," she begged, her voice harsh and ragged.

With a final caress, Haydn dropped her hand. "Then you'd better undress yourself. I don't know if I can keep my hands off you long enough for that." Breathing heavily, she stepped away and undressed, watching Keile do the same. Haydn's eyes blazed as her gaze slowly traversed Keile's strong body, from the tight brown nipples adorning small breasts to the dark curls at the apex of her thighs. She pulled back the covers and climbed onto the bed. "Join me."

Keile complied, on fire at the sight of milky smooth flesh. She stared at Haydn's round breasts, aching to feel them against her hands and mouth. "Can I touch you?" she whispered.

"Please."

Keile's hand trembled as her fingers gently stroked Haydn's soft skin. "You are so beautiful." She cradled Haydn's breasts in her hands and rolled the nipples between her thumbs and forefingers. Licking her lips, she sucked a nipple into her mouth. Her hips twitched involuntarily in response to Haydn's groan. She'd never experienced anything like this before. "So soft, so wonderful," she murmured, almost incoherent as she switched to the other breast. Keile shivered when she felt a soft touch on her stomach. She was almost paralyzed as Haydn's fingers moved slowly down her body. "Hey, you're trying to distract me." The protest was half-hearted at best.

Haydn laughed softly. "Is it working?" Taking Keile by surprise, she wrestled her onto her back.

Keile shivered under the onslaught of Haydn's heated gaze. "Maybe." Holding her breath, she watched as Haydn's lips latched onto her nipple. The touch, when it came, was almost too much to bear. "Oh, yes." She cupped the back of Haydn's head, holding Haydn's mouth to her breast. Her back arched, responding to the fingers stroking her quivering abdomen. Keile moaned and spread her legs, inviting those tantalizing fingers to touch her.

Haydn needed no other invitation. She cupped the wet heat, applying pressure with her palm. "You feel so good." Her breathing hitched at Keile's strangled response. "And you're so wet." Slowly parting the slick folds, she carefully dipped her finger into the moisture, and used the wetness to coat Keile's hardened clitoris. With her gaze trained on her aroused lover, she began to rub gently, then pressed harder on Keile's command.

Keile tightened her legs and bucked her hips as the pressure built up inside. "I'm going to come," she panted, putting her hand on top of Haydn's to hold it in place. With a drawn-out groan, she lifted her torso halfway off the bed as she climaxed. She fell back on the bed, her body still writhing from the aftermath. After drawing a couple of shaky breaths, she slowly opened her eyes. "That was…" She paused, searching for anything that would come close to describing what she had just experienced. "It just was."

Haydn smiled. "You can't even begin to imagine how beautiful you are when you come," she said quietly. She ran her fingers lightly through Keile's damp curls. Keile's hips jerked and she groaned, still caught up in the lingering aftershocks. "And so responsive."

"Come here, you," Keile finally said. "You're trying to distract me again. It won't work this time, Davenport." But she couldn't stop her hips from jerking as Haydn straddled her thighs, and she couldn't stop the hum deep in her throat when Haydn took possession of her lips and almost drove all thought from her mind.

Before she succumbed, Keile twisted her head away. "No fair," she said, breathing heavily. "I want to touch you." Before Haydn could react, Keile adroitly changed their positions. Silently, she studied Haydn's breasts. "So beautiful." She bent and took a pink nipple in her mouth then tugged lightly with her teeth. Someone moaned, and Keile wasn't certain if it was her or Haydn. Switching to the other nipple, she stroked Haydn's curved stomach before slowly drifting down to the top of silky, auburn curls.

Keile's fingers trembled, making contact with Haydn's slick heat. "Oh God, this feels so good," she said as her blood pooled hotly between her own thighs. Loving Haydn was so much more than she'd ever imagined. Taking in the rosy hue that spread from her lover's cheeks to her chest, her breathing grew ragged. "Beautiful," she whispered, and nipped at Haydn's ear. Slipping a finger into Haydn's wetness, she rubbed along the side of the ridged nub.

Haydn flung her head back and raised her hips. "Oh yeah. Right there. Don't…stop," she pleaded, her head thrashing from side to side. She clenched the sheets and her body went rigid. When Keile squeezed her distended clitoris, she came with a shout. Sucking in a breath, she arched her back as tremors rocked her body. Finally spent, she lay flat against the bed and tried to catch her breath.

Keile stilled her movement with Haydn's last gasp, and reluctantly removed her fingers. She stared at her lover in awe. Nothing could compare to the beauty of Haydn in the throes of passion.

"You'll kill me with more experience." Haydn gave a sigh of contentment. Her body was still tingling with the aftermath of her orgasm.

Keile scooted up until her head was even with Haydn's. "Can we do it again?" she begged hoarsely, one hand already attached to a warm breast. She leaned closer and whispered the things she wanted to do with her mouth.

"Not so fast, Griffen." Haydn turned and claimed the lips that were nibbling on her ear. "It's my turn now." She grabbed hold of a hard, dark brown nipple, silencing any protests.

Chapter Twenty

"God, you're like a teenage boy." Haydn grabbed the hand roaming her body, then kissed it to take out the sting of her words. She squinted at the alarm clock and sighed. "It's after eleven, I should go." She turned on her side and propped herself up on her elbow. "Come spend the weekend at my house. I'm not done with you yet." She turned Keile's hand over and slowly licked her palm.

"Ooh. So, do I get to be, like, your love slave?"

"You'll have to come and find out." Haydn dropped Keile's hand and sat up, exposing her naked torso. "And no pun intended," she added quickly at Keile's snicker.

"Yes, ma'am." Keile's tone was meek, but her eyes said something entirely different as her gaze roved hungrily over Haydn's body.

"I've created a monster," Haydn grumbled, dodging Keile's

seeking hands. "Quit fooling around, Frankenstein. The sooner we leave, the sooner we can get to my place."

Keile sighed, affecting a hurt expression. "It's not my fault. Come on, what do you expect when you lead a thirsty woman to something that's way better than water?"

Haydn rolled her eyes and tried to look stern. Swinging her legs over the side of the bed, she stood and reached for the clothing she'd been in such a rush to discard hours ago.

"Why don't you go ahead and check on our boy," Keile suggested, rolling off the bed. "I'll clean up here, throw a few things together and be right over."

Haydn paused in the act of zipping her pants. "You can bring Can too, if you want. He should get used to us."

"Are you sure? I mean, you're not exactly used to having a dog around."

"Keile, he's better behaved than Kyle for God's sake. And then you won't have to come back to check on him."

"We'll be there." A warm feeling settled over her at the thought of the four of them spending time together, so much like a family. *No. Just like a family.*

"And Keile," Haydn said with a wicked smile, "bring the chocolate mousse."

Keile's blood turned to molten mush as her mind flashed to all sorts of interesting new possibilities. "Yes, Mistress," she said, and wiggled her eyebrows.

Keile quickly threw on some clothes and escorted Haydn to her car. "I'll see you in a bit." She buried her face in Haydn's auburn tresses. "I don't want to let you go."

"I know." Haydn nibbled on Keile's chin. "I had a great time tonight, Keile. You do a mean picnic."

"And you do a mean everything else." She caught Haydn's lips for a last long, loving kiss. "Okay, you better go."

"Don't make me wait," Haydn warned, her voice husky. She blew Keile a kiss before she got in the car, already missing the warmth of Keile's embrace. *This is ridiculous. You'll see her in twenty minutes.* With a wave, she backed out the driveway. At the first red stoplight, she pulled out her cell phone and hit the speed dial.

A sleepy voice answered the phone.

"It's me. I just wanted you to know that I'm on my way, in case you and Dani are running around the house naked."

"Been there, done that. We're sitting here fully dressed watching some cop flick Dani insisted on renting."

Haydn laughed when she heard Dani protesting in the background. "I'll be home in a few, and Keile and Can are coming later to spend the weekend," she said, trying to sound casual.

"What! When did this happen? I want details," Edan told her friend.

"Edan."

"What?"

"Bite me."

"I would," she said with mock regret, "but I suspect Keile's already done that."

Haydn turned off her phone, stopping the sound of raucous laughter. She should have known her friend would have something smart to say. Edan had been after her for the past two years to start dating. Now she had done more than that. She'd come perilously close to falling in love. Haydn sighed. She'd been a fool to think the walls around her heart could stand up to Keile. Letting herself fall in love wouldn't take much. She gripped the steering wheel, wondering if she had the strength to open her heart again. Turning on the blinker, she made a right onto her street and exhaled. *Jeez, it's not like she asked you to marry her, Davenport. Take it one day at a time.*

Chapter Twenty-One

The strident noise from the alarm came too soon for Keile Monday morning. She muffled a groan. The hours of work she'd put in after Haydn had fallen asleep every night made getting up to face Monday, and another work week, that much harder. She reached across Haydn and hit the off button. Covering a yawn, she peered at the time. "Ten more minutes," she mumbled and lay back down, snuggling up against Haydn's warm flesh. "Umm, you feel so good." She kissed her smooth back, getting ideas.

Haydn shivered and pressed her behind against wiry curls. "I thought you had to get up."

"I'm up." Keile ran her tongue along Haydn's back. "Just not the way you mean." She began thrusting with her hips to prove her point.

"You're going to be the death of me," Haydn claimed with a moan as long fingers cupped her. "You...don't...have...time for this," she protested, but continued to push into Keile's hand.

"There's always time for this." Keile ran her fingers through Haydn's silky wetness. "You feel so good," she whispered against her lover's ear. Finding the right spot, she increased the movements of her fingers and the thrust of her hips against Haydn's behind. Keile's breathing increased as the pressure within her built.

"I'm…gonna come." Haydn tightened her legs.

"Please," Keile begged, trying to hold back her own release.

"Yes…yes…yes." Her body trembled as the waves of ecstasy washed over her.

Keile, hearing Haydn reach her peak, quickly followed.

They lay entangled, chests heaving, holding each other close in the aftermath of shared passion. *I love you.* Keile held back a sigh. It was too early to say it out loud. She would give Haydn all the time she needed to realize she could trust her heart again. "I'm going to miss you like hell today."

Haydn kissed Keile's shoulder. "Come to dinner."

"Shouldn't I be taking you to dinner?"

"You can take me out another time. I want to be able to kiss you and touch you tonight."

"You make me feel incredibly special."

"Because you are," Haydn softly replied. "Now get your butt up and go to work."

"Slave driver." Keile finally forced herself to leave the cozy cocoon they'd created. Grabbing her overnight bag, she moved to the bathroom. As she stared in the mirror, she wondered if anyone would notice the change in her. She was not the same woman who had left work Friday afternoon.

When she returned, the bedroom was empty. She stopped by Kyle's room and watched him sleep for a minute before dropping a kiss on his cheek. She found Haydn in the kitchen, watching the coffeemaker. Walking up behind her, she parted her hair and kissed the back of her neck. "I guess I have to go." She slid her arms around Haydn's waist. "Parting sucks. There's nothing sweet about it." She sighed. "Have you seen my dog? Although, maybe I should call him Kyle's dog now." Can, after an initial confusion, had adjusted to being around Kyle. Keile suspected it had something to do with the amount of food Kyle dropped on the floor.

Haydn chuckled around a yawn. "I just let him out in the backyard." She put her hands on Keile's arms and squeezed. Gently moving from Keile's embrace, she walked to the coffeemaker, filled a traveling mug and handed it to Keile.

I must be in love. "Thanks." Keile slowly added plenty of sweetener and creamer to her coffee, even though she knew she wouldn't drink it. She was stalling, afraid once she walked out the door she'd discover the weekend had just been a wonderful dream. *This was, no, is real,* she told herself as she stirred her coffee. *Nothing can take it away.*

"Are you okay, Keile?" Haydn looked at her with concern. "What time did you come to bed anyway?"

"I'd be better if I could stay with you." Keile gave her a rueful smile. "Ignore me, I'm being needy."

"Have I told you I like you needy?" Haydn gave her a quick kiss. "But what I love is that you took the coffee without saying a word." She took the mug from Keile's hand and dumped the contents down the drain. "Sorry, I'm not awake." She opened the fridge and pulled out a Dr. Pepper.

"Thanks." It took every ounce of willpower Keile had to leave without admitting her love. She settled for a loving kiss.

An hour later, Keile pulled into the parking lot at work. She climbed out of her Jeep, already counting the hours until she could see Haydn again. Trying to clear her head of pleasurable thoughts, Keile veered into her cube where her attention was immediately drawn to the sheet of paper on her chair. Normally, she would have pounced on it, eager to begin working. Today, she took the time to hang up her coat and stow away her briefcase.

After moving the note to the desk, she plopped into the chair and thought not about work, but the previous weekend. Images of the time she'd spent with Haydn and Kyle flowed through her mind like a slideshow. Keile's heart swelled and she couldn't hold back a big smile. In three weeks her life had been turned inside out. *And I would do it all over again in a heartbeat.*

She retrieved the Thanksgiving photo from her coat. As she positioned it beside her computer monitor, Keile finally understood why her co-workers filled their cubes with pictures of loved ones. It wasn't to remember their faces, it was to remember the feelings they evoked. Still smiling, she reached for the note. The smile slipped as she read, and turned into a frown when she reached the due date. It was going to be a long night.

Promptly at six thirty, Keile rang Haydn's doorbell. She smiled when she heard Marcus holler, "I got it!"

"Hey, Pops," she said when he opened the door.

Marcus held out his arms. "Come to me my long lost child." After a tight squeeze, he pulled back and studied her face carefully. "I think I see it," he said seriously.

"What?" Keile eyed him and stepped away. She used the back of her hand to wipe her cheeks and mouth.

"The good looks that drove my sister over the edge."

Her cheeks grew warm, and she looked away from his knowing smirk. "I…uh…She told you?" Keile gave him a panicked glance.

Marcus laughed. "She didn't have to. It's written all over her face, too." He closed the door and put a hand on her shoulder. "Hey, I think it's great that the two of you got together. Just don't hurt her or I'll have to hunt you down."

"Never," Keile vowed, gazing into eyes almost identical to her own.

"I thought I heard the door." Haydn advanced to the foyer, walked directly to Keile, and gave her a kiss on the lips. "I missed you today," she said softly.

"Not nearly as much as I missed you." She dipped her head, bringing her mouth to Haydn's, careful to keep the kiss chaste. Pulling back even though she wanted more, she said with regret, "I can only stay a few hours. My boss decided to revamp my project, and of course he wants it by tomorrow." Keile worked to hide her bitter feelings that the work she'd squeezed in over the weekend had been for nothing.

"I'll take what I can get. But you owe me." Haydn smiled. "And I don't mean cash," she whispered.

Keile's response was a kiss that left them panting. "Consider that a down payment," she said softly and kissed Haydn's ear.

"Ahem. I'm still here." Marcus laughed when they broke apart. "What a cute couple."

Haydn rolled her eyes. "That's enough of that from you."

"Mama!" Keile and Haydn turned to watch Kyle run in their direction.

"He's talking about you," Haydn said, and watched as Kyle wrapped his short arms around Keile's leg.

After dinner, Keile was assigned the task of wearing Kyle out while Haydn and Marcus cleaned up the kitchen. She took him to the family room where they played chase with the trucks and cars until they both collapsed into a tired heap.

Haydn settled on the floor beside Keile and reached for her hand. "I'm glad you had a few hours to spare for us."

"I want more than a few hours," Keile said softly. "You and Kyle have helped me realize what I was missing. Work and money won't ever be enough for me anymore." She kissed the back of Haydn's hand. "It might take a few days, but work will eventually slow down. Enough so I can take you on another date."

"Dates are nice, but I think I'm happiest when it's just us." Haydn leaned her cheek against Keile's shoulder and placed her hand on Kyle's back.

"I'm pretty happy myself." And she was happy. The only drawback was she would have to leave too soon and go back to working on the Crawford project. She hated that necessity and promised herself work would have to get better.

Chapter Twenty-Two

"You're kind of late this morning, aren't you?" Tom glanced at his watch.

Keile glared at him through bloodshot eyes. Obviously, he'd been watching out for her arrival. "What? Are you my timekeeper now?" she asked, not bothering to keep the disdain out of her voice. After working most of the night to make the changes Rick had requested, she was way beyond caring about Tom, about Rick, about work. "Is there something you need that can't wait until I get to my cube?"

He bristled at her tone. "Rick's looking for you."

She blew out a sharp breath, but it did nothing to ease her irritation. "Fine. Get out of my way and I can go see what he needs," she ground out through clenched teeth and brushed past him.

Keile stopped by the bathroom and splashed some cold water on her face. She looked like she'd only slept for three hours. Praying she'd be able to make it through the rest of the day without saying something she would later regret, she slowly made her way to Rick's office. She knocked on the open door and waited for Rick to look up before entering. "You wanted to see me?"

Rick smiled and pushed away the folder he'd been studying. "Grab a seat. I just wanted to thank you for turning this around so quickly. Good job as always."

She forced a smile. "Thanks for the compliment, but I really could have used that assistance you've been promising me. Any luck with that?" Her stomach tightened as she noticed the almost imperceptible clenching of his jaw.

"I've been busy, and frankly, I thought you'd reconsider."

He's been stringing me along, she thought and swallowed sharp disillusionment. "I haven't changed my mind," she said evenly. "It would help if we could pull someone in just for the rush jobs. I'd be happy to supervise them."

"I'll see what I can do."

Sure you will. "I would appreciate it." Keile barely managed to keep the sarcasm out of her voice. "What time is the project meeting?"

"Don't worry, you can skip this one. You've done enough already." Rick rummaged around on his desk and uncovered a file folder. "Start looking at this until we know the next steps for the Crawford project."

Keile accepted it without a word, wondering what 'you've done enough already' meant. She made her way back to her cube, torn between anger and apprehension. Had her request for help made her less valuable in Rick's eyes? And if it had, what could she do about it?

Polish her resume? Call some of the many contacts she'd made over the years? Quit her job? Her heart literally stopped beating for a fleeting moment at that thought. No she couldn't do that. Her success in this job was why she had a house and why she had things no one could take away, including her professional reputation. Starting over was not an option. Surely Rick would come around after he'd had time to process her request. As her heart returned to its normal beat, she reached for the papers Rick had given her earlier and did what she had always done so well—she focused on the job. She would deal with the bigger picture later.

At six thirty that evening, Keile rang Haydn's doorbell. She'd left work promptly at five, taken Can for a long walk, then invited herself over to Haydn's for dinner. Her heart raced when Haydn opened the door, dressed in a tight T-shirt and low-riding sweat pants. "Hey."

"Hey, back." Haydn gave her a quick kiss before stepping back, allowing Keile and the Whole Foods bag she was carrying to enter the house. "I'm glad you decided to come over."

Keile grinned. "It probably didn't hurt that I promised to bring food, huh?"

"You brought food?" Haydn feigned surprise. "You shouldn't have." They shared a laugh. "We should put the food in the kitchen so you can give me a proper welcome."

"Then lead the way, Ms. Davenport." Keile followed Haydn to the kitchen. When her hands were free, she reached for Haydn and kissed her thoroughly. "I missed you," she whispered against Haydn's neck.

"Already? It hasn't even been twenty-four hours," Haydn teased.

Keile nipped at her ear. "Okay, so I missed seeing you naked."

Haydn shivered. "How hungry are you? Edan and Dani aren't due back with Kyle for an hour."

"I'm very hungry." Keile's voice was rough with desire as she snaked a hand under Haydn's shirt and stroked her stomach.

Haydn raced up the stairs, with Keile close on her heels. "You've turned me into a sex fiend," Haydn said as she reached for the hem of Keile's shirt and pulled it over her head. "Ooh, no bra." She licked each nipple, then skimmed her fingers down Keile's bare stomach and slipped them inside her loose-fitting jeans. "I wanted to do this last night."

Keile put her hands on Haydn's hips, and sucked in a breath when Haydn pressed lightly against her clit. "That's good... right?"

"As long as you're prepared for the consequences." Haydn removed her hand and pushed Keile back onto the bed. She unsnapped the jeans, then pulled down the zipper. "Are you?" she asked, tugging on the jeans.

"What?" Keile raised her hips and used her hands to push at the jeans. "Am I ready? Oh, yeah." The huskiness in Haydn's answering laugh made her quiver. "I want to feel your skin against mine." She sat up, kicked off her jeans and boxers before helping Haydn get undressed. Keile lay back down and watched with pleasure as Haydn straddled her body. "Have I mentioned how much I adore your freckles?"

Haydn leaned forward, rested her weight on her elbows and dropped a teasing kiss on Keile's lips. "Maybe."

Keile fastened her fingers in Haydn's hair and slipped her tongue inside Haydn's mouth. Their tongues did a sensual duet as Haydn pressed her hips against Keile's heated flesh. Haydn broke off the kiss and trailed her lips to Keile's sensitive neck. Keile's hips jerked in response and she let out a hum of pleasure.

Haydn maneuvered her leg between Keile's thighs and applied more pressure to Keile's hard clit. When Keile's breathing became ragged, she pushed a hand between their bodies and entered Keile. "So soft, so wet." She met the rhythm of Keile's rising hips with sure thrusts, and much too soon, she heard her hoarse cry and felt the contractions squeezing her fingers.

Keile ran her hands along Haydn's back and tried to catch her breath. "You tear me up," she said, breathing hard. "But I like it."

Haydn laughed. "It's all about consequences."

"Then let's see if I can exact some of my own." Keile flipped Haydn onto her back and lowered her mouth to lave one rosy nipple, then the other. Her fingers danced down Haydn's stomach and dipped into her satiny wetness. Keile brought her wet fingers up to her nose and breathed in deep. "You smell almost as good as you taste." She looked into Haydn's eyes as she slid her fingers into her mouth.

Haydn's eyes turned into slits and she arched her back. "Touch me."

Keile's mouth followed the trail her fingers had blazed. She took Haydn into her mouth and sucked gently before applying pressure with her tongue. At Haydn's urgent request, she entered her and timed her thrusts with the movement of her tongue.

Haydn thrashed her head back and forth, practically sobbing in pleasure. She gritted her teeth, but couldn't stop the release that rushed through her body like white heat. She caught her breath and lifted half off the bed, crying out Keile's name.

Keile rested her head against Haydn's stomach. "Being with you is always so sweet."

Haydn opened one eye and crooked her finger. "Come here, you."

Keile kissed her way up Haydn's body, nestled against her chest and sighed deeply. "I'm not sure how I lived without you. I love you." She raised her head, her heart in her throat, at Haydn's indrawn breath. "I'm not trying to push," she said quickly, taking in Haydn's almost panicked expression. "And I don't expect an answer. It's just..." Keile smiled. "It's just you take me places I never knew I wanted to go. Thank you."

"I...I'm—"

Keile stopped her with a kiss. "You don't have to say anything. It's enough for me to be here with you, like this. Please believe me."

Haydn gave Keile a shaky smile. "You never cease to amaze me."

Keile's heartbeat returned to normal. "Good. My plan is working." She sat up and tapped Haydn's nose. "We'd better get up before they get back."

"I guess you're right." Haydn looked away. "Are we okay?"

Keile hugged her and tried not to wish Haydn had been able to say *I love you* back. She was being greedy. With time, it would happen. "Yeah. We're okay."

Chapter Twenty-Three

Keile smoothed back the strands of hair that had escaped from her ponytail and pushed open the door to Jake's Bar and Grill. For a Thursday night the place was fairly empty and quiet. She peered around the dark, narrow room, with booths on one side and a bar along the other, until she spied Dani sitting at the far end of the bar. "Yo." She tapped Dani on the shoulder, then draped her coat on the back of the stool next to Dani's. "It's hot in here."

"Not as hot as you," Dani said with a grin as she took in Keile's black sleeveless T-shirt and tight black jeans. "I've never seen you in all black. What's the occasion?"

"I could say it fits my mood but really I need to do laundry. Between work and other things I haven't gotten around to it."

"Other things?" Dani laughed when Keile shrugged and looked away. "Maybe I should ask about work instead, huh?"

"Work sucks," Keile said, then ordered a Coke from the pierced and tattooed bartender.

Dani looked at her in surprise. "This is the first time I've ever heard you bad-mouth the job. What the hell is going on at Planning Associates?"

"Oh, I was sort of demoted." Keile tried to sound off-hand as she raked her fingers through her bushy ponytail.

"What?"

If Keile had been in a better mood, she would have laughed at Dani's comical expression. "It's a big mess. And in a way I'm not even sure I'm in the right anymore. What I do know, is after yesterday morning I've lost all respect for Rick."

"Rick, as in your boss Rick?"

"Yeah, the one I *used* to think was so great," Keile said bitterly. She nodded a thanks when the bartender set her drink in front of her. "I was stupid."

"I doubt that." Dani took a long swig of beer. "What happened yesterday morning?"

"Rick put someone else in charge of the project I've been working my ass off on." Keile shook her head in disgust. "I wouldn't be so frustrated except the asswipe he put in charge couldn't direct traffic, much less a big project like this."

"Hold up, I'm confused. Maybe you should start at the beginning."

"You, me, boy, park." Keile watched as Dani's eyes lit up with understanding. "Yeah because of that, for the first time ever, I pressed Rick for help on a project. My fault was thinking... Hell, I don't know what I was thinking." She took a deep breath and bit on her lip, fighting the anger and frustration she'd felt all day. "But in my defense, Rick seemed to realize this project had grown in complexity and offered the help first. All I asked for was someone part-time. Instead of assigning someone to me, he throws Tom at me. And with Tom as lead, I know at some point I'll be doing my job *and* his." Keile slapped her palm against the bar. "And Rick knows it, too!"

"Damn." Dani patted Keile's thigh. "Sounds like your

proverbial rock and hard place."

"Not to mention Tom is making sure everyone knows he's supervising *me*." Keile took a sip of the watered down Coke, hoping to control the quiver in her voice. "After only two days of putting up with this crap I'm so pissed my head's ready to explode. I hate feeling this out of control. I hate it!" She exhaled and unclenched her hands. She hadn't felt this angry since she'd found out her mother died.

"Hey, after all the work you've put in, you have a right to be pissed. Does this affect your title or salary?"

"Not yet. I think this is Rick's way of letting me know he's in charge."

"After all the hours you've given him, how can he do that? And just because you asked for a little help? You're right, that sucks big time. What are you going to do?"

"Hope my resume will convince another firm to give me a job. I've already applied for one position, but I can't exactly count on a glowing reference from Rick."

"Don't give them his name."

"The consulting community in Seneca isn't that large," Keile said with a grimace. "I wouldn't be surprised if Rick hasn't already had a call. I also wouldn't be surprised if I end up having to look farther, like in Atlanta."

Dani frowned. "Damn! That's beyond sucks."

"That's life. You kind of need money to keep a house," she said and forced a smile when smiling was the furthest thing on her mind. Only the thought of being broke and going to Haydn empty-handed had kept her from quitting a couple of times today alone. "I do hate the idea of an hour-and-a-half commute each way."

"You wouldn't move up there?"

Keile shook her head and found some pleasure at the relieved expression on Dani's face. "There's too much in Seneca for me to leave."

"And I thought we weren't going to talk about *other things*." Dani nudged Keile with her shoulder.

"Hey." Keile returned the nudge. "Consider yourself included in the other things keeping me here. Now, didn't you promise me food? And don't think I've forgotten we still have to dissect your life."

"What are you doing still awake?" Keile asked softly. She and Haydn were snuggled up in bed, winding down from another weekend spent together. "I must be losing my touch if I didn't put you to sleep."

"Your skills are still up to par," Haydn replied, clearly amused. Her head rested against Keile's bare chest. "I'm enjoying this twilight time between being fully awake and asleep. It's nice to be worn out and know I don't have to move any time soon."

"Yeah. It's—"

"Sweet?"

"Hey, I wasn't going to say sweet…this time." Keile tightened her hold on Haydn. "I was going to say very nice. I wish I could have devoted more time to you and Kyle instead of work." She sighed. "These extra hours are getting frustrating."

"It's okay, Keile. Besides, I got to see you when Kyle decided you needed a break from your computer." Haydn chuckled. "You're such a sucker where he's concerned."

"And you," Keile said, stroking Haydn's arm. "Don't forget I'm your personal sex slave."

"Hmm, there is that. You've become quite an adept student."

"I had a wonderful teacher, in more ways than one. I'm glad you let me hang around."

"Come on, you do more than hang around. Kyle and I wouldn't know what to do without you." Haydn reached for Keile's hand and brought it to her lips. "Your patience with him astounds me. What were you like as a child?"

"Determined."

"You." Haydn pinched. "I'm serious. I bet you were a cute kid."

Keile tensed. She wasn't one for reminiscing about her

childhood. Her starkest memories were of the times she'd been removed from her mother's care. A mother who went from loving and playful to silent and distant for no reason a young Keile could figure out. She'd been nine when they took her away from her mother for the last time.

"Hey, did you fall asleep?" Haydn asked with a nudge. "Or are you ignoring me."

"I would never ignore you. I was thinking about how uncute I actually was." She forced a smile. There was no need to bring Haydn down with her. "I went through puberty early, meaning I was taller than anyone in my class. I spent sixth grade tripping over my own feet. I still suffer from lingering embarrassment."

Haydn shuddered. "Tell me about it. I got teased because of my flaming red hair and freckles. I think I've successfully destroyed all photographic evidence from that time period."

"I thought we agreed I like the freckles."

"I'll concede that point, Ms. Griffen. But I stand by my assessment that you were cute and adorable as a child."

Keile kissed the top of Haydn's head. "Far be it for me to stop you from declaring a surly, uncoordinated bookworm adorable."

"I'm glad you realize it's my right." Haydn changed position so they were eye to eye. "See, it's not that hard to talk about yourself."

Keile pulled her close for a tender kiss. Maybe years from now she would share everything.

"No, really it's okay," Haydn said in a soothing voice, for the third time. It was Wednesday afternoon and she was seeing her last client of the day. Mrs. Sampson was one of the elderly, low-income clients referred to her by Marcus that she assisted for no charge. They were in the conference room Haydn shared with three other small businesses on her side of the floor.

She resisted the urge to rub her temples. "I understand you got confused and brought me the wrong folder. What happened to your daughter today? I thought she was going to accompany you."

"She thought we were supposed to meet next Tuesday and scheduled something else today," Mrs. Sampson explained with a worried smile as she pulled on the straps of her pocketbook. "I had to call a taxi to get here. I can't drive myself anymore, you know."

"Why don't we do this," Haydn suggested, putting a hand on Mrs. Sampson's arm. "Since you're my last client today, I can take you home, pick up the right folder and then get back with you once I've reconciled your bank statement."

"Oh, I don't want to impose."

"It's no problem," Haydn assured her with a smile. "I go that way to pick up my son from day care."

"Well, if it's no trouble." Mrs. Sampson was clearly relieved. "I don't like to trouble anyone. Especially my daughter."

"I promise you're not causing any trouble." Haydn locked up her small office, and assisted her client to the front door of the building. "You wait here where it's warm, while I go get the car." Haydn had only taken a few steps before she pulled up the collar on her coat and reached for her gloves. Looking at the cloudy gray sky, she wondered if they were going to get the freezing rain the weather people had predicted. She silently prayed that it wouldn't happen until after she made it to Keile's place.

As she drove to the front of the small office building where her office was housed, she was warmed by thoughts of being iced in with Keile. She could see them on the blanket in front of the fire, sipping wine, talking, kissing and more. Keile's face, glowing red as she begged for release, flashed through her mind. *You have it bad.* Haydn jumped out of the car and this time she was glad for the cold wind that slapped her in the face, calming her thoughts.

After dropping off her client and picking up the correct folder, Haydn proceeded to the day care center, located in the basement of a Methodist church. She pulled into the parking lot, looked at the darkening sky and grabbed an umbrella. Battling the wind, she hurried into the brick structure and made her way down a single flight of stairs.

"Good afternoon, Ms. Davenport," the cheerful young woman behind the desk called out as soon as Haydn entered the front area. "I hope it hasn't started to rain."

"Not yet, Trish," Haydn said with a shiver. "But it looks like it's coming."

"I hope I can get home first. Most parents are picking their kids up early." She hit the buzzer that unlocked the door leading to the rooms where the children spent their days. Haydn smiled her thanks and pushed the door open. Whereas the front space was designed with adults in mind, the hallway and the rooms in the back were for the kids. They were decorated in bright colors with sturdy child-sized furniture, plenty of toys and books.

She walked down the hall to Kyle's room, passing the other rooms with the top part of the door open. She stopped at the next to the last door on the right and looked in, easily spotting her son sitting by himself, jabbering at a furry-headed stuffed creature. "Kyle."

He looked up, and a big grin transformed his face. Pushing himself up, he ran to the door yelling, "Mama!"

Haydn waved at Kyle's main teacher before lifting the safety latch. After making sure the door was closed securely behind her, she squatted and hugged her son. She held him close for the brief minute he allowed, letting go when he pushed away.

"Tee, tee," he said, shaking the creature in his hand.

"Yes I see. It looks like a Wild Thing," she said slowly, pointing to the stuffed toy. "Wild Thing."

He laughed, then said something only a mother would think sounded like wild thing before holding out the creature for her to kiss. With a big grin, Haydn gave it an air kiss and handed it back to Kyle, who mimicked her actions. She sent him to put the doll up while she conferred with his teacher.

"Okay kiddo, let's break out of this joint." As had become his habit, he insisted on walking. "Come on Kyle, let me carry you. We're going to go visit Keile and Can tonight."

"Mama." Kyle grinned, clapping his hands. "Do."

"Yes, Can will be there, too." She held out her arms.

"Mama, Do." He grabbed her hand and pulled her toward the exit.

"Determined is good," she mumbled under her breath. When they entered the front office, she crossed to the counter where the sign-out book was located.

"Ms. Davenport, I forgot to remind you earlier that we need you to check your authorization release form. We've run into some problems lately, so we ask that every parent revisit their form."

Haydn accepted the proffered form. Currently, the only alternative name was Marcus. She thought about the past week and made a quick decision. "I may need to add a name later. Is that okay?"

"Sure. For now, put your initials at the bottom to show you reviewed the form."

Haydn's cell pone rang before she pulled out of the parking lot. She looked at the caller ID and smiled. "Hello," she said, her voice soft and husky.

"Do you know how sexy you sound?"

"No, but thanks for telling me."

Keile whimpered. "Okay, stop with the sexy voice. I'm still at work."

"You're not calling to cancel are you?"

"I'm calling to suggest that I come over to your place tonight because of the weather. I promise to pick up Chinese before I come."

"You're planning on *coming*, are you?" Haydn taunted with a wicked grin.

"Who knew you were such a naughty little girl?" Keile chuckled. "I love it. I'll try to get to your place by seven."

"I'll see you then, sweetie." Smiling, Haydn dropped the phone on the seat next to her. Getting iced in at her place would work as well, if not better. Kyle would be asleep upstairs while she and Keile snuggled in front of the fire. She could hardly wait to see Keile again. To touch her again. She was quickly reaching the point where simply talking to her on the phone wasn't enough anymore.

Haydn thought back to the Friday after Thanksgiving when she'd realized how easily she could fall in love. *Could?* She laughed without humor. She probably already was. *Then why can't I admit it?* Checking in the rearview mirror before backing out, her glance fell on Kyle. *Reagan.* She sighed. It always came back to her ex-lover. Reagan had been the one to push for a child, going so far as to convince Marcus to donate his sperm.

She eased into traffic, reminding herself that she was over Reagan and the heartache she'd brought. And that she no longer harbored any secret desire for Reagan's return because her mind was filled with Keile. *Then I should stop being an idiot and act like it.* No more holding back.

Haydn was surprised to find Edan's gold sedan in the garage when she arrived home. It wasn't even four and Edan usually didn't get home until after five. That was on the days she didn't stay at Dani's place.

"What are you doing home so early?" she asked Edan, who was sitting at the kitchen table, mug in hand.

"Oh, yeah. This is your first winter in Seneca." Edan grinned. "Around here, the threat of ice or snow puts a lot of people in a panic. My boss let us go early. Seems he was caught in a big snowstorm in Atlanta years ago and it still haunts him. But you won't catch me complaining."

"Now that I think about it, Trish at the day care did mention parents were picking up kids early." Haydn removed Kyle's jacket and watched him run to greet Edan before he went to his toys. "Have you checked the forecast lately? Keile's supposed to stop by and bring dinner. Sounds like she'll be lucky to find anything open."

"Last I heard we were still in the path of the storm. I got tired of the weather people salivating over the threat of bad weather. Most of the time they make it seem worse than it is."

"True." She pulled out the chair next to Edan.

"You seem pretty sweet on Keile these days. Everything still progressing?"

Haydn nodded. "Things are going good. She doesn't push me. I like that."

"Don't you worry that means she's not interested in taking things further?"

She frowned and gazed at her friend. "Is this about Keile or Dani?"

Edan wrapped her hands around the mug of coffee and grimaced. "Dani. Every time I try to talk about the future, she changes the subject or kisses me silly. It's driving me crazy but I'm afraid it's too early to press. That maybe I should just be glad we're together."

"I don't know. The times I've seen the two of you together, she acts like you're all that and more. Give it a little more time. Maybe she's scared to let go of that tiny chunk of armor left guarding her heart."

"Oh, Haydn, is that how you feel?" Edan reached for her hand. "I thought for sure you were past that."

"I should be. I want to be. And maybe Dani does too. One minute I'll look at Keile and think, this is it, I'm in love. Like today, I had to review a form at the day care and I almost added her name as an authorized pickup person for Kyle. How is it I can trust her implicitly with my child, but I can't extend that same trust to include my heart?"

"Do...Do you ever wish for Reagan's return? Is that what's holding you back?"

"No! She killed the love I had for her. I don't think I can ever forgive her for what she did to me. It cut too deep." She shook her head, wanting to get rid of the memories. She didn't want to think about the bad days when it hurt to live. "I think I'll have some of that coffee. Kyle, are you ready for some juice?" She moved to the cabinet above the dishwasher and removed one of his cups without waiting for a response. The simple act of providing for him soothed her nerves.

"So where does that leave me?" Edan asked once Haydn was seated again. "What should I do about Dani's shield?"

“Ask her about it someplace public. I assume she hasn’t kissed you senseless in the middle of a restaurant,” she said with a smirk.

“No telling what desperation may drive her to do,” Edan said glumly.

“Then maybe you need to tell her what you see as your future and hope she catches a hint.”

“Have you ever thought of doing the very same thing with Keile? She’s probably as frustrated as I am.”

“Nobody could be as short of patience as you, Edan. And Keile knows my limitations and she accepts them.”

“For how long?” Edan challenged.

Haydn put down her mug. “She doesn’t pressure me, why should you?” She exhaled. It wasn’t Edan’s fault she couldn’t let go of the past. “Look, my situation with Keile is nothing like what’s happening between you and Dani. We’re not trying to overcome a joint history.”

“I know. So where does that leave us?” She gave Haydn a semblance of a smile. “You up for another deal?”

“What kind of deal?”

“I’ll talk to Dani if you talk to Keile?”

Haydn held out her hand. “You’ve got yourself a deal.” She waited until after they shook hands to add, “Is now a good time to tell you I was already planning to have that talk with Keile?”

Keile was clearing up her desk, getting ready to head out when Tom stuck his head in her cube. “Sorry this is late, but Rick and I need to go over some changes with you,” he said, affecting the superior air he’d developed since being made project manager.

Haven’t I jumped through enough hoops today? She bit back an expletive. “Will it take long?” she asked, pointedly glancing at her watch. “I have an obligation.”

“You might want to reschedule.”

“Just great!” Keile pinched the bridge of her nose as the niggling pain behind her eyes blossomed into a full-blown headache. She’d already wasted the day making one unnecessary change after another. Though Tom claimed the changes had been approved by Rick, she knew better. She exhaled sharply, an inch away from quitting on the spot. "I'll be there in five."

Keile stormed into her cube twenty minutes later and threw her pad on the floor. As expected, the work she'd done today was useless, and it would take her a good portion of the night to get her where she needed to be by mid-morning. She paced until she calmed down enough to be coherent, then phoned Haydn.

Keile swallowed the disappointment the sound of Haydn's voice brought her. After dealing with Tom, she'd been looking forward to the comfort of Haydn's presence. "It's me." She squeezed her eyes shut and continued. "I won't be able to make it tonight," she said slowly, striving to keep her voice steady. "I'm sorry, but I just got dumped with another last-minute assignment that's due tomorrow morning."

"I understand. These things happen."

She cringed when she heard the unspoken disappointment in Haydn's voice. "God, I'm sorry, Haydn. If there was any chance I could stop by, I would." She stopped, hearing the raw emotion in her own voice.

"Keile, what's going on? Is everything okay at your job? You're not in trouble are you?"

"No. Work's okay." She closed her eyes and gathered her thoughts. "It's nothing. I'm disappointed because I was really looking forward to spending time with you and Kyle. You know, cuddling up in front of the fire and enjoying some of that wonderful coffee you brew."

"You're full of it, Griffen."

She was warmed by the open affection in Haydn's voice. "Full of you, Ms. Davenport."

"That's all I can ask for. Maybe tomorrow?"

"For sure," Keile promised. "I'll call you in the afternoon."

"I'll be waiting. They changed the forecast to rain, but you be careful driving home, okay?"

"I will. I'll dream of you. Naked of course."

"Sweet talker," Haydn with a soft laugh.

"That's me. I love you." Keile replaced the receiver and bit her lip till it stung. She was stuck doing what she hadn't wanted to do—working extra hours and missing time with Haydn. Damn Rick and damn Tom. As she reluctantly retrieved and opened the folder, she vowed to make time for Haydn and Kyle tomorrow no matter what.

Chapter Twenty-Four

Haydn looked at the clock on the kitchen wall in surprise when the doorbell pealed. Keile must have gotten off early to make up for the extra hours she'd put in the day before. Smiling, she hurried to the front door, and pulled it open without checking. "Hey, you're…" Her smile faltered, then turned into a frown. When her heartbeat returned to normal, Haydn's first instinct was to slam the door and lock it. She was too late. Reagan Darrow had already entered her home.

"Surprise." Reagan's smile was brittle. "Sorry to come by without calling, but I only had an address." She tucked thick golden strands of hair behind her right ear.

The nervous gesture didn't go unnoticed by Haydn. "What are you doing here? Haven't you done enough already?"

"I deserve that," Reagan said, flinching under Haydn's baleful glare. "I…I came to apologize. Something I should have done before now."

After three years and three thousand miles, how had Reagan turned up on *her* doorstep? And curse it all, why now? Haydn closed her eyes briefly and took a deep breath. Memories that were never too far away returned, and her heart ached. Bracing herself against the pain, she studied Reagan without saying a word. Reagan still had the slim athletic build and the gorgeous blue eyes she remembered too well. "I don't care anymore, Reagan."

Reagan swallowed. "Would it help if I said I haven't gone a single day without missing you?"

Her lips twisted in a bitter smile. "Funny, I used to miss you too. But I had to get on with my life after you so callously destroyed all my dreams."

Reagan reared back as if she'd been slapped.

"What the hell did you expect from me? Did you really think I'd welcome you with open arms and smiles?" Haydn threw her hands up. "You didn't even have the guts to tell me to my face we were through. That makes you a fucking coward in my book." Haydn steeled herself against the hurt in her ex-lover's eyes. Whatever Reagan was feeling now couldn't compare to the pain she'd experienced.

"I'm sorry I did that to you." Tears pooled in Reagan's eyes. "Please understand. I had to get away or go crazy."

"And you couldn't talk to me about it? I wasn't only your partner. I thought I was your best friend." Haydn couldn't hide the hurt she'd thought was long gone.

"I was wrong. I should have told you. I was scared I'd let you talk me out of going, and I needed to go."

Haydn wiped her eyes with the back of her hand. She didn't want to spend any more time or effort grieving over Reagan. "I guess you got what you wanted." Her voice was monotone. "Now I want you to leave and never get in touch with me again."

"Please, I really am sorry. Give me a chance to explain," Reagan begged.

"I heard you, Reagan. I'm just finding I don't want to hear

any more. Do me a favor and do what you do best…leave."

She barely gave Reagan time to clear the doorway before she slammed the door. Turning the lock, she let loose a muted scream. Haydn covered her mouth with her hands and sank to the floor, her shoulders shaking from the sobs wracking her body.

She cried until the tears tapered off. Wincing at the ache in her head, she pushed herself off the floor and stumbled to the bathroom. She patted her red, swollen eyes with a wet cloth as the scene with Reagan replayed through her mind like a video. *So it was all my fault.* Somehow, someway it had been her fault.

Haydn closed her eyes and thought back to the weeks before Reagan left. Again she came up empty. Nothing out of the ordinary had happened. They had been getting their lives together in preparation of parenthood. How could she have been oblivious to her partner's suffering? *What does that say about me as a lover, a partner?* She bit the inside of her cheek against a new kind of pain.

It wasn't until four forty-five that it hit Haydn: Keile was due for dinner. *I can't see her now.* She dialed Keile's office number and almost cried in relief when she got voicemail. "It's Haydn. I know it's last minute, but I…need to cancel tonight. Uh, something came up. I'll call you when I'm ready to reschedule." She turned off the phone, praying Keile wouldn't call or drop by after she heard the message. In her current state she didn't want to see or talk to anyone. She was grateful Edan had convinced Dani to go away for a long weekend, and couldn't see her swollen eyes or comment on her red, blotchy face.

Haydn clenched her teeth and tried to stop another bout of tears. The moment she thought she had her emotions under control, something would set her off. Even Kyle had picked up on her mood after he woke up from his nap. He refused to let her out of his sight despite her assurances that everything was okay.

She couldn't blame her son for doubting her. Every time she looked at him, her eyes filled with tears as she was reminded that at one time Reagan had wanted to be Kyle's birth mother. And remembering brought feelings of hopelessness, anger and now, shame to the forefront. Haydn flinched when the doorbell rang. *Oh God, I waited too late to call.*

"Mama!" Kyle's face became animated. He had come to expect Keile to be on the other side of the door every time the doorbell sounded. "Mama."

Despite her nervousness, Haydn smiled at the look of excitement on his face. When the doorbell pealed again, she followed him to the foyer, this time checking to see who was there. She would have ignored the summons if Kyle hadn't been beside her. Taking a deep breath, she opened the door.

Kyle barged around his mother's legs. "Mama!" He took a hasty step back when he got a good look at the woman on the doorstep. "No!"

Reagan's mouth fell open in surprise as she looked from Kyle to Haydn.

"I thought I told you not to come back." Haydn was forced to keep her tone gentle in deference to her son, who was clinging to her leg. "The conversation is finished."

Reagan's gaze returned to Kyle. "It took me a long time to get to this point. Please hear me out, and I'll leave peacefully. Please."

Haydn crossed her arms over her chest. "I guess the minute it takes you to tell your side won't hurt." She waited for Reagan to enter before closing and locking the door. Briefly resting her forehead against the door, she took a deep breath and prayed for calm.

"I see you went ahead with our plans," Reagan said, her voice suddenly husky.

"Yes. *I* did go ahead with our plans. This is *my* son, Kyle." She put her hands on his shoulders.

"He's adorable." Reagan's expression showed regret. "Obviously, Marcus went ahead with the plan to be the donor."

"Yes," she said curtly. "That's not what you came here to tell me."

"May…maybe we could sit down," Reagan suggested.

"As you wish." She ushered Reagan into the family room, knowing Kyle would feel more comfortable there. "Have a seat." Haydn motioned to the sofa before she dropped into the nearby recliner. Kyle quickly climbed onto her lap.

Reagan sighed and curled her shoulder-length hair behind her ears. "This is hard for me," she began.

"Just get to the point, Reagan. I have things to take care of."

"Must you be so hateful?" Reagan blinked her eyes rapidly.

Yes, she wanted to shout but didn't. "The clock is ticking."

"Fine. I started to panic after I quit my job so we could try to get pregnant. Everything was about you, Haydn. It got to the point where I didn't exist anymore outside of you."

"I want to thank you for coming back to let me know what a monster I was. Will you please leave?" She stood up with Kyle in her arms, signifying the end of the discussion. "Let me make this clear, Reagan. There is nothing you have to say that I want to hear. Ever!"

Reagan stood, battling against tears. "For what it's worth, I'm sorry that I dealt with the situation the way I did."

Haydn glared. "It's not worth a damn thing. I don't need you coming into my life making me feel everything was my fault. I'm not the one who didn't think what we had was worth fighting for."

"You don't understand! I had to fight it alone." She wiped at the tears, streaming down her face. "I didn't want to do it, but in the end, I had to."

"What is it you want from me? I'm not a priest. I can't absolve you of your sins."

"There's no need to be sarcastic."

"I'm not being sarcastic!" Haydn shot back. "You come to me three years too late with a sob story, and what? I'm supposed to say I understand you had to go find yourself? I'm supposed to say I forgive you for leaving me so damn depressed I didn't want to get up? Am I supposed to say I understand you didn't mean it when you cut out my heart and stomped on it? What am I supposed to say?" She ground out the last sentence slowly.

"Mama?" Kyle's lips trembled.

Haydn's anger was quickly replaced by remorse. "It's okay, baby." She kissed him on the forehead, then rested her head against his. "Mama's sorry she yelled," she said, rubbing his back.

"I'll go now," Reagan said quietly. "I'm sorry I bothered you."

Keile hurried away from the conference room, looking forward to grabbing Can and heading to Haydn's place. The new assignment Tom had given her could wait until after Haydn was asleep. She smiled faintly, wondering if he realized how simple it was to make the changes he wanted. *I'll never tell.*

In her cube, she listened to her messages while packing her briefcase. Her hands stilled when she heard Haydn's voice. Keile quickly replayed the message. It sounded just as bad the second time. She massaged her scalp and thought about their conversation the day before. Haydn had sounded disappointed that Keile had to work, but she hadn't sounded upset. So what could she have done between now and then?

Swallowing hard, Keile sank into her chair. What the hell had she missed? She stared at the phone, debating ignoring Haydn's request not to call. *Don't push. She said she'd call when she's ready.* Closing her eyes, she told herself everything was all right. That Haydn was having an off day, and she would call tomorrow to make arrangements for them to spend time together. Everything would be fine. *I haven't done anything wrong.* Keile blew out a sharp breath. It was time to go home.

As she walked through the rapidly emptying parking lot, she couldn't help feeling lonely. *Which is ridiculous*, she thought, rummaging around for her keys. She'd spent plenty of evenings alone. Tonight wouldn't be any different. But it would. Had she grown dependent on Haydn's company? Maybe not dependent, but she'd certainly come to enjoy the time they spent together.

And you will enjoy it in the future. Keile unlocked the door to her Jeep. She needed to shake off the feeling of doom and enjoy an evening, virtually free of work. If she hurried, she and Can could get to the park in time for Can to have other dogs to play with.

Chapter Twenty-Five

"I hope you didn't think not answering the door was going to keep me…" Marcus stopped in the doorway and peered around the dimly-lit family room. "Hey, what's going on? Are you sick?" He crossed the room to where Haydn was sitting.

"I feel crappy today." She looked away from his concerned gaze, afraid the tears would return. "What time is it anyway?"

"Around eight thirty. You should have called me earlier. Kyle and I could have been doing manly man things together."

Haydn's smile was fleeting. "Kyle yes, you no." She rubbed her eyes. "I'll be fine by tomorrow." She didn't want Marcus to worry about her. He'd done enough of that three years ago. "What are you doing here anyway?"

"I got worried when I couldn't reach you. I've been trying to call you all afternoon about Mrs. Sampson."

"Oh." Yesterday seemed so far away. She swallowed and

dropped her hands. "I forgot about that. Can we discuss it later?"

He gave her a probing look. "No problem. Are you sure there's nothing wrong? Did something happen with you and Keile?"

Yes! Haydn shook her head and squeezed her eyes against the burn of tears. "Bad day, okay?"

"Have you eaten dinner yet?"

"I wasn't hungry when I fed Kyle."

"At the risk of sounding like Mother, you need to eat. Why don't you go wash up while Kyle and I fix something."

"I don't—"

"Come on, Hay. It'll make you feel better."

"Hay is for horses." She smiled in exasperation when she realized she'd automatically responded to the dreaded childhood nickname. "I swear, I'll be a hundred and you'll still be bugging me."

"Yup." Marcus smiled sweetly and tousled her hair. "So get used to it."

Haydn sighed. "Okay." She pushed herself out of the recliner and trudged upstairs. If she made it through today, tomorrow would be a little easier, and the day after that, easier still. Eventually, she would be back to equilibrium. But would she ever be back to where she was yesterday?

The throbbing in her head drove Haydn to the bathroom, where she downed a couple of aspirin and pressed a cold washcloth against her eyes. *Damn her! I finally had a chance to be happy again.*

She had wasted the afternoon driving herself crazy replaying her last weeks with Reagan and still she hadn't been able to come up with a single clue hinting Reagan was unhappy enough to leave. How could she, who'd known Reagan better than anyone, possibly have missed the signs? *If I didn't know her, I'll never know anybody.*

Haydn turned away from the mirror and the haunted look in her eyes. Keile's face sprang to mind and she swallowed hard.

She should never have gotten involved with Keile. Reagan's appearance had proven she wasn't over the betrayal. Keile, with her sweet, innocent ways, deserved more than she could give.

"What's this?"

Haydn jerked, surprised by the harshness in Marcus's voice. "What's what?"

"This." He thrust a card in her face. "When did you get this?"

Looking at the name on the card, she groaned. "I never actually got it. Reagan must have left it behind earlier."

"What was she doing here?"

"Foolishly seeking absolution."

"And you let her in?"

The accusation in Marcus's voice riled her anger. "I didn't have a choice! Kyle was there, and I didn't want to cause a scene in front of him. We exchanged barbs and she left. End of story."

"Sorry. I didn't mean to accuse you of anything." He ran his fingers through his hair. "I can't believe she had the nerve to show up here."

Haydn watched his jaw tighten and tried to distract him. "What about my food?"

"Did she really expect you to want to see her after all she did?" Marcus continued as if he hadn't heard her question. "And what about Kyle? What did she say about him?"

"Does it really matter?" She sighed loudly when he nodded. "She thought he was cute. Can we leave it alone now? It's over and done."

He looked at her and shook his head. "If it was over and done, you wouldn't be moping. What did she say to you?"

Haydn clenched her teeth, but it didn't hold off the tears. "Please drop it. I can't talk about her anymore."

Marcus's expression softened. "Okay. But if you ever want to talk, I'll be there."

She nodded and wiped her eyes. "I'll be down in a minute. I promise."

"Good." Marcus suddenly stopped on his way out of the

room. "I'm sorry," he said softly, and walked away before she could reply.

"Me too," Haydn whispered. She wasn't hungry, but if eating would put her brother's mind at rest, she was willing to do it. He'd been at her side when her world fell apart. This time, she would go it alone, without her brother and without… Rubbing her chest, she frowned at the sour taste in the back of her throat. *I'll think about that later*, she thought and hurried downstairs, to distraction.

"Mama." Kyle left his toys to run to his mother.

Feeling guilty, Haydn swung him up into her arms and kissed his cheek. "Hey, bro, where's my food?"

"Sit, I'll bring it to you." Marcus returned moments later with a tray.

Haydn couldn't stop a teary smile. He'd fixed her favorite comfort food—a grilled cheese sandwich and cream of tomato soup. "Thanks." She inhaled, feeling the warmth of the soup against her nose. "Smells good." Dipping the spoon into the creamy mixture, she took a swallow. "Tastes good, too."

He bowed. "Campbell's thanks you." He sat down beside her and pulled Kyle onto his lap. "Do you want me to stay here tonight?"

Haydn turned her head so he could see her eyes. "Thanks, but no. I'll be fine once the shock of seeing her wears off."

"Will you… Are you going to see her again?"

"There's no need. We said everything there was to say."

"Then can we talk about someone dear to my heart?"

Haydn choked on the soup. Grabbing the napkin, she wiped her chin before taking a sip of water from the glass Marcus thrust at her. Oh God, she wasn't ready to talk about Keile. "Thanks," she said once she got her coughing under control. "That went down the wrong way. I didn't know you were seeing anyone."

Marcus snorted. "I'm talking about me. I think I may be able to finagle a copy of my birth certificate."

"What?" Her eyebrows inched up her forehead. "How?"

"Very convolutedly, if that's a word. A friend of a friend of a friend dates someone who works in the Records department. It sounds so clandestine, doesn't it?"

"Yeah." Haydn pushed the bowl to the side, unable to eat another spoonful. For her brother's sake, she hoped he and Keile were related. But for her, she wasn't ready to deal with the implications or any future relationship with Keile until she worked through Reagan's return.

Marcus interrupted her thoughts. "Yeah, I'm excited and leery at the same time." He gave a nervous laugh. "I'm not sure what I want to find."

"What do you mean?"

"If Kyle Griffen's name is on the birth certificate, then I can't very well pretend anymore he didn't know I existed." He leaned back against the sofa and ran his fingers through Kyle's soft curls. "And who wants to be related to someone who can walk out on their kid. I can't imagine anything that would make me walk away from Kyle."

"That's tough. I hadn't thought about it like that." Haydn placed a hand on his arm. "Whatever happens, I'm still your big sister."

"Thanks, Hay…den." Marcus gave a satisfied smile when she glared at him.

Chapter Twenty-Six

Keile raised her hand to ring the doorbell and quickly lowered it, her heart hammering wildly. When she first heard Haydn's message, she'd been too happy to hear from her to pay attention to anything else. After listening to the message again, she began to worry. There had been something in Haydn's voice she couldn't place. Now, she was here at the prescribed time and afraid of what was to come.

She raised her hand again and gave a start when the door opened before she could ring the bell. "Hey," she said with a nervous smile. "I'm glad you called." Her smile faltered as she took in Haydn's swollen eyes. "Did something happen? Is it Kyle?" She stepped forward to give her a hug.

"Uh…he's fine," Haydn said, almost stumbling over her feet as she quickly backed away. "Come on in, we need to talk."

With a feeling of dread, Keile swallowed around the knot in

her throat. She'd been right to worry. "Maybe afterward I could take you and Kyle out to dinner," she said, with only a slight quiver in her voice. "I lost track of the number of meals I owe you."

Haydn was silent as Keile hung up her coat. "Let's go to the kitchen," she said and led the way. "Can I get you anything to drink?"

"I'm fine for now." Keile, copying Haydn's actions, took a seat at the table. "Can…can I ask what's going on? If I pushed you too hard, I'm sorry." She looked at Haydn, pleading for understanding.

"It's nothing you did." Biting her lip, Haydn blinked rapidly. "It's me. Reagan showed up and I'm all confused about everything." She took a shuddering breath. "I need some space away from us to figure out what's going on in my head."

"Space?" was all Keile could think to say.

"Just so I can sort out what's happening. I need some time."

Keile closed her eyes against pain unlike anything she'd ever felt before, as she realized yet another part of her life was collapsing. The phrase, *I need time*, sounded so much like *Your mother needs time*, the words the social worker had used to comfort Keile when she was separated from her mother for what would be the last time. *She's breaking up with me*. Fighting back bile, she opened her eyes, unmindful of the tears. "Do…do you still love her?"

"No! This is about me and who I am. Reagan and I were finished a long time ago."

I don't think we'd be in this situation if you were, she wanted to shout. "That says it all. I guess it's time for me to go."

Haydn wiped at her face with the hem of her shirt. "I can't tell you how sorry I am, Keile, but I need time for me." She reached for Keile's hand.

"No!" Keile jerked away from Haydn's touch as if it were fire. Haydn's rejection, on top of all the shit she'd been getting at work, was too much. She'd endangered her job and now some woman she hadn't even met was taking Haydn and Kyle away from her. Maybe she should have been more concerned with the fact that Haydn hadn't yet said *I love you* back. Shit! She'd just been somebody to have around until life got too complicated. Tears streamed down her face as she shook her head, saying, "No, no, no." Keile stopped because she realized she was losing control. "I've got to go," she said, and ran from the kitchen.

Keile was at her car before she remembered her keys were in her coat, inside. Looking at the door, she knew returning was not an option, so she started walking. Her only intent was to get away from pain that felt like a vise grip around her heart. She ignored the cold tears falling off her face and the wind ripping through her clothes, too busy fighting demons of rejection, which should have been laid to rest.

When the chill finally penetrated her consciousness, she looked around to get her bearings. Somehow, her subconscious had brought her to the park where it had all started. Curled up in a ball on the cold grass, she cried for the little girl whose mother never had the time she needed to get herself together. She cried for the woman who had just been dealt a severe blow, and she cried because everything in her life was falling apart and it was beyond her control to fix it.

Eventually the tears slowed, leaving Keile shivering. When she looked up and saw the swings, she was reminded of her first meeting with Kyle. A meeting that had turned her world inside out. Attempting to bring back those early moments of joy, she scuttled to a swing hoping the motion would numb her pain.

As she swung back and forth, she tried to figure out where she had gone wrong with her job, with Haydn, with her life. Scenes flashed through her mind like a roller-coaster ride, but there was never a point at which the ride stopped at a clear exit. At some point, the uncontrollable shivering of her body filtered to her brain. Freezing to death wouldn't solve anything. When she stood, Keile felt the full force of the cold. Teeth chattering, she stuffed her hands in the pockets of her jeans and trudged for home.

The walk seemed to take forever as cold seeped into her

bones, making her feel lethargic. Keile stumbled to the backyard where she kept an extra key hidden. She had to blow on her hands in order to get her stiff fingers to grasp the key. Unlocking the door, she disabled the alarm and mumbled a greeting for Can before heading to the bathroom.

She started the water running for a bath, then sank to the floor to wrestle her boots off. She sat on the floor shivering violently as her body started to warm up. She wrapped her arms around her legs and rocked back and forth, telling herself she was okay.

Can slunk into the bathroom with his tail between his legs. He propped his head on her knees and licked her face. She gave him a tearful smile and hugged his body close. They stayed in that position until the water level in the tub was close to overflowing.

"I'll be okay, boy." *One day.* She slid into the warm water, grimacing at the stinging sensation as her flesh thawed out. Closing her eyes, she rested her head against the back of the tub and tried to clear her mind. It didn't work. The words 'I can't see you anymore' resounded through her brain. She had known something was wrong. But this?

Keile sank deeper into the tub as the tears started up again. *Damn Reagan!* Why did she have to come back now? Now, when their relationship was going so well. Now, when she'd begun to hope Haydn was falling in love with her. "Life sucks!" She brought her fists down repeatedly, splashing water everywhere. Can ran from the room, whimpering. "I'm sorry, boy."

Shit! I can't do anything right. Pressing her fingers against her eyes, Keile took a deep breath and let it out slowly. She was tired of crying. Crying hadn't brought her mother back, nor had it helped when kids teased her about her crazy mother, about her height, about everything. It was time she got off her ass and stopped feeling sorry for herself. Haydn's feelings were beyond her control, but she could damn well do something about the job she hated. Flipping burgers until she secured another job was preferable to being Rick's whipping boy or having to answer to Tom.

Resolute, she stepped out of the bathtub. Tomorrow she would tender her resignation. *Then what?* She considered her options while she dried off. After working her two weeks notice, she could take some time off and go somewhere away from Haydn and this intense agony. A month would help take the edge off. Keile had no doubt the pain would linger for a long time, but surely it wouldn't always hurt to breathe.

Shivering despite the warmth, Keile pulled on some sweats and thick socks. She wandered into the kitchen with Can on her heels, searching for something to make her feel better. As she reached for a packet of hot chocolate, she couldn't help but think of Haydn and the nights they'd snuggled in front of the fireplace. A sob caught in her throat. She wanted so badly to hate Haydn. But hate couldn't be forced. *And apparently, neither can love.* The best thing to do was to get on with her life. "I can do that," she whispered. "I can." She rested her head against the cabinet as sobs wracked her body.

Keile was up early the next morning, despite the lack of sleep. When her brain wouldn't shut down the night before, she'd left the bed and typed up her letter of resignation, then followed that with an expanded job search. There were a few offers in Atlanta she was going to follow up on. But now she was eager to take the first step in her new plan. The next steps were still vague, but she had two weeks to flesh them out. By the time she walked out of her bedroom in her running gear, Can was sitting by the front door, leash in his mouth.

Keile stroked his silky coat, comforted by his steadfast loyalty. "You still love me, right boy?" She clipped his leash on, then reached in the closet for the hooded sweatshirt that was perfect for running in colder weather. Tears sprang to her eyes when she noticed the absence of her coat. She wasn't ready to face Haydn. *It's not like you have a choice*, she told herself sternly. She couldn't do without her wallet or her car. Ignoring the tightness in her chest and the tears in her eyes, she pulled on the sweatshirt and took Can for a brisk run.

When she returned home, Keile drew out her regular morning rituals. After straightening up the already clean kitchen, she could delay no longer and pulled out her phone. Her heart started pounding when the phone was answered.

Keile's throat closed as the huskiness in Haydn's voice brought back memories of other early mornings. When Haydn repeated the hello, she was forced to clear her throat to continue. "Keile here," she said briskly. "Sorry to disturb you so early, but I need to come by and get my coat." She kept her voice level and steady. "It has my wallet and keys."

"Huh?"

Keile cleared her throat again. "I just need to get my coat, and then I'll give you all the *space* you need." She gritted her teeth, striving to maintain her composure. *I will not cry anymore!*

"Uh…sure."

Keile wasn't sure if Haydn had heard a word she said. *Maybe I wasn't the only one who couldn't sleep last night.* The thought brought her no comfort. "I'll be there in thirty minutes to get my things," she said slowly, and disconnected the call. The tiny part of her heart that had hoped Haydn would change her mind died. *It's really over.* She leaned against the counter, huffing hard, desperate to stop the tears from returning. Clenching her teeth, she forced herself to think beyond the pain. No matter how hard she was hurting, life still went on, and she would too, as she always had.

Keile spent the thirty-minute walk to Haydn's house convincing herself she felt nothing. Despite that, she stood in front of the door for five minutes before finding the courage to press the doorbell. Hearing the clatter of small feet, she couldn't help but smile. She would never have Haydn's heart, but she had Kyle's.

Haydn opened the door. With a strained smile, she stepped back to let Keile enter.

Seeing the ravages of tears on Haydn's face, Keile stuffed her hands in her pockets to keep from reaching out. "Sorry to bother you," she muttered.

Haydn reached out a hand. "I'm—"

"Don't!" Keile said more harshly than she'd intended. Sucking in a breath, she let it out slowly.

"Mama!" Kyle launched himself at Keile's leg. "Do?"

"Can's at home." She bent to pick him up and kissed his warm cheek before resting her head against his. For a brief moment, she lost herself in his clean baby scent and dreams of what-if. He felt like the only solid part of her life and she didn't want to let him go. "I'm Keile, remember?" she said, smiling despite the tears in her eyes. "Keile," she repeated slowly.

"Kee," he said with a wide grin and patted her cheek. "Kee."

"Yeah, Kee," she agreed with a gentle smile. After a final hug, she set the protesting boy on the floor. "I have to go to work, Buster." Keile ruffled his curls. "I'll see you again," she promised solemnly. It wouldn't be here. She couldn't come back to this house, which had so many memories, both good and bad.

"I put your coat on the foyer table," Haydn said. "I'm sorry," she added before Keile could stop her. She looked away from the hurt blazing in Keile's eyes.

"Yeah, me too." Keile gently untangled Kyle from her leg, grabbed her coat and walked out the door.

"Keile, wait!" Haydn called.

She stopped, but didn't turn around because doing so would shatter her fragile composure.

"Please know I'm not doing this to hurt you," Haydn said, her voice pleading for understanding.

Keile stopped in front of Nicole's desk, clutching her letter of resignation. "Good morning. Does Rick have a second for me?"

Nicole smiled. "I'm sorry. He had an early meeting in Atlanta and I'm not sure when he'll be back." She checked her computer screen. "Most of his afternoon is taken up as well. I can put you on his schedule for four thirty. Would that work?"

Keile felt the weight of the envelope in her hand. Leaving it for Rick to find was not enough. She needed to see his expression when he realized she wasn't going to play his game anymore. "That works for me." She sketched a wave before returning to her desk. Only two more weeks and she would be free of this place. Some other poor sap would have to deal with Rick and Tom. If there was any justice in the world, the project, along with Tom as manager, would be a big flop. And it wouldn't hurt if Rick's shining record went with it. With that uplifting visual in her head, Keile reached for the ringing phone. "Hello, Keile Griffen speaking."

"I need to see you in the conference room immediately," Tom said and disconnected the line.

She replaced the receiver and grabbed the project folder. The next two weeks were going to be interesting. "You rang?" she said as she sauntered into the conference room as if she didn't have a care in the world and pulled out the chair opposite Tom.

He slid a piece of paper across the table. "I did some brainstorming and this is what you need to do next."

Keile studied the tasks impassively. It was going to be another wasted day, but what did she care. "Is this all?"

"Why? Is there something else you think we should be doing?"

"*You're* the project manager, Tom. You tell me." She saw his lips tighten and smirked.

"I want this finished before you leave today." Tom pushed back his chair with more force than was necessary and stormed from the room.

Keile watched him go, feeling none of the tenseness or anger that had plagued her the past week. Deciding to resign was a good thing. Maybe one day she would feel like thanking Reagan for giving her the impetus to end this farce. The all too familiar pain tugged at her chest. Maybe not.

Pressing her fingers against her eyes while taking deep breaths, she managed to stave off tears. Now was not the time. Back at her desk, Keile put away her problems and worked steadily on Tom's list. As long as she focused on work, she could keep her mind off of her personal problems. When her phone rang at four twenty-five, she was halfway done. "Hello, Keile Griffen speaking."

"Hi Keile, Rick wants to know if he can push your meeting to five thirty. His meeting with Tom is running over."

"Okay."

"I'll let him know to expect you."

Keile swallowed hard as she replaced the receiver. Wiping her palms on her pants, she tried to refocus on work. It was no use. The confrontation with Rick loomed too large, overshadowing every other thought. She looked at the envelope. It appeared so plain to contain one of the biggest decisions of her life.

I'm in the right, she told her pounding heart. *He can't do anything worse than he's already done.* The pep talk didn't stop her heart from racing, nor did it have any effect on her churning stomach.

An hour later, Keile strode to Rick's office, her mask of confidence firmly in place.

Nicole was locking up her desk when Keile arrived. "You can go right on in, he's waiting for you. Have a good weekend."

"You, too." Keile managed to smile before she entered Rick's office, clutching her resignation letter like a lifeline.

Rick looked up as soon as she entered. "Have a seat. Sorry you had to wait. This day has been hectic. I just finished with Tom and he'll have something new for you on Monday." He sat back in his chair and rubbed his eyes. "What did you want to see me about? Having second thoughts?"

"Well, I have come to a decision, Rick." She placed the envelope on his desk. "Consider this my two weeks notice." She wanted to laugh at the look of consternation on his face. Obviously, she'd trumped his ace. When he didn't immediately respond, she sat quietly, waiting.

He pushed away the folder of materials he'd been studying and reached for Keile's resignation letter. "I wasn't expecting this quite so soon. So I have to ask myself what you expect to get out of this maneuver."

"Rick, what are you talking about?"

His smile was closer to a smirk. "I think this is retaliation for forcing you to report to Tom. While I see nothing wrong with making him the project manager, I am willing to shift him to a different project, leaving you in charge. I'm also willing to put you in for a promotion." He raised a finger. "But it will be on my terms. I need you to commit to giving one hundred percent again."

Her blood began to boil. He had some nerve. She jumped out of the chair without conscious thought. "No! You want me to commit to two hundred percent! Like a fool, I did that for too many years. And when I had the audacity to want something other than working 24/7, you stabbed me in the back."

"You need to calm down and remember who you're talking to."

"Like I could forget!" she shouted, then quickly got control of feelings that were slipping away. "I'm talking to the man who's losing the best damn employee he has. And the worst part is that it didn't have to be this way. You could have worked with me. But no, you had to chastise me by putting Tom in charge and making a mockery of me, leaving me no choice *but* to leave. So think of my resignation as doing what you wanted me to do."

Rick's mouth was a thin hard line. "Are you finished?"

She nodded curtly. "I've said it all."

"Then let me tell you that this is a dangerous game you're playing, Keile." He steepled his fingers and raised them to his chin. "I hope you don't expect me to give you a favorable recommendation? Officially it wouldn't be prudent to say anything negative, but who knows what might slip out over a friendly lunch. I should let you know I've already received inquiries."

"This isn't a game!" Keile slapped her hands on the desk, leaned forward and looked him in the eye. "You do what you have to do, Rick," she said slowly. "If you feel you can't give me a favorable recommendation, then obviously I've outlived my usefulness here. I need to go to a firm that can appreciate what I have to offer." She took a deep breath and tried to still her anger. Rick had proven he wasn't worth getting upset over.

"I expect you to finish out two full weeks. Anything I have to impart to you will come through Tom, your supervisor."

First you'll have to teach him how to pull his head out of his ass. "Understood." She couldn't get away from Rick fast enough. To think she'd once respected that asshole.

Keile's steps slowed as she neared her cube, and she smiled. Rick had given her carte blanche to do nothing for two weeks. What was he going to do, fire her, or worse yet, give her a bad recommendation? She gave a one-finger salute to the work she'd been doing for Tom, gathered her belongings and left the building. As she reached for her keys, she laughed, imagining the look on Tom's face when he realized she hadn't met his stupid deadline.

Chapter Twenty-Seven

The next morning Keile stood in front of the bathroom mirror fluffing her hair. She was still startled by the short-haired stranger who stared back at her, but the ease of care couldn't be beat. "Can, I should have done this years ago." He whined and nudged her leg. She smiled. "I know, all you care about is going for a walk." Dropping to her knees, she wrapped her arms around him and squeezed. *Woman's best friend*, she thought, remembering her breakdown two nights before. With a deep sigh, Keile attached his leash. "Let's go."

Her cell phone rang as she unlocked the front door. Keile removed it from her pocket and noted with interest the caller's name.

"Hi, Keile, it's Charles Newman."

"Hey, Charles. How are you doing?" She had worked projects with him on a couple of occasions and he had always gone out of his way to let Rick know what a good job she'd done.

"Good. Listen, I have something I'd like to run by you. Would it be possible to meet me at the park this morning?"

"Sure," she said, doing her best to hide her surprise and at the same time, wondering if Steve had finally won the coin toss over who fetched the bagels. "Can and I were about to leave the house."

"Buzz and I can meet you there in about twenty minutes. Will that work for you?"

"Uh…yeah. I'll see you then." Keile stared at the phone thoughtfully. Her mind churned with possibilities until Can whined. "Okay, let's go."

Keile let Can set the pace and tried not to think about the significance of their destination. Periodically, she rubbed the back of her neck, unused to the sensation of cool air against her bare skin. After leaving work, she had given in to an impulse and stopped at The Cut Zoo. Although a haircut hadn't been on her new action plan, she thought it was apropos for the new her.

New hair, new job…new life. Feeling the prickle of tears, she blew out a sharp breath. After the past two days, she was surprised, and dismayed, that she had any tears left. *I've got to do better than this*, she thought, blinking her eyes rapidly. At the rate she was going she'd have to start using makeup to cover the damage. And that would be hell.

Shuddering, she slowly became aware of her surroundings and was relieved to see Can had steered them away from the playground entrance to the park. She wasn't ready to face the swings and what they represented. She bit her lip and wondered when the pain would become bearable.

She took a deep breath and let it out slowly, reminding herself, yet again, that it was time to look forward. Releasing Can, she pulled her sunglasses from her jacket and slipped them on. With effort, she redirected her thoughts to her future. It was time to plan a vacation. Twenty-eight years, and she'd never left the State of Georgia. As the wind picked up, thoughts of sunny beaches came to her mind.

"Keile."

She gave a start when a hand touched her arm.

"Sorry. I didn't mean to startle you." Charles Newman let his arm drop.

"That's okay." Keile removed her sunglasses and forced a smile. "I was lost in thought. I have a lot on my mind these days."

He gave her a searching look. "Should I admit I've heard rumors?"

She shrugged. "Should I start singing 'It's a Small Consulting World After All'?"

Charles laughed. "Steve told me you have a wicked sense of humor."

"I may add that to my resume. Think anyone would hire me?" She was only half-joking.

"In a heartbeat." His handsome, dark brown face grew serious. "Actually, that's the reason I wanted to talk with you. It's come to my attention you may be ready to spread your wings. I recently received a promotion and I'd be *very* interested in having you on my team."

"I tendered my resignation yesterday." Keile grimaced and watched Can and Buzz nip at each other. Saying it out loud made it seem more real. "You should know Rick made it clear he won't give me a positive recommendation."

"That sounds like something he would pull." Charles made no attempt to hide the disdain in his voice. "You forget I used to work with him. Not that it matters, Keile. Your work speaks for itself. I'd love to sit down for dinner early next week and discuss options."

Keile gave him her full attention. "Just like that?"

"Like I said, I know what you're capable of accomplishing and I want it to be for me. What do you say?"

A glimmer of a smile touched her lips. "I'm available any night next week."

Charles's white teeth gleamed as he smiled. "Why don't we shoot for Tuesday? I want to beat the rush."

"Tuesday works for me. But I don't think you have to worry about a rush of job offers. Rick knows a lot of people in this town."

"You'll see. Let's plan for Manos at seven. If anything comes up, give me a ring and we'll reschedule."

"Will do. Can I get a non-work number?" Keile asked, reaching for her cell phone.

Charles removed a card from his coat pocket. "I was hoping you would ask for this. Here's my card with all my numbers."

"I want you to know I appreciate the opportunity to sit down and talk, Charles." She wanted to clutch the card to her chest, but instead slid it into her pocket, then held out her hand. "I look forward to talking with you Tuesday."

"This will be an opportunity for both of us, Keile," he said, returning the handshake. "By the way, I *love* what you've done with your hair. It suits your face." He grinned and said conspiratorially, "This will be another thing for Steve to work himself into a tizzy over."

She laughed. This was a side of him she'd never seen. "Thanks. Tell him *hey* for me." Almost overwhelmed by relief, Keile watched him collect his dog. Pulling out the card, she stared at it, nonplussed. It seemed another door had opened. Squinting against the brightness of the sun, she looked at the sky. *I sure hope you gods know what you're doing.* Before she received a sign, her phone rang. For a brief moment, hope flared, then died when she saw who was calling. She hesitated a moment before answering. "Hello, Marcus Davenport."

"Hello, my lovely daughter. How are you doing on this great and glorious morning?"

"Don't tell me you've been drinking already?"

Marcus laughed. "Not yet, I'm an after twelve kind of guy. I have someone with me who wants to know if you can come out to play. He said 'pretty please with sugar on top'."

"Aw. I'm a sucker for sugar. You guys headed to the park?"

"What other place is there? Can you meet us anytime soon?"

"I'm already here. Can and I will meet you by…the swings."

"Okay. Hey, since Haydn canceled your afternoon plans, would you have time to meet again later on with just me? There's something I want to talk to you about."

What did Haydn tell him? "Uh…sure. My day is wide open."

"See you in a few."

"Gotcha." Keile put the phone away, frowning. Obviously Haydn hadn't told her brother about needing space. Was that task going to fall on her shoulders?

Ten minutes later, Keile and Can were sitting by the swings. As much as it hurt, she couldn't turn away from the sight of a mother cuddling her blanket-wrapped baby. The look of love on the mother's face was poignant. She'd seen that same look on Haydn's face the day they'd met. Tears filled her eyes and rolled down her cheeks. When the other woman gazed her way, Keile turned her head.

"Mama, Kee!"

Keile wiped her face as she scrambled to her feet. "Buster!" Smiling, she held out her arms to the boy riding on Marcus's shoulders. "I missed you, big boy." Her heart leaped when his arms snaked around her neck and hugged her tight. The feeling was bittersweet. *One Davenport loves me.* "I see you missed me, too."

"Excuse me, do I know you?" Marcus ruffled what was left of Keile's hair.

"Hey." She jerked her head back. "Do you know how long it takes me to get it just right?"

"Five minutes?"

"More like two." They shared a grin.

"It looks good. Almost as good as me." His gaze touched on her eyes before moving back to her hair. "When did this transformation take place?"

"I've been thinking about it for awhile." Keile shrugged. "Last night seemed like a good time for making changes."

"Let me tell you, the new you is fantastic. Haydn will be in for a nice surprise. You're okay with her needing a little space, right? I'm sure it's just for a little while."

She nodded, directing her attention on Kyle. "It must have been tough seeing Reagan again."

He kicked at the grass. "I wish I could have been there. Three years later and I still feel angry for what she did to Haydn."

"I know you'll help her all you can."

"As much as she'll let me, you mean. I get the sense she's going to try and go this alone. What did she say to you?"

"Not much. No offense, but I'm not comfortable discussing Haydn behind her back." She smiled to take any sting out of the words.

Marcus nodded. "No offense taken. I'm glad she has you in her life."

Kyle saved her from making a reply. Letting go of his stranglehold, he said something while pointing in the direction of the swings. "Looks like somebody is ready to play."

A little over six hours later, Keile entered Got Beans, a popular coffeehouse off the downtown square. She'd come close to canceling three times, not ready to dodge more questions about her relationship with Haydn. In the end, she'd decided Marcus and Kyle were two people she wanted to keep in her life, and now was the time to make the effort.

She spotted Marcus right away, nursing a large cup of coffee. After a quick wave of acknowledgment, Keile purchased a fruit drink, then joined him at a little table. The suddenly serious look on his face made her want to leave. Had Haydn told him after all? "What's up?"

"There's no easy way to say this," he said, pushing a folder toward her. "We have the same sperm donor."

She was momentarily speechless. Opening the folder, Keile quickly scanned the birth certificate. Her eyes got wide when she saw not one, but two familiar names. "Christ!" She looked up in disbelief. "You're not going to believe this."

Marcus stared at her, unblinking, waiting.

"We have the same mother, too." Tears welled up in Keile's

eyes. The past week had been so stressful and now this. She had a family, and given the way Marcus was looking at her, this one wouldn't be ripped away from her anytime soon.

Neither one of them moved until Marcus whispered, "*What?*" He slowly reached for the folder as if he hadn't already read the birth certificate a thousand times. "How…why…" He leaned back, obviously stunned. "I can't believe it. We have the same mother?"

"Funny how when we were talking about mothers, neither one of us mentioned names." She raked her fingers through her hair, unused to the lack of length.

"I always thought if we were related, it would be through Kyle Griffen."

"Oh God, I have a *brother*." Keile grinned and reached for Marcus's hand.

Marcus returned the grin. "And I have a baby sister to boss around."

"Wait, I'm not sure if I like that part." She pretended to give it some thought. "I guess it's okay, since a nephew comes with the deal. I'm going to miss calling you daddy."

He smirked. "I'm sure Haydn won't mind if you call her that at the appropriate moment."

Keile laughed along with him, hoping hers didn't ring hollow. "Does…she know?"

"I wanted to tell you first. I didn't really believe it until I got the copy in the mail today and saw it with my own eyes."

"I'm confused." She leaned forward and rested her elbows on the table. "I thought you knew who your mother was. Wasn't that from your birth certificate?"

He shook his head. "It was from a letter she wrote me, just signed Mom. Original birth certificates are sealed after adoptions are final. And you don't want to know how I got a copy of it," he added before she had the chance to ask the question.

"My brother the criminal." She lightly socked him on the arm.

"Do you suppose there are other siblings running around?"

She frowned. "I don't know if I want to know. For now, it's enough to have you and Kyle."

Marcus picked up the almost empty coffee cup and drained it. "I'm thinking of trying to find Griffen. I know you're not interested, but I wanted to let you know. Probably nothing will come of it."

"Do what you think is best," she said even as her mind recoiled at the thought. "I… Well, I hope you understand I'm not ready to embrace him with open arms."

"I don't know that I am either." He gave a humorless laugh. "But there are things I'd like to know. Do you have a picture of your mother?"

"Our mother." Keile pulled out her wallet and removed a battered-looking photo. "I have a few more at home, but this is my favorite."

He carefully studied the young woman mugging for the camera. "I don't see much of us in her," he said quietly.

"I always thought we had the same-shaped eyes," Keile said in response to the longing she heard in his voice. "You should come by sometime and look at the other photos. I got them after…you know?"

"I'd really like that." Marcus placed his hand on top of hers. "I hope this is okay. I mean…does it feel strange having to share her with me?"

Keile shook her head and gave him a sad smile. "I never really had her. But I'm glad to have you."

"Enough to let me follow you home?"

"Come on, you big goof." As they left the shop, it hit her that not only did she have a brother, she really did have a nephew. She was immediately sobered by the thought that it wasn't the preferred way of having Kyle become family—without Haydn.

Chapter Twenty-Eight

Haydn settled on the sofa and eyed her brother warily. She was too tired to fight off his questions, and not yet ready to talk about Reagan or Keile, or the fact that she wasn't any closer to figuring out what her choices were. What she did know was she didn't want to keep feeling the way she did now—guilty. Guilty for whatever she'd done to make Reagan leave and guilty for giving Keile hope. "Okay, why are you really here? I know you didn't just drop by on a Sunday night to help me put Kyle to bed. And before you ask, I'm doing okay."

"You don't look it," Marcus said bluntly. "But I didn't come here to talk about that. You made it clear yesterday you weren't ready."

She eyed him warily. "Then what are we talking about?"

"My birth certificate."

Haydn sighed and pressed her hands together. His tone told

her all she needed to know. "Kyle Griffen is your father, right?"

"Yeah, and Cynthia Marcus is my mother. Now that wouldn't mean anything, except Cynthia Marcus is Keile's mother. And now we know why my name is Marcus."

She blinked slowly, frowned, then shook her head vigorously. "No way! Does Keile know?"

"She's the one who pointed it out after seeing my birth certificate. It's incredible really. Keile shared some photos with me." He paused, a melancholy expression on his face. "I thought I would feel some sort of…I don't know, connection. I didn't."

"I'm sorry." Haydn rubbed his arm. "That must have been hard."

"It was at first, but after talking with Keile I realized my expectations were unrealistic."

All she heard was Keile. "How…how is she?"

"You could call her and find out for yourself," he said pointedly. "She tried to hide it, but I could tell she's worried about you. It's been five days since you saw Reagan. Don't you think that's enough space?"

"What did she say?" she asked, not sure she wanted to hear the answer.

"That she didn't feel comfortable talking about you behind your back." He gave her a level look. "You're obviously miserable." He held up a hand when it looked like she would interrupt. "I'm sorry, but it's true. Why would you shut out the people you love?"

Biting the inside of her cheek, she looked away from the intensity of his gaze. She took a deep breath, feeling like she was seconds away from a meltdown. Tears were never far away these days. "You don't understand," she said quietly as tears rolled down her cheeks. "I feel like I'm going through the grieving process all over again. I just need more time."

Marcus reached for her clenched hand. "I'm sorry I keep pushing. I worry about you, sis."

"I know, but the only thing you can do right now is stop talking about it." She blew out a sharp breath. "There are some issues I have to figure out for myself."

He squeezed her hand. "I won't bring it up again."

"Thanks." She used the back of her hand to wipe her cheeks. "When are you going to tell Mom and Dad?"

"I hadn't thought that far ahead." He rubbed his chin. "They'll be okay with this, right?"

"Of course. Let's call them now," Haydn suggested, eager to put the spotlight on someone else.

"I can't. I sort of have a date."

"How does one *sort* of have a date?"

"It's a blind date kind of thing. If he's cute it's a date, if he's not it's not."

"Marcus, Marcus, Marcus. You are so shallow," she said with affection.

"Maybe, but I bet he's saying the same thing about me."

Haydn smiled, slapping at his leg. "You're horrible. Where are you meeting?"

"We agreed to meet at Turner's. Then if it doesn't work out, there'll be plenty of other guys around."

"My brother, the ever-practical thinker," she said dryly. "Call me and let me know how it went."

He stood and held out a helping hand. "Will do. I can spell you sometime with Kyle if you need it. I don't have a lot going on at work this week."

Haydn nodded. "Speaking of work, what happened with Mrs. Sampson's case? I sort of dropped the ball on that," she said with a grimace. Once she'd gotten around to reviewing the file, it had been easy to pinpoint the reasons for the bounced checks—Mrs. Sampson's daughter.

"That's right, I forgot to tell you. The situation's been somewhat resolved."

"What have you volunteered me for now?" She crossed her arms over her chest and gave him a threatening look.

"I thought you could go back to working with her monthly. She really likes you."

Haydn gave an exaggerated sigh. "Okay. But I don't want to

have anything to do with the pilfering daughter."

"Not a problem. Seems she decided to move on. Now I have to get home and get pretty." Marcus pulled her to the front door and gave her a bone-crushing hug. "Take care."

"I promise. Thanks for being concerned." She kissed his cheek.

"That's what pesky little brothers are for."

Haydn locked the door behind her pesky little brother and bit her trembling lip. If Marcus had known she felt worse than she looked, he never would have left. Her world was caving in on her and she felt helpless to stop it. She hadn't been this depressed when she came home to find Reagan's letter. Only the need to maintain some sense of normalcy for Kyle kept her going.

She pulled out a tissue to soak up the tears that were starting to fall in earnest. Everything was a mess, made all the worse because she was to blame. *If only…* Haydn shook her head. There was no 'if only'. She had loved Reagan with all her heart, and that still hadn't been enough. What chance could she and Keile possibly have to make a go of it? None. *Then why can't I bring myself to tell her it's over?*

Chapter Twenty-Nine

The following Wednesday evening, Keile crossed the room at Got Beans, hot chocolate in hand, and pulled out a chair. "We have to stop meeting like this."

Marcus looked up from the magazine he was reading. "Is the FBI still on your tail, sis?"

"No, but people will think I like coffee," she said, sitting down. "I have a rep to protect."

"You're full of it." He swatted her hand with the magazine. "Well tell me, how did it go with Charles last night?"

"Good." She couldn't suppress a big grin. "He offered me a great job and it pays more than I make now. I'm psyched."

"Good? That's great! Now you can tell those pricks at your office to kiss your ass."

Keile shuddered. "I wouldn't want those lips touching me. And there's a good chance I'll have to work with them in the future. I don't want to screw up before I start."

"Too bad. When do you start?"

"Two weeks to a month." She blew on her chocolate before taking a sip. "Originally I'd planned to take some time off, but now, well, I think I need to work." Keile shook her cup and watched the hot chocolate swirl around. "To help keep my mind occupied."

"Ah. Hang in there, Keile. You're the best thing to happen to Haydn since Kyle. It may take a couple more days, but I'm sure she'll figure that out."

"We'll see," she said, knowing he was wrong and not having the heart to correct him. He should hear the truth from Haydn. After all, it had been Haydn's choice. Keile just hoped it was soon because not telling Marcus was starting to feel a lot like lying—the worst way to start off a new relationship. "But in the meantime will it still be okay to hang out with you and Kyle on Saturday mornings? Only if it's okay with Haydn, though."

"God, yes!" Marcus leaned forward and sandwiched her free hand between his. "Haydn would be the first to suggest it and he *is* your nephew, remember?"

She smiled. "You're right. Can I be Aunt Kee now?"

"As far as Kyle's concerned, you can be anything. He'd go nuts if he didn't get to see you. You know how stubborn he is."

"Determined."

"Okay, so he's determined enough to break free and try to find you and Do. He thinks you live at the park."

"We'll work on that," she said and took another sip of her drink. "So, big brother, do you believe in fate?"

"I do now. It can't be a coincidence that because I overbooked, Kyle got loose and found you." Marcus let go of her hand to take a sip of his coffee. "And you'll see, things *will* work out with Haydn."

Keile raised her cup. "To my brother the optimist. I'll always be grateful you and Kyle came into my life."

"Stop, you're going to make me cry. How can I look macho with the sheen of tears in my eyes?"

"Hey, real men cry. And real men care about their sisters."

"That I do. I care about both of my sisters."

"I know." Keile squeezed Marcus's arm. "Now tell me more about this guy you've been seeing."

"He's to die for. But I can do better than that." Marcus glanced at his watch. "He should be here any minute. You can judge him for yourself."

"Don't think I won't. I can't have just anybody going out with my big brother."

"Behave. You don't want to scare him off already."

Keile smiled sweetly. "I never had a brother, but I think little sisters are supposed to be pests. I have years to make up for."

"Hush, here he comes now." Marcus gave her the evil eye before he stood and watched the handsome, brown-skinned African American man walk to their table. "Hello."

"Hey."

Keile looked on as Marcus and his new flame shared a warm smile, wondering how long it would be before they remembered her existence. Marcus certainly had great taste in men. The new arrival was a couple of inches shorter than Marcus, with a slender build and big brown eyes. Keile cleared her throat, feeling like a voyeur. "Should I leave?"

"Not before George has a chance to talk to you. He wants your signature."

"What?"

George smiled and held out his hand. "I'm George Stanton. I took the photo of you and Kyle."

"Seriously?" She ignored his hand, turning to look at Marcus, amazed. "Doesn't this all seem too weird to you?"

"It's a small world. And am I glad." Marcus blew her a kiss. "Actually, he came up to me after I ditched my blind date. At first I thought he was trying to pick me up because well, it is all about me. Turns out he thought I was your brother and wanted your permission to use the photo in a contest. I told him if he went out with me, I could talk you into it."

Keile turned back to George and finally shook his hand. "Do

you know what you're getting yourself into?"

"I hope to." The look he shot Marcus practically sizzled.

"It's really hot in here," Keile said, wiping her forehead with the back of her hand. "I'll leave you to it."

"No, don't go. We'll behave." Marcus put a hand on her arm. "Come to dinner with us."

"I can't. Rick's trying to work me to death before I leave."

"Blow him off, you already have another job."

She smiled, thinking about the outcome of the meeting she'd had with Rick and Tom first thing Monday morning. "I don't mind. I'm getting paid overtime for the hours I put in over forty. It's nice to have him by the balls for the first and last time."

"Girl, I hope you're wearing gloves."

Keile threw back her head and laughed. "I love you, Marcus."

Haydn smoothed out the crumpled card on the kitchen table. Over a week had passed since Reagan showed up on her doorstep and she was tired of pretending everything was back to normal. That facing each morning hadn't increasingly become a chore without Keile in her life. Keile. Haydn pressed her fingers against her eyes. Last night it had finally sunk in that in order to make a life with Keile, she had to truly let go of the past. It was time to stop letting what happened with Reagan control her. Blowing out a pent-up breath, she reached for the phone and quickly punched in Reagan's number, then held her breath waiting for the phone to be answered.

"Hello, Reagan. It's Haydn."

"Haydn?"

She tightened her grip on the receiver and swallowed. "Surprise. I'm sure you weren't expecting to hear from me."

"You're right. Still, I'm glad you called," Reagan said in a rush. "I'd like a chance to talk."

"When would be a good time? I'm sure I caught you at work."

"Actually, I haven't left Georgia. I'll be driving down from

Atlanta this afternoon and planned to spend the night in Seneca. Can we meet somewhere public this evening? I'd like the chance to apologize in person," she added softly.

"We could meet at your hotel around five thirty."

"That would be fine. I'm staying at the Marriot Suites on the Square."

"I know where that is. There are plenty of places to go to around there. I'll see you then." Haydn disconnected the call and let out a shaky breath. She'd taken the first step. *Now to find someone to watch Kyle.*

Haydn speed-dialed her brother. "Hey, Marcus," she said when he answered the phone. "I know it's Friday night, but I need a huge favor. If you already have plans, I understand."

"What time do you need me?"

"A little after five. I should only be two hours at the most."

"Perfect. George isn't available until later."

"A third date? You guys are practically married."

"Only if we were lesbians."

She laughed. "True. When do I get to meet Mr. Wonderful?"

"Anytime you want. I know you haven't felt much like company these days."

"I...I'm hoping to change that soon," Haydn said quietly. "I'm tired of just existing." She heard him release a sigh and could picture the look of relief on his face. "Maybe we can have a long talk this weekend. I think I'm ready to spill my guts."

"Count on it. I'll see you later, sis. Take care."

"You too." Haydn stared unseeing out the window of her home office, feeling better than she had in days. In six hours, she would try her best to listen to everything Reagan had to say, without letting anger cloud her hearing. She hoped she was up for the task.

"Daddy's here," Haydn called out when the doorbell sounded.

"Dada!" Kyle raced for the front door with a wide grin.

"Mama, Kee? Do?"

The smile left Haydn's face. "No, sweetie. Keile's not coming today." She opened the door. "Come on in."

"Dada, Kee?" Kyle repeated.

"Not today, big guy. It's just you and me." Marcus lifted Kyle above his head and was rewarded with a big smile. "Hey, sis. Wanna tell me where you're going?"

A fleeting smile curved her lips at the look of concern in her brother's eyes. "I'm going to see Reagan. I need to let go. And this is the only way I know how."

Marcus stroked her cheek. "Then take as long as you need."

Haydn nodded. "You boys be good." She kissed Kyle on the cheek. "I'll see you later."

Once on the road, she directed her thoughts to her upcoming meeting with Reagan. She still wasn't sure what to expect. *The most important thing is to remain calm,* she told herself, drumming her fingers on the steering wheel as she waited impatiently in a long line of cars making a left into the busy parking deck nearest to the hotel. She castigated herself for forgetting about the popular Friday night Happy Hour specials at the restaurants and bars around the square. *You're only a little late. Calm down.*

A nervous-looking Reagan was waiting for her outside. Her blond hair fell loosely around her shoulders and she matched Haydn in jeans and a casual top. "Hi. Thanks for seeing me," Haydn said.

Reagan smiled. "No, thank you. I thought we could go to the hotel bar and grab a drink. It's fairly quiet."

In a booth in the bar, Reagan took a deep breath. "Haydn, I can't tell you how much I *still* regret taking the coward's way out. After all we'd been through together, you deserved better than that from me."

Haydn stopped pretending to read the menu and leveled her gaze on Reagan. "What did I do wrong?" she asked softly.

Reagan closed her eyes briefly as if she were in pain. "It's all so complicated. I know it sounds like a cop-out, but I can admit now I made a lot of mistakes."

"Was…" Haydn turned her head away. "Was I one of them?" She blinked her eyes rapidly against the familiar pre-tear burn.

Reagan was silent a moment too long.

"I was," she said, dejectedly and slumped back against the booth.

"It's not that simple, Haydn. Looking back I was so damn arrogant, thinking I knew what I wanted and what I wanted you to want. You always had the better job and made more money but I still felt in control. After I quit my job to get ready for the baby that changed. I changed."

"This is about money?"

"God, no." She ran her fingers through her hair. "You have to understand. It felt like I was waiting all day for you to get home and make me feel like I was worth something. And I knew it would only get worse after we had a kid. Then I really would be a nobody. Only your wife and the mother of your child."

Haydn slapped her palms on the table and fixed her former lover with a glare. "Christ, Reagan! I did what *you* wanted. You're the one who went to Marcus. You're the one who decided to quit your job. You're—"

"I know that, okay?" She blew out a sharp breath and looked away. "I was wrong all the way around. But I didn't know how much I resented your success till I no longer had a job. Till I had to listen to you go on and on about this new contract or that new client every day. And after awhile, there was no me. There was only you."

"You're right, I was the problem," Haydn said, her voice shaking with anger. "I foolishly thought we were a team. That I was making money for *us* and our soon-to-be baby. But for you it was all about the power." She rested her head in her hands and wanted to cry. She'd wasted three years grieving for something that hadn't existed. Taking a deep breath, she let herself think that just maybe not everything in the world that went wrong was her fault.

"I did love you, Haydn."

She raised her head. "Bullshit! Why did you really come back here? To rub my face in it?"

"No! I'm trying to explain. That's how I felt. Right or wrong." Reagan pressed her fingers against her eyes. "At the time I didn't see any other way out. And once I was gone there was no going back."

Haydn exhaled. "I wish you would have told me this three years ago. It would have saved me from wasting time and energy on something I had no control over. God, I was a fool." She shook her head when Reagan opened her mouth. "I forgive you for not knowing me at all. I guess I should be thankful I now know what I was up against. Goodbye, Reagan." She slid from the booth and walked away without looking back.

Chapter Thirty

Keile rolled away from Can's wet nose and grabbed her head. "Oh God, give me a second, Can," she mumbled, "I think I'm blind."

"Blind drunk was more like it." Dani smirked and poked her again with an ice cube.

Keile opened one eye and found herself looking into Dani's baby blues. "I've died and gone to hell," she said and closed her eye.

Dani pried the eye back open. "Tsk, tsk. You only wish you had died." She ran the ice cube down the side of Keile's face.

Keile pulled away and tried to sit up. "Shit!" Moaning, she grabbed her head and lay back down. "Why are you here, Devil?"

Dani laughed. "You were a bad, bad girl last night. Welcome to the family."

"Leave the poor girl alone, Dani."

"Edan?" Keile cracked an eye open again. "If you loved me, you'd take this maniac home. After you help me up that is."

"Keile, Keile, Keile. You only have yourself to blame. In your drunken state, you agreed to go to Susan and Jo's cabin. Now get up so we can go hit the mountains." Dani pulled back the covers. "Don't make me get my nightstick."

Mumbling about false friends, Keile stumbled to the bathroom, downed a couple of painkillers and sat on the toilet waiting for her head to stop pounding. Once she was able to have a coherent thought, some of the events of the night before came rushing back. The evening had started out as a quick drink after work with Sam, Patti and a couple of their friends. When Sam offered shots in honor of Keile's resignation and subsequent job offer, things had gotten out of hand. *More like I got out of hand.* Slowly unbuttoning her shirt, she looked down at her chest and sighed. The fire-breathing, green dragon was still permanently inked above her left breast.

She rubbed her temples, calling herself all kinds of a fool. After a horrible week spent hoping against hope that Haydn would call, and being the figurative punching bag for Tom, getting drunk had seemed like the answer to her problems. So as she'd matched Sam drink for drink, she'd cursed Rick for being stupid, Tom for being inept, Reagan for coming back and Haydn for being so damn lovable. But most of all, she'd cursed herself for hoping Haydn would change her mind, when life had already taught her hope was what she could least afford to have.

Keile blew out a sharp breath and rubbed her eyes. Hope was a hard notion to kill. Apparently, tequila shooters didn't change that.

"Keile! You awake in there?" Dani pounded on the locked door.

She jumped and almost fell off the toilet. "Give me ten minutes. I need to grab a shower."

"Hurry up. We want to have lunch on the deck."

"Okay," Keile replied with tired resignation. Life had been

coming at her fast, catching her with her protective shields down. Last night she'd hit rock bottom with a vengeance, so there was nowhere to go but up. Maybe a couple of days away from the city would help her get her head in the right place.

Dressed in sweatpants and a long-sleeved shirt, she walked into the kitchen fifteen minutes later. Though she was starting to feel like she could make it through the day, she snarled at Dani and Edan and grabbed the bottle of Dr. Pepper off the table. "You guys suck," she said, leaning against the counter.

Edan grinned. "I haven't had a woman complain yet. It's not our fault you were stupid enough to let Terri lead you astray. Camera phones are nothing short of miraculous."

Terri? Camera phones? Keile's eyes narrowed to slits as she tried to remember more from the night before. So much of it was a jumbled blur. "Edan, bite me. I'm too tired for puzzles."

Dani smirked. "Sounds like you're ready to go. Your bag's already in the car, so grab Can from the backyard and let's hit the road."

Keile sighed. "Why don't you just shoot me?"

As Dani backed out of Keile's driveway, Marcus was approaching Haydn's front door. He rang the doorbell, then used his key to enter. The sound of footsteps brought the usual smile to his lips. "Hey, squirt." He set down the bag of goodies, lifted Kyle high in the air and swung him around, making airplane noises until they were both dizzy. "Let's go find your mama before I fall down."

"Pa," Kyle said and grinned. He scrambled to get down and toddled off to the family room flapping his arms. "Mama, pa."

Haydn sat up, pushing her hair off her forehead as her son ran into the room. "You're a plane." She watched as Kyle twirled around in a circle until he dropped to the floor giggling. "What energy." She turned to Marcus. "How are you?"

"Surprisingly, more awake than you." Marcus removed a cup of coffee from the Dunkin' Donuts bag and handed it to Haydn. "You look like you might need this. Rough night?"

"I always need coffee." She took a sip and moaned with pleasure. "I woke up at midnight and couldn't get back to sleep. The good news is that I got a decent amount of work accomplished while I was up." She squinted at the clock before giving up. "What time is it anyway?"

"Almost nine. I take it you're not going to your office today?"

"I should, but..." She shrugged. "I might go later and if I do, I'll take Kyle with me. Sorry, I should have called and let you sleep in."

"That's okay." Marcus opened the box of doughnuts. He broke one into pieces, and handed a piece to Kyle. "I wanted to talk some more about last night."

Haydn searched through the box and snagged one of the powdered doughnuts. "Coffee and doughnuts, you must really want something."

Marcus laughed, watching her stuff half of the doughnut into her mouth. "You're too easy. And I don't want anything...*today*."

"Okay, I'll bite." Haydn wiped her mouth. "What else do you wanna know? I already hit the highlights."

"Were you serious about not having any feelings for Reagan?"

"None that are positive. Why?"

Marcus rubbed his chin. "It's hard for me to know how much to say. I mean, I have to think of both of you."

"Is it...about, Keile?" Haydn didn't dare hope.

"Tell me why you want to know?" Marcus replied, looking into her darkened green eyes.

Haydn sat up and straightened her shoulders. "Because I want her in my present and in my future. And because I know now I *can* be the partner that she needs."

"All that from your talk with Reagan?" Marcus asked, not unkindly.

"Keile hasn't been out of my mind for a second. The more I tried not to think about her, the more I thought about her. But until I talked to Reagan, I was convinced there was something wrong with *me*. And that…that something drove Reagan to leave. And I would drive Keile away just the same way, unless I knew what I'd done wrong." Haydn was surprised to feel tears on her face. She wiped her face and quickly checked to make sure Kyle was otherwise occupied. "I've done a lot of thinking and realized with Keile I'm equal and it's not something we have to work at, or compensate for. We don't have to spend time processing our needs because we do want the same things. I don't think I ever had that with Reagan—I thought so, but Reagan didn't and foolishly I never asked. I'm better with Keile in my life and so is Kyle. Ironically, being a mother has made me a better listener and more focused on the basic priorities. Home. Love. Little moments that mean so much. Keile seems to want those things, too, so my job going forward is to make sure that's still true." Her lips twisted in a wry smile. "The problem is I don't know if she wants those things with me anymore."

"Okay. Keile called me last night. She was pretty drunk, and all she said was that she couldn't kill hope. I have to think she was talking about you, but there's only one way to find out."

"I know, I know. I have to call her." Haydn gripped her thighs. "Do you know how hard this is for me? I'm terrified I destroyed what we had. Terrified she won't be able to trust her heart to me again. And then what?"

Marcus pulled her into his arms. "The first thing you need to do is get some sleep. Then after you're rested, go see Keile. She deserves that."

"Oh, God, and tell her what? That I'm a complete idiot?"

"If you want to, but if it was me, I'd tell her your fears. She'll understand. She's special that way."

"She is." Haydn used a napkin to wipe her face. "And so are you, little brother."

Marcus snorted. "It's about time you noticed. And speaking of notice, I think someone may be getting upset," he said quietly.

Haydn immediately felt guilty. She'd promised herself she wouldn't to cry in front of Kyle anymore. Forcing a big smile, she turned to Kyle, who was studying them intently. "Mama's okay, baby" she said, noticing the slight quiver in her son's bottom lip. He got up and brought her the truck he'd been playing with. "Thank you, sweetie." She pulled him close, dropping a kiss on top of his head. "Are you ready to leave your grumpy Mommy and go do something fun with Daddy?"

"Dada, tee." He grabbed his truck and handed it to his father.

"I'll take that as a yes." Marcus accepted the truck. "You're going back to bed before you call, right?"

Haydn squared her shoulders. "Yes."

"And what if she says no?"

She shrugged, raising her hands. "Then I'll improvise. I promise I won't accept no for an answer."

"That's my girl." He patted her shoulder and gave her an encouraging smile. "Kyle and I are going to that new place on Madison with the indoor play thingie. Call me if you need anything."

After seeing Marcus and Kyle off, Haydn returned to the family room and stretched out on the sofa. Thirty minutes later, she gave up any attempt to sleep. Tired or not, she couldn't possibly sleep until she tried to fix things with Keile. "Now or never." With her heart pounding rapidly, she made her way to the kitchen and quickly dialed Keile's number. Haydn disconnected when the voicemail picked up. "Either she's not awake or she doesn't want to talk to me." For her sanity, she chose to believe the former.

An hour later, she tried again with the same results. Haydn banged the receiver against the counter and paced around the kitchen for a few minutes before she came to a decision. She had to know if she still had a chance. Not knowing was killing her. Suddenly calmer, she left a note for Marcus and made her way upstairs to get dressed.

During the drive to Keile's house, Haydn practiced what she wanted to say. But no matter how many times she said the words out loud, they sounded lame. *Please let her give me a chance to explain.*

She noticed Keile's Jeep in the driveway before she reached

the house. Her heart sank as she slowed and gripped the steering wheel. *Maybe she's sleeping in*, she thought, even though that didn't mesh with the Keile she knew. Wetting her dry lips, she pulled into the driveway. "Now or never, remember?"

The walkway leading to the front door seemed to get longer with each step. Haydn ran her fingers through her hair and rang the doorbell, expecting to hear Can's bark. She was met with silence. After waiting a minute, she rang the bell again, listening intently for any sound of movement. Haydn stood in front of the door, indecisive, when it hit her. "I'm an idiot." Keile and Can would be at the park. She gave a nervous laugh of relief and returned to her car. Her brother had been right. She was too tired to think straight.

Haydn's newfound relief evaporated after her second circuit around the park. Keile and Can were nowhere to be found. She pulled out her cell phone and called Marcus. "Have you talked to Keile today?"

"No. Is she not answering her phone?"

"Nor her doorbell it seems. God, maybe she really doesn't want anything to do with me anymore." She turned her back to a passerby, unwilling for them to see the tears in her eyes. "Shit, I messed it all up."

"Where are you?" Marcus demanded. "I'll come get you."

"No! I don't want Kyle to see me like this again. He's had enough already." Haydn bit her lip hard. "Can you keep him for most of the day?"

"You don't even have to ask, but I think you're overreacting. Keile's probably crashed at Dani's place oblivious to the world. Give it a couple more hours before you panic."

Haydn felt a thread of hope. "Okay, I'll try again later this afternoon."

"Or try calling Edan. She'll know what's going on."

"No," Haydn said, wiping her face. "I don't want to put her and Dani in the middle. Not when they finally reached an accord. This is my mess to fix."

Chapter Thirty-One

Keile watched the flames lick against the pine logs, releasing sparks that popped. She absently petted Can who was trying to inch his way up onto the pullout sofa.

"How's it going?" Lynn asked.

Keile looked up with a hint of a smile. "Better than this morning. Is it your turn to deal with the emotional cripple?"

"Don't. I won't let you put my friend down. Got it?"

Keile nodded, then gave a humph when Lynn plopped down in her lap. She stole a quick glance to the kitchen area where Terri, Jo and Susan were preparing dinner.

"Don't worry, she won't consider this a trespass," Lynn gently teased. "Don't forget she still owes you for last night. I don't know what I was thinking, sending Terri to rescue you. That overgrown kid can't rescue herself."

"In that case." Keile put her arms around Lynn's waist and

kissed her cheek. "Now admit you've been sent to deal with me."

"I'll admit they think that's what I'm doing. Really, I'm getting out of kitchen duty." She grinned and scooted down, dropping her head on Keile's shoulder.

"But you're the best cook," Keile whispered with a furtive look at the chefs.

Lynn laughed. "I already did the hard stuff. I figure I deserve to cuddle up with a cute babe and rummage around in her brain."

Keile let out a mock groan. "I knew there had to be a catch. And I hate to break it to you, but there's not much left upstairs."

"What about here?" she asked, pointing to Keile's heart. "Anything left of Haydn in there?"

"You don't want to know how much I wish there wasn't." Keile sighed. "Somehow wishing hasn't worked for me."

"Maybe you're not wishing for the right thing. What makes you so sure it's over with Haydn? From what you've said, she only admitted to needing space, and that's hardly surprising given her circumstances."

"She hasn't tried to contact me in over a week, Lynn. I don't need everything spelled out for me. It's over all right. I have to learn how to accept her decision and move on."

"I'm still not convinced, but you know her better than I do." Lynn turned to be face-to-face with Keile. "I want you to promise me that if she calls, you'll hear her out. And I want you to promise you won't be a stranger after this weekend. We're your friends, let us help you."

Keile could only nod and clench her jaw against that tiny shred of hope. There was no way Haydn would call.

"Is that a promise for both?" Lynn asked, her eyes alight with sympathy.

"Yes. I've learned my lesson. I don't have to suffer alone anymore. Not when I have good friends to call on. Thanks for not giving up on me."

"Now you'd better stop making this femme's heart flutter, or

Terri will come kick your ass." Lynn kissed Keile's cheek.

"Hey Lynn, I don't think that's the kind of consoling my sister had in mind," Jo yelled across the room.

"You be quiet," Susan said in a threatening tone, shaking an oven mitten in Jo's direction.

Lynn rose gracefully and crossed the room to where Terri was leaning against a counter. "Do *you* have a problem with my methods, baby?"

Shooting her twin a dirty look, Terri replied, "No, dear."

"Good." Lynn fisted Terri's shirt and kissed her passionately.

Keile watched the interaction between Lynn and Terri with a heavy heart. She thought back to Thanksgiving, reliving that special feeling of being part of a family within a family. Now she was with her family but once again she was the lonely one without an inner family. When she couldn't hold back the tears, she turned away from the display of affection and watched the flames as the wood popped and sparked.

Before dawn the next morning, wide awake, Keile folded her hands behind her head and listened to the unfamiliar silence, grateful Dani hadn't given her a choice about coming to the cabin. Away from the cause of her heartache, her mind was clearer. It was time for a master plan that wasn't based on her youthful fears.

She smiled when she heard the clinking of Can's tag as he stood and stretched. "You ready to go out, boy?" she asked softly, reaching down to pet his head. At his muffled bark, she threw back the covers, shivering as the cold air struck her warm body. Quickly pulling on chilly sweats, she let him and Jo's two dogs out.

Keile grabbed the comforter off the sofa and made for one of the three wooden rockers on the front porch which was on the second level since the cabin was built on a hill. She looked up at the stars, their sheer numbers a wonder for someone used to a night sky virtually obliterated by city lights. She found herself wishing she had come out the evening before to catch the first star. She had never wished on one, but given the way her life was going, last night would have been a great time to start.

Unbidden, her mind flashed to her conversation with Lynn. If she'd made a wish last night, would she have asked for the right thing? The answer formed almost instantaneously. *Yes!* More than anything she wanted to still be an integral part of Haydn and Kyle's inner family. Everything else paled in comparison.

Breathing in the crisp early morning air was almost painful. The most important goal in her life and she had no control over achieving it. Studying and working hard wouldn't help in this instance. Haydn had said she needed space and time. Maybe she had let her tenuous relationship with her mother lead her to the wrong conclusion. Maybe she, too, had needed some space and time to sort out her own stuff. After all, she'd let one bump in the road send her into a tailspin.

Keile groaned. Admittedly, she'd been looking at the situation from her own selfish perspective. But what if she stepped back from her knee-jerk reaction and considered the woman she professed to love? Wasn't it understandable that Reagan's sudden appearance would cause Haydn to question herself again? *God, I'm a self-absorbed ass.* Her one week of misery was nothing compared to the three years Haydn had struggled to get over Reagan's desertion.

Her heartbeat sped up as she became filled with hope. She tried to ground herself with the reminder that Haydn hadn't been in touch, not even to congratulate her on having found a brother. But even that couldn't squelch the hope, that perhaps, just perhaps her goal was attainable. The first thing she needed was patience. Lots of patience, and maybe a little bit of the faith she'd lost long ago. She'd gotten through to Haydn once, she could do it again. "I will do it again," she whispered fiercely and returned her gaze to the stars, seeing them and her own inner universe from a different perspective.

The sky was starting to lighten when the dogs returned from their morning adventure. At Can's urging, Keile returned inside. She grabbed a Coke, started a fire, then sat and mapped out a plan to woo Haydn. Thirty minutes later she heard the first stirring in the kitchen.

"What has you looking so pensive this morning?" Dani asked, holding her hands toward the warmth of the fire.

Keile looked up at Dani. "Partly my fascination with flames. I think I was a fire starter in another life."

"You certainly weren't a coffee starter." Dani pointed to the Coke can in Keile's hand. "So," she said, nudging Keile with her slippered foot, "what else were you being pensive about?"

"Well, Friday night of course," she said, not ready to share her early morning discovery. "I can't believe I got drunk."

"Between work and other things, you were due." Dani put a hand on her shoulder. "Most of us got it out of the way when we were younger. You're just a slow learner."

"Thanks, Dani. I could have easily gone through my life *without* it happening to me." Keile covered her face with her hands. "Why the hell did I let Terri and Sam goad me into getting on a table to show off my new tattoo? And that was *after* I let them psych me into getting the damn thing in the first place. That's just not me."

"Not the sober you. Don't worry about it, Keile. It wasn't that bad, really." Dani whipped out her cell phone and scrolled through the photos. "Here, look at this. I would hardly call this indecent."

Keile groaned, but didn't remove her hands from her face.

Dani dropped down to sit next to Keile. "It's over and done with. Let it go." She slung an arm around Keile's shoulders. "Or better yet, consider it a learning experience."

"I learned a lesson." Keile uncovered her face. "Never drink with Sam and Terri again."

"Not that one. I'm referring to the one where you talk to your friends *before* you feel like everything is falling apart. I know I was out of pocket, but you could have called me anytime. That's what friends are for."

"You're not the first person this weekend to point that out." Keile leaned her head against Dani's shoulder. "I'm used to going it alone. And I didn't want to give you any excuse not to finally talk everything out with Edan."

"Let me worry about that next time, okay? I have to have someone to practice my parenting skills on."

"Parenting skills?"

"Don't look so surprised. Surely you knew being around Edan and Kyle would wear me down. But we'll talk about that later. For now, we need to get you fixed up."

"I hope you have a super mechanic on call."

"You're not that broken. I know it doesn't seem like it now but eventually the pain dulls to a bearable level. Then before you know it you'll be ready to try dating again." She ignored Keile's loud snort. "And when you are, I bet I know just the place to start."

"No," Keile said, shaking her head. "Don't say it."

"Come on. Terri said your table dance was quite the hit with the ladies and the fellows. But maybe next time you could wear a skimpier bra."

"I'm gonna kill Terri." Keile thought for a moment. "And Sam, and Patti, and—"

"I think the coffee's ready," Dani said and scrambled to her feet.

Edan fumbled around in the bag at her feet, searching for the ringing phone. She answered and then passed the phone to Keile, who was in the backseat. "It's Marcus."

Keile smiled. "Hey, bro. What's up?"

"You're a hard woman to reach. I was starting to worry. Especially after your call Friday night."

She cringed. "Sorry about the call. We've been in the North Georgia Mountains. Dani kidnapped me but she forgot to kidnap my wallet and cell."

"I knew there had to be a good explanation."

"What's going on? Kyle's okay, right?"

"He's fine, but somebody else isn't. She's been trying to reach you since yesterday morning."

For a second, Keile's mind went blank. This could not be happening. It was too easy.

"Keile, are you there?"

"Yeah," she said quietly. "You're talking about Haydn. She wants to talk to *me*?"

"Don't sound so surprised. Since you haven't returned her calls, she's convinced you don't want anything to do with her."

"No!" She ran her fingers through her hair, trying to pull her thoughts together. "Nothing could be further from the truth. Could you let her know it finally sunk into my thick skull why she needs time, and that I'm willing to wait."

"I could, but it would be so much better coming from you. She's really desperate to make things right."

"I can do that," she said slowly.

"I'm available if you need me, kiddo."

"Thanks. You're a good brother." She closed the phone and tapped it against Edan's shoulder.

"Well?" Dani demanded.

"Haydn's been trying to call me." She rested her elbows on her knees and propped up her head. "I almost don't believe it."

Edan twisted around and faced Keile. "Why not?"

"I'm always leery when I get what I wish for. It's too easy to have it snatched away again."

"Sometimes you get lucky and the second time around is better than the first," Dani said with a quick glance at Edan.

Edan smiled and squeezed Dani's thigh. "She's right, Keile. If Haydn's ready to talk, she's faced the past and she still wants you. That's some powerful magic you have."

"I hardly think I'm magical."

"You didn't know how Haydn was before. I do and let me tell you, there's a big difference and it's because of you."

"You're a miracle worker, Keile. Deal with it," Dani said, glancing in the rearview mirror. "Now you have two hours to come up with something romantic to say."

Keile rolled her eyes and suppressed a smile. Friends—a pain in the ass, but you had to love 'em.

Keile shut the rear door of Dani's Explorer and walked around to the passenger side window. "Thanks for the kidnapping, guys. Wish me luck."

"You got it," Dani said.

"Remember, Haydn's probably more scared than you are," Edan said. "You'll do fine."

After a wave, Keile joined Can on the porch. "I can do this, right boy?" When he barked, she wasn't sure if he was agreeing or urging her to open the door. She unlocked the door and smiled as he raced to the kitchen to begin his search for intruders. *That answers my question.*

Thirty minutes later, Keile's smile was long gone and she was ready to hit something. She'd searched the house and still couldn't locate her cell phone or her wallet. Closing her eyes, she tried to remember when she'd last seen either of them. All she had was a vague memory of calling Marcus. Keile sank down on the bed and grabbed her head. "God, I'm pathetic." Can nudged her leg. "You still love me even if I'm a…an idiot!" She pushed off the bed. "Hell, I know where she lives."

Keile pulled the front door open and stopped short at the sight before her. Even with swollen eyes, Haydn was a sight to behold. *She came to me.* Without conscious thought, Keile trailed her fingers across Haydn's cheeks. "I love your freckles," she said, her voice husky with want and uncertainty.

Haydn's laugh sounded close to a sob. "You never did play fair, Keile Griffen."

"Good girls finish last, and I want to finish first and forever with you." She slid her arms around Haydn's waist and pulled her close. "Is that what you want?"

"Forever sounds like it might just be enough time with you." Haydn leaned into Keile and sighed. "I've been so worried that I'd blown everything. That you didn't love me anymore."

"Not possible." Keile breathed in her familiar scent and brushed her lips against Haydn's temple. "I tried to move on and ended up a candidate for an intervention. That's where I was this weekend and the outcome was that I realized I didn't want to move on. You and Kyle are locked in my heart forever."

"You do say the sweetest things. If we weren't on your doorstep, I'd kiss you."

Keile backed them up until they were clear of the door, then shut it with her foot. "You made me forget where I was."

"Good." Haydn threaded her fingers through Keile's hair and brought their lips together. The kiss they shared was a declaration of forever. "Oh, God, I've missed you. Missed us." She captured Keile's lips in a kiss that was hard and fierce. When Haydn rested her head against Keile's chest, her heart was pounding. "How did I last so long without you?"

"I hope that's a rhetorical question," Keile said before taking Haydn's ear lobe between her teeth and tugging. "I love you so much."

"I love you with all my heart. I should have said it before and I'm sorry you had to go so long without knowing that. And I'm sorry for the—"

Keile stopped the apology with a kiss. "We'll talk more later. For now it's enough that you came to claim me." She rested her forehead against Haydn's, then couldn't resist giving her a kiss. "You did come to claim me?"

"How could I not? With you is where I belong."

"I'm glad." Keile closed her eyes briefly, savoring the moment. "Kyle may have found me, but you found my heart and gave me a chance for a real life."

Epilogue

"Mama Kee, me up," Kyle demanded, holding up his arms.

"Please," Keile said as she tightened her grip on Can's leash. When Kyle parroted, "Peas," she hoisted him into her arms. They were on their way home from their ritual Sunday morning walk. It was one of the traditions Keile had started in the six months since she and Haydn had combined households, giving her and Kyle time together and Haydn the chance to sleep late or take a long soak in the tub.

In five minutes, they entered the house to the smell of cinnamon. Keile breathed in deeply. "Smells like French toast, Buster. Someone loves us."

"Mama, cook," he said and ran for the kitchen with a big grin on his face. Keile was right on his heels.

The kitchen was the only room in the house that was virtually the same. Every other room had benefited from Haydn's touch and to Keile it turned her house into their home. She stopped in the doorway and watched as Haydn deftly added a piece of toast to the stack, then patted Kyle on the head. The scene warmed her heart as always.

"What?" Haydn asked as she turned off the front burner.

"Just happy." She crossed the room and gave her a warm welcoming kiss.

"Hey, love. How was the walk?"

"Great. It's beautiful outside. Kyle and I decided we should go to the park this afternoon."

Haydn smiled. "Kyle or you? Are you ever going to get enough of that park?"

"Never. Who knows when I'll run into another cute tyke and his beautiful mother," she teased, and got the expected smack to her stomach. "Let me wash my hands and I'll set the table."

"Worry about getting Kyle cleaned up."

"Are you sure? I don't want you to have to do everything."

"Hey, you get to clean all this up."

"I can do that."

When they returned, Keile placed Kyle in his high chair, then cut a piece of toast in bite-size pieces for him and drizzled it with syrup. "This looks delicious, honey," she said as reached for the scrambled eggs with cheese and turkey sausage.

"Edan called to check in while you were out."

"So they made it back from San Francisco, huh? I wonder if Dani liked the cable cars as much as Kyle and I did."

"You can ask her yourself. I invited them for dinner."

"Cool."

"Don't you look domesticated," Dani said, as she joined Keile on the patio.

Keile turned her attention away from the kabobs on the gas grill. "Just taking advantage of the last of fall. You look rested."

"Vacations do that." Dani handed her a beer. "Haydn thought you might be ready for this."

"So what's the news? Is it what I think it is?"

Dani laughed. "God, you look like an excited puppy," she teased. "And yes, Edan has a bun in the oven."

Keile slung an arm over Dani's shoulder. "How crude. You're going to have clean up that language now, you know."

"I'm so looking forward to it. I can't believe I used to be afraid having a baby would change us. Make us not us, you know? Guess I needed those three years from Edan to mature and learn to trust her."

"Well congrats. We've both gone through a lot of changes this past year. I have a wife, a child and a life. I never thought I could be this happy, Dani."

"I hear you." She raised her bottle. "A toast to loose kids in parks."

"And chance."

Publications from
Bella Books, Inc.
The best in contemporary lesbian fiction

P.O. Box 10543, Tallahassee, FL 32302
Phone: 800-729-4992
www.bellabooks.com

WALTZING AT MIDNIGHT by Robbi McCoy. First crush, first passion, first love. Everybody else knows Jean Harris has a major crush on Rosie Monroe, except Jean. It's just not something Jean, with two kids in college, thought would ever happen to her. $14.95

NO STRINGS by Gerri Hill. Reese Daniels is only in town for a year's assignment. MZ Morgan doesn't need a relationship. Their "no strings" arrangement seemed like a really good plan. $14.95

THE COLOR OF DUST by Claire Rooney. Who wouldn't want to inherit a mysterious mansion full of history under the layers of dust? Carrie Bowden is thrilled, especially when the local antique dealer seems equally interested in her. But sometimes secrets don't want to be disturbed. $14.95

THE DAWNING by Karin Kallmaker. Would you give up your future to right the past? Romantic, science fiction story that will linger long after the last page. $14.95

OCTOBER'S PROMISE by Marianne Garver. You'll never forget Turtle Cove, the people who live there, and the mysterious cupid determined to make true love happen for Libby and Quinn. $14.95

SIDE ORDER OF LOVE by Tracey Richardson. Television foodie star Grace Wellwood is not going to be golf phenom Torrie Cannon's side order of romance for the summer tour. No, she's not. Absolutely not. $14.95

WORTH EVERY STEP by KG MacGregor. Climbing Africa's highest peak isn't nearly so hard as coming back down to earth. Join two women who risk their futures and hearts on the journey of their lives. $14.95

WHACKED by Josie Gordon. Death by family values. Lonnie Squires knows that if they'd warned her about this possibility in seminary, she'd remember. $14.95

BECKA'S SONG by Frankie J. Jones. Mysterious, beautiful women with secrets are to be avoided. Leanne Dresher knows it with her head, but her heart has other plans. Becka James is simply unavoidable. $14.95

PARTNERS by Gerri Hill. Detective Casey O'Connor has had difficult cases, but what she needs most from fellow detective Tori Hunter is help understanding her new partner, Leslie Tucker. $14.95

AS FAR AS FAR ENOUGH by Claire Rooney. Two very different women from two very different worlds meet by accident—literally. Collier and Meri find their love threatened on all sides. There's only one way to survive: together. $14.95